**LAVISH PRAISE FOR
THOMAS H. COOK'S**

THE INTERROGATION

"TIME IS A SILENT, LOOMING CHARACTER IN *THE INTERROGATION*. . . . A GREAT STORY TICKS ALONG RELENTLESSLY TO A SURPRISING CONCLUSION." —*The Wall Street Journal*

"AN INCREDIBLY INTENSE READ, CULMINATING IN A TRUE SHOCKER OF AN ENDING."—*Booklist*

"Compelling . . . The Edgar-winning Cook makes the most of that brief period of time, not only braiding the intricate elements of the crime but laying open the secretive, troubled lives of [his] characters. . . . Down to the cleverly hatched, melancholy ending, COOK AGAIN TAKES READERS DOWN A DARK, TREACHEROUS ROAD INTO THE HEART OF HUMAN FALLIBILITY AND STRUGGLE." —*Publishers Weekly*

"BRILLIANT! A MELANCHOLY, BEAUTIFUL and—above all—SUSPENSEFUL meditation on guilt and the nature of time." —*Time Out New York*

"A TAUT AND TENSE PROCEDURAL THAT TAKES READERS ON AN UNEXPECTEDLY EXCITING RIDE AS IT RACES TOWARDS ITS CLIMAX . . . This one gets better and better the deeper it goes." —*San Francisco Chronicle*

"DARK AND ENTHRALLING . . . COOK'S COMPLICATED BOOK IS A KEEPER." —*Fort Worth Star-Telegram*

PLACES IN THE DARK

"With its passionate characters, compelling family-driven narrative and surprising conclusion, *Places* presents irrefutable evidence that it sometimes pays not to be afraid of the dark." —*People*

"[The story] is swept along by Cook's artistry, his insights into broken people, his austere imagery of the barren landscapes that attract them." —*The New York Times*

"Cook writes very well; his tone is sad, even foreboding, yet almost elegiac, as he weaves . . . an intricate fabric of tragedy." —*The Boston Globe*

"A serpentine tale of long-buried secrets leading to murder and betrayal . . . Reminiscent of John Fowles' *The French Lieutenant's Woman.*" —*The Orlando Sentinel*

"A strong, suspenseful story . . . Cook accomplishes what he consistently does so superbly: He sets the tone, creates characters, [and] engages the reader." —*The Houston Chronicle*

"Mr. Cook springs his share of effective plot surprises. . . . Maybe the greatest is the wonderfully redemptive ending." —*The Wall Street Journal*

"Skillfully blends flashbacks with current action and his deftly drawn characters invoke both empathy and pity. In sum, a splendid performance by a gifted artist." —*The San Diego Union-Tribune*

INSTRUMENTS OF NIGHT

"[A] once-in-a-lifetime masterpiece." —*Kirkus Reviews*

"Probably no other suspense writer takes readers as deeply into the heart of darkness as Cook. . . . As always, Cook's prose is precise, his storytelling slow and deliberate. This is one powerful story." —*Chicago Tribune*

"Although it's easy to miss the very real clues that Cook drops so artfully into the story, there's no ignoring his savage imagery, or escaping the airless chambers of his disturbing imagination." —*The New York Times Book Review*

"Cook's last book, *The Chatham School Affair*, won the 1997 Edgar Award for best novel, and his haunting new one, *Instruments of Night*, could be a contender. . . . The denouement took me by surprise and disturbed me for days." —*Los Angeles Times*

"An enthralling tale that cannily uses elements of the Gothic thriller." —*The Seattle Times/Seattle Post-Intelligencer*

"Hypnotic prose and fresh scenarios set [Cook's] suspenseful fiction apart. . . . If you've not yet been haunted by a Thomas Cook novel, now is a fine time to start." —*Star Tribune,* Minneapolis

"Cook teases readers throughout the narrative with tantalizing bits from Graves' own past. . . . But he also saves the best—and most shocking revelations—until practically the last page." —*The Orlando Sentinel*

EVIDENCE OF BLOOD

"In [his] previous novels . . . Cook has shown himself to be a writer of poetic gifts, constantly pushing against the presumed limits of crime fiction. . . . In this fine new book, he has gone to the edge, and survived triumphantly." —Charles Champlin, *Los Angeles Times Book Review*

"Gripping southern drama, with its byzantine family trees, old wives' tales, and overheated memories." —*Kirkus Reviews*

BREAKHEART HILL

"Haunting, lyrical . . . a mesmerizing tale of love and betrayal." —*Alfred Hitchcock Mystery Magazine*

"Intense . . . Impossible to put down." —*Rendezvous*

"Cook has crafted a novel of stunning power, with a climax that is so unexpected the reader may think he has cheated. But there is no cheating here, only excellent storytelling." —*Booklist*

"Cook's writing is distinguished by finely cadenced prose, superior narrative skills, and the author's patient love for the doomed characters who are the object of his attention. . . . Highly recommended." —*Library Journal* (starred review)

MORTAL MEMORY

"Cook builds a family portrait in which violence seems both impossible and inevitable. One of [*Mortal Memory*'s] greatest accomplishments is the way it defies expectations . . . surprising and devastating." —*Chicago Tribune*

"Haunting . . . Don't pick this up unless you've got time to read it through . . . because you will do so whether you plan to or not." —*Alfred Hitchcock Mystery Magazine*

MORE PRAISE FOR THOMAS H. COOK

"Cook's night visions, seen through a lens darkly, are haunting." —*The New York Times Book Review*

"A gifted novelist, intelligent and compassionate." —Joyce Carol Oates, *The New York Review of Books*

ALSO BY THOMAS H. COOK

FICTION
Peril
Places in the Dark
Instruments of Night
The Chatham School Affair
Breakheart Hill
Mortal Memory
Evidence of Blood
The City When It Rains
Night Secrets
Streets of Fire
Flesh and Blood
Sacrificial Ground
The Orchids
Tabernacle
Elena
Blood Innocents

NONFICTION
Early Graves
Blood Echoes

THE INTERROGATION

THOMAS H. COOK

BANTAM BOOKS

This edition contains the complete text
of the original hardcover edition.
NOT ONE WORD HAS BEEN OMITTED.

THE INTERROGATION

A Bantam Book

PUBLISHING HISTORY
Bantam hardcover edition published April 2002
Bantam mass market edition / October 2002

ISBN 0-553-58250-X

Published simultaneously in the United States and Canada

PRINTED IN THE UNITED STATES OF AMERICA

OPM 10 9 8 7 6 5 4 3 2

FOR OTTO PENZLER

Though we talk of all Time smothers,
And all that Age affrights,
Yet with joy in one another,
Laugh through these New York nights.

THE
INTERROGATION

City/Autumn/1941

The morning headlines reported that the Germans were closing in on Leningrad, but Detective Norman Cohen was focused on the more immediate task of cracking a murderer. He knew in his heart that Klemper had strangled Martha Dodd thirty-six hours before and he planned to prove it.

Jack Pierce entered the detective bull pen, humming "Chattanooga Choo-Choo."

"So how's the new father?" Cohen asked.

"Sixteen hours, twenty-three minutes, and four seconds old," Pierce replied, glancing at his Timex. "We named her Debra." He glanced down the corridor toward Interrogation Room 3. "I saw Klemper cooling his heels in Room 3. This trap of yours better work."

Cohen saw the door of Martha Dodd's apartment, the velvety white flowers that twined from the wooden trellis beside it. "It'll work," he answered confidently. "You know why?" He gave Pierce a thumbs-up. "Because we, my friend, are the good guys."

Pierce laughed and hung his hat and coat on the wooden rack just inside the door. "I'm ready."

Cohen glanced at the clock. Six fifty-eight A.M. "Okay. Let's do it."

"Ready."

They walked together up the corridor to Interrogation Room 3.

Klemper was seated at a square wooden table, back erect, hands folded neatly before him. "How long will this take?" he asked, smiling genially when the two detectives entered. "I have to be at work by eight."

Klemper was a bookkeeper for a shoe factory on Dawson Street, and to Cohen's eye, he looked the part. His dark hair glistened with Brilliantine. His gold-rimmed glasses had lenses so thick they magnified the calculating eyes behind them. His suit was pressed, his vest buttoned, the crimson bow tie an unexpected gout of color. Everything was properly placed . . . and to Cohen all of it rang as false as two sets of books.

"I don't know why I'm being questioned again," Klemper told them.

"Because you have a record, for one thing," Pierce replied. "That little matter of attempted murder, remember?"

"That was over twenty years ago."

"The girl you tried to kill was the same age as Martha Dodd," Cohen reminded him.

"The method was the same, too," his partner added. "Strangulation."

"I was twenty-four, for God's sake." Klemper looked offended by the very notion that such an old offense was being used against him now. "And besides, I paid my debt to—"

"Martha Dodd worked for Dawson Shoes," Cohen interrupted.

"There must be forty or fifty girls in that factory," Klemper scoffed.

"Have you ever been to Braxton Apartments?" Pierce asked.

"Never."

"But you know where they are, don't you?" Cohen asked.

"No, I don't."

"Martha Dodd lived in 8-D."

"So you've told me." Klemper drew a shiny watch from his vest pocket, and flipped the lid. "I really need to be going. . . ."

Cohen sat across the table from Klemper. He looked him dead in the eye. "Tell me, Art, you want to live or die?"

"That question is absurd."

"The chair, that's what we're talking about." Pierce leaned over to take the watch from Klemper's fingers. "Whether you fry in it or not."

"You're wasting your time with these outlandish—"

"What'll it be, Art?" Cohen broke in sternly. "Life? Or the chair?"

Klemper brushed his right sleeve. "If you have some reason for keeping me here, Detective, I'd like to hear it. Otherwise, I intend—"

"Remember Patricia Clayborn? Eileen McDowell? Both strangled in their apartments." Cohen dropped the easy banter. His voice turned as wintry as his eyes. "You and Patty Clayborn both worked at Lambert Hospital Equipment. Patty was murdered. The same with Eileen McDowell, only that was at Klein Metal Shelving."

"Coincidences. So what?"

Cohen leaned forward. "Here's the deal. You tell us exactly what you did to Martha Dodd, or we'll tell you exactly what you did to her. If you put us to the trouble of doing that, the D.A. won't settle for anything less than death. If we tell you first, you'll go to the chair. It's that simple." He waited for a response, and when none came, he said, "There's this old German movie. A guy kills a kid, and somebody finds out, and the guy who finds out takes a piece of chalk and writes a great big M on the killer's coat. M—for 'Murderer.' You ever see that movie, Art?"

"This is nonsense." Klemper lifted his head haughtily. "If you have nothing further, I'd like to be on my way."

Cohen drew an envelope from his jacket pocket and tapped it lightly against the table. He opened the envelope and scattered a few pink specks onto the battered surface of the table.

Pierce raised his wrist and glanced at his Timex. "You have sixty seconds, Klemper."

"To do what?" Klemper demanded.

Cohen was studying the specks on the table, no longer looking at Klemper. "To tell us what you did to Martha."

"Do you honestly believe that—"

"Fifty-five seconds," Pierce said.

Klemper glared at Pierce. "You can stop that melodramatic countdown."

"The apartment building where Martha lived is owned by Robert Braxton," Cohen said, nudging one of the specks with his fingertip.

"Fifty-one."

"Mr. Braxton is something of a horticulturist."

"Everyone needs a hobby," Klemper said with a slight chuckle.

"Forty-five."

"He grows rare flowers," Cohen continued. "There's a particularly rare one right at Martha's door. A vine. It has big white flowers, remember?"

"I was never anywhere near that girl's apartment," Klemper said evenly.

"Thirty-five."

"Braxton gave me the scientific name, but that doesn't matter. What matters is that those flowers are the only ones in the city."

"Thirty."

"That's why we got a warrant to search your apartment this morning," Cohen continued. "Our guys are there now."

Klemper's face tensed.

"Looking in your closet."

"Twenty."

"Looking for pollen from those big white flowers. Seems it's real messy, that pollen." He raised a pollen-smeared finger and turned it toward Klemper. "Sticks to anything the wind blows it on. Like your coat, Art. Or your shoes."

"Ten."

"Your clothes are marked," Cohen said ruthlessly. "Just like that guy in the movie."

"Five."

Klemper shifted in his seat. "Listen, maybe—"

"Marked by pollen." Cohen blew gently on his fingertip, sending a fine pink spray into the air.

"Four."

"Stop it!" Klemper snarled at Pierce.

"Three," Pierce said evenly.

"So what's your choice?" Cohen inquired, as if willing to do Klemper a very big favor.

"Two."

"Live?" Cohen asked.

Klemper stared around frantically.

"Or fry?"

"One."

"Live!" Klemper yelped.

Cohen's gaze swept over to Pierce, caught the satisfaction in his partner's dark eyes. He turned back to their prisoner. "Don't leave anything out, Mr. Klemper, or our deal is off."

Klemper was blinking frantically behind his thick lenses. "Pollen," he whispered.

Cohen looked down at the face powder he'd borrowed from one of the secretaries. He thought of the small gust that had stirred the sterile white blooms, a little breeze, nothing more, but one he suddenly imagined as rising from deep within the scheme of things, a gift to the good guys, dropped from on high into their outstretched hands.

City/Autumn/1952

PART I

Are we alone in this?

6:00 P.M., September 12, Trevor and Madison

Eddie Lambrusco pressed down on the brake and steered Siddell Carting Truck 12 over to the curb. Five metal garbage cans stood in a sloppy line at the edge of the street. All were swollen with the day's refuse, but Terry Siddell, Eddie's shift partner for the night, made no effort to deal with them.

"Well, you getting out or not, Terry?" Eddie asked.

Siddell didn't move, but that didn't surprise Eddie. Siddell wasn't used to taking orders. Eddie was used to nothing else. Except when he was with his daughter, Laurie, saw himself reflected in her adoring gaze and suddenly felt like a man again. He thought of Laurie now, the way her eyes had followed him out the door of her room that morning. *Don't go, Daddy*. Any man would do anything for such a sweet kid, Eddie thought. Anything he had to do to make her happy. And yet he'd not been able to stay with her. He knew that other fathers would be with their kids tonight, all curled up on the family sofa, watching Sid Caesar or Uncle Miltie. But not Eddie Lambrusco. Old Man Siddell would never have given him the night off just because his daughter was sick. With that bitter recognition, Eddie returned his thoughts to the job at hand.

"Look, Terry, we got a full twelve-hour shift," Eddie said, making sure that the raw hostility he felt for Terry Siddell didn't show.

Siddell peered morosely into the night. "Twelve hours," he griped. "Twelve fucking hours."

It wasn't just the hours, Eddie knew. It was that Terry had to spend them with a guy like Eddie, a little guy, going nowhere, without power or influence, a guy who could never make Siddell pay for anything he did, which Eddie yearned to do . . . just once.

"Nobody likes a twelve-hour shift," Eddie said. Again he thought of Laurie. Her sickness. Her fever. The way she'd vomited through the night. Then his mind shifted to her mother, snatched from the secretarial pool, screwed, and tossed aside. He'd scooped something out of her, the guy who did that, so that she'd collapsed from the inside, abandoned her husband and daughter, leaving nothing behind but the lingering smell of her afternoon gin.

The terrible loss that had been inflicted upon his life abruptly swept down upon Eddie Lambrusco, a grown man who couldn't hold on to a wife or stay home with a sick daughter or say "Go fuck yourself" to anyone at all, not even the little punk who sat whining at his side.

"So, you getting out?" he asked.

"Okay, okay," Siddell answered sourly. He grasped

the door handle, jerked it up, and pulled himself out of the truck, leaving the door open behind him.

"Fucking wimp," Eddie growled under his breath. He leaned over and violently jerked the door closed, imagining Siddell's right hand smashed by the impact, screaming for him to open the door, release him, gazing in horror at his mangled fingers when he did. The only problem was that such vengeful fantasies were brief, and in their wake Eddie felt only smaller and more powerless.

In the wide rearview mirror, he watched as Siddell lumbered toward the bulging cans. Christ, he thought, what a lousy break. A twelve-hour run ahead of him, every second of it with a rich kid who'd be his boss in five years, another jerk he'd have to answer to. He imagined Terry Siddell behind a big desk, dressed in a suit and tie, pinkie ring on his finger, puffing a big cigar as he handed him the pink slip. *Sorry, Eddie, but we just can't keep you on.*

In the old days he'd been partnered with Charlie Sweeney, and the two of them had laughed the night away. If Eddie hadn't lost his job with the city, they'd have still been partners, gotten the work done, cleaned up the whole area around police headquarters, the park, Briarwood, where the big Dumpsters bulged with the dreadful garbage of Saint Vincent's Hospital, and finally the crumbling tenements of Cordelia. They'd have laughed their way through the whole damn thing because Charlie was a jokester, a guy who made faces and could imitate the people he saw on the street. Charlie moved the clock forward one gag at a time, lightened the load for everybody else. Every shift run, Eddie decided, needs a comedian, and he knew that without Charlie, tonight would be long, the work arduous, and there'd hardly be a moment when he wasn't brooding about Laurie, chewing at the fact that he wasn't with her, despising himself for leaving her alone.

A clatter sounded behind the truck, the intentionally vicious noise Siddell always made, rolling the cans back and forth and banging them against the metal sides of the truck as if trying to get even with Old Man Siddell for making him work for his supper. Amazing, Eddie thought, what some guys feel entitled to. He reached in his pocket and drew out the battered pocket watch he'd inherited from his father, a laborer's timepiece with its chinks and scratches and slightly skewed hands that circled turgidly around the yellowing dial. After a lifetime, he thought, this.

Siddell groaned as he crawled back into the truck. "Okay, let's get out of here."

Eddie glanced in the mirror. A trail of garbage lay strewn across the wet street. "Next time try to get some of it in the truck, Terry," he said, relishing what he knew would be only a fleeting moment of authority over Terry Siddell.

Siddell's lips jerked into a scowl. "Fuck you, asshole."

Eddie gave no indication that he'd heard Siddell's insulting reply. After all, what could he do about it? Punch the little shit's lights out and get fired for it? No. He couldn't do that. He'd gone that route before, been fired by the Parks Department and the Sanitation Department and even the private carting service where he'd worked before being hired by Old Man Siddell. No, he had to control himself now. For Laurie's sake. Because she needed things.

And so he swallowed his rage, grasped the black knob of the gearshift, stomped the clutch, and stirred the truck back onto the deserted avenue, his eyes locked on the street ahead, where, at the end of it, the great stone facade of police headquarters loomed.

As the truck lurched forward, Eddie let his gaze drift up the side of the building. On the top floor, he could see a solitary figure in a lighted window, staring down at the darkening street, head bowed, shoulders slumped, as if beneath a weight he could not carry anymore.

6:12 P.M., *Office of the Chief of Detectives,* 227 *Madison Street*

Chief of Detectives Thomas Burke peered through the arched window of his sixth-floor office, hands clasped behind his back, staring down at the city's tangled streets. At the corner of Madison a garbage truck made a clumsy rocking turn, a spume of trash blowing behind it. Is that what dooms us in the end, he wondered, a million small neglects?

He had no answer to this question, and he looked out across the city, where lights had begun to flicker in the distant apartment houses as the day workers returned to their rooms like birds to their nests. The image, he knew, was from one of his son's poems. What had Scottie called the city? *A rookery of scars*.

He closed his eyes briefly, tried once again to fathom his son's fall. Where had it come from, Scottie's utter lack of nerve, the way he'd curled into a ball of defeat and let life squash him like a can in the street? A little spine would have saved him, Burke thought, but there'd been no sign of that. No sign of muscle, sinew, the strength required to take a punch. He thought of Rocky Marciano, the championship bout that was coming up. That's what Scottie had needed, a touch of the fighter in his soul. But Scottie had hit the mat in the first round, and never gotten up.

When Burke opened his eyes again, the great bridge

rose mutely before him, its stone ramparts towering above the unreflecting waters of the harbor. The bridge was often lost in spooky fogs, but this evening, as night fell, it glowed in a pale blue light. Burke thought of ghost ships in the mist, of the coffin boat that had disgorged some half-starved ancestor at the harbor door a century before, a scullery maid or landless tinker. Scottie had failed to grow the thick hide and sharp fangs of these wolfish forebears. If subjected to some final interrogation, Burke wondered what answer his son would give to the one question he should have asked him. *Why didn't you fight back?*

A knock at the door.

He turned to face it. "Come in."

It was Commissioner O'Hearn, tall and erect in the doorway, all but gleaming in his dress uniform, the police-brass equivalent of a tuxedo. His luxurious black coat was folded neatly over his crooked arm, his cap held delicately in recently manicured fingers, and in that pose the Commissioner looked decidedly aristocratic, like an old European military man, trusted adviser to the Kaiser or the czar. Only the lilt of his voice betrayed his shanty-Irish roots.

"Did you ever figure, Tom, that I'd end up wearing a monkey suit like this?" the Commissioner asked.

"No, never," Burke replied.

What he remembered were two kids from the slums, throwing rocks in the river, leaping off the pylons, racing across the bridge fast as the wind that hummed through its steel cables, playing them like massive harp strings. They'd sneaked into movie houses, stolen apples from peddlers' carts, both of them orphaned by fathers dead from drink and raised by mothers increasingly bitter, looking every day more ragged and used up, like the clothes they washed. Then the Dealer of the Cards had unexpectedly switched the deck and sent them Officer Horace Miles, the beat cop who'd taken two street urchins under his wing, offered a way they might escape the iron grip of Harbortown. *You two don't have to end up like the rest of this scum, you know.*

"I've never learned to like them, Tom." The Commissioner shook his head. "These fancy balls and dinners. Me? I'd rather go home, put my feet up, maybe listen to a Patti Paige record, smoke a cigar. That's my idea of a good way to spend the evening."

It was a lie, but Burke let it go, for it was harmless enough, a boy from the slums claiming against all evidence that some part of him remained loyal to the people who still toiled there. In fact, as Burke knew, the Commissioner felt nothing for the old neighborhood. Once lifted from the pit, he'd never looked back into its teeming depths. Even so, Burke could say nothing against the life his old friend had forged. Francis O'Hearn had worked hard to get where he was, a detective shield at twenty-six, Commissioner Dolan's hand-picked successor by thirty-six, Commissioner himself a short eleven years later. But more than that, Francis had put three daughters through college, a doctor, a lawyer, and an aide to the mayor. He'd reared strong, determined children, kids with grit and fortitude, and in Burke's view, once it could be said of a man that his children bore his steel, little could then be said against him.

It was a badge of honor he would never wear, Burke knew. He thought again of Scottie, this son of his who was a sneak-thief, beggar, dope addict, mercifully dying now, soon to be cremated. A fitting end, he thought, to a life reduced to ashes.

"It's the shindigs they throw at the art museum I have the most trouble with," the Commissioner added with a hearty laugh. "It's something the nuns never taught us, isn't it, Tom, that you need the rich if you want to get anything done." He drew in a deep breath. "I'm afraid I don't have the best of news for you tonight. This fellow we have. He's got to be released by six tomorrow morning. The D.A. says that's all the time we've got. You can't hold this guy forever, Tom, without some evidence. So I'm having him brought here for a final interrogation. He should arrive within the hour."

"Another interrogation won't do any good," Burke said. "We've been over everything with him time and again. All we get is evasions, denials. How he didn't do it, has no idea who did."

The Commissioner draped his uniform coat over one of the chairs in front of Burke's desk and lowered himself into the other. "True enough. But sometimes even the toughest of them will crack under the right questioning. You've seen that, Tom. You know what a good interrogation can do."

Burke well knew what a good interrogation could do, hammer home the incriminating evidence, wind the suspect in coils of lies and contradictions, force him to see under the ruthless light of inquisition that there was no escape from what he'd done. But he also knew that no interrogation could ever find the toxic spring that had finally boiled out into the world, poisoning everything it touched.

"Are you telling me that you see no purpose in any further questioning of this fellow?" the Commissioner asked.

"No, I just think that there are limits to what we can get out of him," Burke answered.

"That's the sin of despair, wouldn't you say, Tom?"

"You sound like a seminarian, Francis."

"Do I? But it was you who once considered the priesthood, wasn't it, Tom?"

"Not for long," Burke said. He shook his head. "Look, what we really need is evidence. Something that physically links Smalls to the murder. Without it, we can't—"

"The man's a child killer, pure and simple," the Commissioner interrupted. "We found the murder weapon in that hole he lived in, remember?"

Burke remembered. It was a two-foot coil of wire with a strand of long dark hair clinging to it, but otherwise washed clean by rain and mud, with no prints of any kind to link it to Albert Smalls. Nor had it actually been found "in that hole he lived in," but a full fifty feet away, near a worksite littered with pipes, bricks, other strands of the same rusted wire, any one of which could have been snatched from the ground, used to strangle a child, then tossed back into the debris.

"I don't want this fellow back in the park, Tom," the Commissioner said resolutely.

Burke was in the park now, the trees that bordered it in a thick green wreath, the gravel paths that wound through it, a playground filled with laughing children, and finally the child they'd found in the grass near the duck pond, her dark hair wet with the rain that had washed over the city, a trickle of blood at the corner of her mouth.

"What I'm telling you is, we've got to get results," the Commissioner added.

"We'll do our best," Burke said. "Pierce and Cohen know the case inside out."

The Commissioner adjusted the cuffs of his dress uniform. "Cohen has never seemed all that serious to me."

"He's gotten more serious since he got back from the war," Burke told him.

"I'll take your word for it," the Commissioner said, although he did not seem convinced. He glanced at his watch, rose, and gathered his coat and cap. "You'll be here at headquarters too? During the interrogation?"

Burke knew this was not a question, but an order. He nodded. "I have to go over to Saint Jude's, but I'll be back by the time Pierce and Cohen get here."

"Saint Jude's?" the Commissioner said with a chuckle. "Is it hopeless cases you're praying for tonight, Tommy?"

Burke felt the rookery stir beyond the window, heard a million hapless crimes. "Every night," he said.

6:23 P.M., 212 Morgan Street, Apartment 7

A plain white roll, boiled ham, a slice of cheese, a dab of mustard. His daily bread.

Detective Jack Pierce ate hunched over a square table balanced on aluminum legs, one of the few pieces of furniture he'd bought for the place during the three years since his wife had left him. In the background, the radio played scratchily, tuned to the low-watt station Jenny had preferred and Pierce had never bothered to change, so that it simply droned on, a memory both of her and of the daughter they had lost.

He snatched the evening edition from the chair beside the table and glanced through it. Charlie Chaplin was heading back to America and Nixon was trying to explain some cash he hadn't told Ike about. There were ads for Coca-Cola and Kaiser cars and a new kind of toaster that popped the bread out when it was done. So what? he thought, folded the paper, and tossed it on the chair.

He'd turned thirty-three a month before, but there'd

been no party. He'd been unable to celebrate anything since Debra's death, but at the same time he was aware that he could not drift forever in his grief, live the way Jenny did, with Debra's murder always in his mind. And yet, after four years he couldn't pull himself out of it. Even Costa's drowning death a year after the murder had done nothing to relieve his burning sense of loss. At times he'd tried to imagine Costa's stubby fingers clawing desperately at the wooden pylons as he labored to pull himself from the oily water, but he could find no solace in the final terror of the man who'd slaughtered his daughter. Instead, Costa's death had faded, and in its place he'd seen Debra in the summer grass, then the dank basement where Costa had maintained his museum of child murder, files bulging with newspaper clippings, photographs taped to poster board, even a "toy" scaffold just high enough to hang a child, a hideous contraption Costa had dismissed with a snicker as a "little joke."

"When I think of children," Costa had freely told police during his first interrogation, "I like to think of them as dead." Then, with a mocking smile, "There's no law against having a sick mind, is there?"

No, no law at all. And so, with no evidence against him, Nick Costa had been set free, and in that instant Pierce had felt a fiery bitterness consume him, charring everything that had ever promised peace.

Pierce washed the last of the sandwich down with a gulp of stale coffee, then lit a cigarette and thought of Anna Lake. During the last few days, the terrible thing they had in common, a murdered daughter, had created a bond between them. More than anything, Pierce wanted to keep the promise he'd made to her during the first days of the investigation, a pledge that her daughter's killer would not go free.

The phone jangled.

"Hullo."

It was Chief Burke, his voice hard and authoritative. "Pierce, you're needed downtown. Be here by seven. Do you know where Cohen is?"

"At home, probably."

"Get in touch with him. Tell him to be downtown by seven." A pause. "Prepare to stay the night."

"Yes, sir," Pierce said. "Is this about . . . ?"

But Chief Burke had already hung up.

6:31 *P.M.*, *1272 Hilton Street, Apartment 5-B*

Norman Cohen trudged up the stairs more slowly than he liked or wanted to admit, hoping the young woman who lived in Apartment 4-A had not peeked out the peephole in her door to see him standing, wheezing, on the fourth-floor landing. He put Ruth Green's age at somewhere in the mid-twenties, and he thought that had she known his true age, forty-one, she might have stifled any further interest in him, never again stopped on the landing or paused to chat when she met him on the street.

Ruth Green had no idea of her power, Cohen thought as he glanced down the stairs, hoping to see her materialize there, beautiful as she peered up at him, hesitantly speaking the words he now imagined. *I've been thinking about you.* He shook his head, embarrassed by his adolescent yearning. *Fantasy,* he told himself as he turned from the empty stairs and slid the key in the lock. *You're living in a dreamworld, Norm.*

He walked into the kitchen and placed on the table the bag of groceries he'd just lugged up the stairs. Then he opened the small, rumbling refrigerator. Someone had left a beer from the card game two nights before. The first swig went down cold and easy, the second had no taste. How some of the guys on the job could down a dozen beers in a single sitting at Luke's Bar amazed him. A *goy* thing, he decided, remembering how Ralph Blunt had stared at him glumly from the other end of the bar. *You people don't like beer, huh, Norm?*

You people.

Cohen remembered the things he'd seen at the Camp's liberation, skeletal faces behind barbed wire, mounds of bodies bulldozed into a pit. Had they not liked beer? he wondered. Is that why they'd been killed in such vast numbers, because in a few insignificant ways they had been different from their neighbors? And if this were their only crime, was there nothing to prevent their wanton slaughter?

No answer to these questions came, of course. Nor did Cohen expect any. His father, the great rabbi and respected leader, had told him that in no uncertain terms. *God is not one of your criminals, son. He will not subject Himself to interrogation.*

He parted the blinds and scanned the street below, now thinking he might get a glimpse of Ruth Green as she made her way home from the public school where she taught second grade. Mid-twenties, he thought, wondering how she'd managed to stay single. But what did that matter? he asked himself. For why would she ever want to marry him? He was a loner now, solitary, divided from Ruth Green less by age than by what he'd seen in the war, the haunting, irresolvable questions it had left him with. A strange darkness had descended upon him during those long years, dense and heavy, a black ink poured into his life. Find something good when you get back home, he'd told himself over and over during that time, find something good and cling to it. But for all his effort he had discovered nothing that could remove the dark stain that marked him. Randomness was all he saw, life and death decided by a throw of the dice in the stone-cold dark.

The phone rang.

"Norm," Pierce said. "Jack. I got a call from the Chief. I think they've decided to let Smalls go, and he wants us to take one more crack at him before they do it."

"Are we alone in this?"

"Yeah, I think we are."

"How long do we have to question him?"

"Till dawn, I think."

"Okay, I'm on my way," Cohen said, all other questions, large or small, now silenced for the night.

Why is this happening to me?

"Hello, Tom."

Chief Burke looked up from where he sat near the back of the church. The priest stood above him, Sean Paddock, another escapee from the old neighborhood, motionless in his black cassock, one hand holding the other, like someone upright in a coffin.

"'Evening, Father," Burke said.

"How's Scottie?"

"It won't be much longer." Burke rose from the pew, started to leave.

Father Paddock placed his hand on Burke's shoulder. "Sometimes a child just goes astray, Tom. I've seen it a thousand times. A child starts out fine, then goes astray."

Burke saw his son as he'd appeared in the emergency room five days before, clothes foul and filthy, stinking of sweat and the sourness of stale urine, deranged, clawing at his own belly as if it were a mound of earth.

"He wanted to die," Burke told the priest. "When they found him, that's all he wanted. Just for the doctors to let him die. And do you know something, Sean? I couldn't find a single reason why they shouldn't."

The priest nodded silently. "Come," he said. "I'll walk you out."

The two men drifted down the central aisle until they passed through the door and out onto the wide marble steps of the church. In the distance, through the last light of day, Burke could make out the southern border of the park. He thought of the duck pond, the small, twisted body found lying in the mud nearly two weeks before, a girl named Cathy Lake, blood oozing from her swollen lips, a heartbreaking question in her open eyes. *Why is this happening to me?*

"I've been thinking of leaving the force, Sean."

"Why's that?"

"I don't know that I'm doing any good anymore." He thought of Cathy Lake, alone in the park, her killer watching her. Where did it come from, he wondered, the evil it took to destroy a child? "That little girl, the one who was killed in the park. The man who killed her will be released in the morning."

"Is that what's troubling you, Tom?" the priest asked. "Raising doubts about staying on the job?"

"Part of it, I suppose."

"Well, don't let it. Because it's a noble calling. What you do." Again he placed his hand on Burke's shoulder. "You're the questioner of Cain, Tom."

Burke nodded, but it didn't seem true. What had he

ever really questioned? Not his faith. Not his work. Not his life. Not that he'd known best for his son, guided him away from useless studies, useless thoughts, those poems he scribbled incessantly, when he should have been thinking about his future, the place Burke had prepared for him on the force, his duty to take up the banner of the blue.

"You should read *The Silver Chalice*, Tom. A book of faith. Everybody's reading it."

"I'm not much of a reader, Father."

The priest nodded. "Other things on your mind, I know. Scottie. That little girl. Murdered. Terrible."

"Yes," Burke said. He saw the moon-splashed waters of the pond, the people at that very moment strolling obliviously around its shadowy path. They had never seemed more vulnerable. All of them, in the end, were as helpless as Cathy Lake had been on her last day on earth, no more aware than she of what menace lay in wait. No more able than she had been to defend herself against it.

"They have no idea what's out there, Father," Burke said. "The harm that can be done to them."

"And that's God's gift to them, Tom, the things they don't question," Father Paddock replied. "And the questioning of these same things, that's the gift He's given you."

6:57 P.M., *Office of the Chief of Detectives*

Pierce sat alone in Chief Burke's office. While he waited, he recalled other interrogations he'd conducted, trying to find something within them that he might use during the one he was about to begin. Sometimes suspects would simply grow tired or too confused to keep up their denials. Sometimes they would be overwhelmed by the sheer weight of the evidence against them. The only thing that never broke them was an unbearable guilt for what they'd done. If you looked into their eyes, all you saw was the regret of the caught for getting caught, nothing more.

"Don't get up, Detective Pierce," Chief Burke said as he strode through the door. "Where's Detective Cohen?"

"He's on his way, sir."

Burke sat down behind his desk. "The order has come down straight from the Commissioner himself. We have until six A.M. to get something solid. Or we have to let Smalls walk."

Before Pierce could protest, Norman Cohen knocked and came into the office.

"I was just telling Detective Pierce that you have until six to get something on Albert Smalls," Burke told Cohen. "He's being brought here. The Commissioner thought a change of scenery might shake him up a little." He nodded toward the open door. "As you can see, he's just arriving."

Pierce and Cohen looked down the corridor to where Albert Jay Smalls, Municipal Jail Inmate 1407, shuffled toward Interrogation Room 3, hands cuffed, ankles shackled, a uniformed officer at his side. He seemed lost inside the striped prison uniform, but there was a sense that no clothes would have fit him any better. His body looked as if it had been made from separate parts of other bodies, his head a bit too weighty for the narrow shoulders, a bit too large for the stringy neck. His hands were small, delicate, and oddly feminine. Despite his slenderness, he seemed curiously fleshy, some residue of baby fat still clinging to his bones.

"What a creep," Pierce said.

Cohen nodded. But it was not just his creepiness that set Smalls apart, he thought. There was also the deep melancholy he had observed over the last ten days, a lacerating inner suffering that separated Smalls from every other criminal he'd ever known, marked him as utterly alien, a creature dropped to earth from someplace that glimmered dimly in the far reaches of the firmament—dark, cold, profoundly inhospitable to life. The suspect never laughed and he never wept, allowed himself neither comfort nor release.

"But being creepy isn't a crime," Burke told the two detectives authoritatively. "And if we can't prove by six tomorrow morning that he murdered that girl, he must be released."

"But he knew Cathy, we know that much," Pierce argued. "He admits it."

"He admits *seeing* her," Burke corrected Pierce. "Recognizing her. But what does that prove? The fact is, we don't have any evidence that he ever touched the murder weapon. We have a witness who saw him within a few yards of where Cathy's body was found, but that was quite some time after she'd already been murdered, and even if Smalls had been seen in the area at the time of the murder, his presence could be purely circumstantial, particularly since he was living in a drainage pipe not far away."

Pierce leaned forward, still intent on making his argument. "But what about the drawings? Where we found them, doesn't that prove—"

Burke shook his head. "We need more. We need physical proof. Evidence. A confession. You have until six. That's just eleven hours. Any questions?"

There were none.

"All right, you may go."

With that, Pierce and Cohen left the Chief's office and headed down the corridor, walking shoulder to shoulder until Pierce stopped and turned toward Interrogation Room 3.

"Maybe we should let him stew for a few minutes. Maybe the Commissioner's right. Maybe a change of scenery could shake him up."

Cohen offered no objection, and so they entered the observation room that adjoined Interrogation Room 3, where, through its rectangular one-way mirror, they could see Inmate 1407 sitting stiffly at the room's scarred wooden table.

"How do you want to do it this time?" Cohen asked his partner.

"Hit and run," Pierce answered. "Throw out the time line. Keep him off-balance. Hope he'll trip up somewhere and give us an idea of what he did with the locket, or some other little detail."

"Or maybe just an idea of where he came from." Cohen kept his eyes on Smalls. "He has to have come from somewhere, Jack. That's the one thing we can be sure of about this guy. Everybody has a past."

7:05 P.M., Criminal Files Room

"Good evening, sir."

Chief Burke nodded to the young officer who stood behind the counter. "Bring me the Catherine Lake file."

The officer vanished into a labyrinth of metal shelves so packed with bulging manila envelopes, they drooped beneath their weight.

A metal table stood a few feet from the counter, four chairs placed neatly around it. Yellow pencils lay scattered across the table's surface, along with notepads and a few ashtrays. How many hours had he sat at that table, Burke wondered, first as an eager young officer, then as a no less eager rookie detective, and finally as Chief of Detectives? To gain the gold badge had been his sole ambition. He recalled the long struggle he'd made to win the shield, at work when Scottie had been born, at work at all but two of his son's birthdays, at work as Scottie's mood darkened with adolescence and the raging quarrels began, at work on the day Scottie told his weeping mother he'd had enough of "this tyranny" and left home for good.

"Here it is, Chief."

Burke faced the counter and saw himself in the guise of Officer Jimmy Day, the blue uniform impeccably pressed, every speck of lint scrupulously picked off, the polished silver badge winking in the naked bulb that hung above him. The abyss that separated his own experience and the young officer's struck him as impossibly wide.

"In my spare time I read the cold-case files," Officer Day remarked as he handed Burke a manila envelope. "When I got this assignment, Sergeant Philips said I should read them, because when you had this job, you solved one of them, Chief. The Lorna Dolphin murder."

Burke had first seen her in crime-scene photographs he'd randomly pulled from the cold-case file his third day at the front desk. Lorna Dolphin, aka Sheila Kanowski, sprawled in one of Harbortown's filthy alleys, her fleshy legs dangling over a ragged pile of fish nets and scrap metal, blood snaking down them to drip from her thick ankles and gather in a sticky pool beneath her feet. She'd been shot once in the chest, after which she'd lived long enough to scratch something in the oil-slick muck in which she'd died. One word: BLADE. An odd word for her to have chosen, Burke had thought, for she'd been shot, not stabbed. This more than anything else had given Burke the sense that there were stones still unturned in this cold case.

And so he began to look through the file more closely, and after that to explore beyond the file, using off-duty hours to make inquiries in Harbortown, where Sheila Kanowski had lived her last days, and finally moving backward into the life that had preceded it.

He discovered that in her youth Sheila Kanowski, known then as Lorna Dolphin, had partied with the uptown crowd, an extraordinarily pretty young hooker who'd been passed from one white-gloved hand to another until age and familiarity had stolen her allure. After that she'd worked as a fish packer in one of the local markets by day and haunted the dockside bars by night, a loud-mouthed sot often picked up by foot patrolmen, tossed in the nearest drunk tank, and left to dry out overnight.

And so she might have lived out her days, then been found dead beneath the bridge or in some harbor shanty, one of hundreds like her.

But at thirty-seven Sheila Kanowski took up prostitution once again, turning tricks in Harbortown, usually dockworkers or old sailors so bleary with drink, they hardly saw the body they pawed.

On the night of her death, the cold-case file concluded, Sheila Kanowski had likely taken one of her customers to a garbage-strewn back alley, where the tryst had suddenly turned lethal, probably because Sheila had at some point during the proceedings opened her famously abusive mouth.

But it was not that simple, as Burke uncovered, for Sheila Kanowski had done more than return to a life of prostitution. True, during her last days she'd plied her trade in Harbortown. But in the weeks immediately preceding those days, she'd seemed seized by a deluded determination to recapture the beautiful young woman she'd once been. Sheila had returned to an old identity, as if by will alone she could revive the party girl who'd once been the toast of Broad Street, a compact pleasure palace much admired by the well-heeled middle-aged club men of fashionable Winchester Heights, men who'd used her for a time, then unceremoniously dropped her from their circle.

And for fifteen years she had, in fact, disappeared from their lives. Then, abruptly, Sheila Kanowski had dyed her hair flaming red and bobbed it in the style of the days of her youth. She'd pulled her old clothes out too, let out the seams to their full measure, and slipped into them again. She'd become a grotesque, overweight flapper, complete with the long black cigarette holder that had once been the emblem of Lorna Dolphin.

All of this could be dismissed as the theatrics of an old whore who'd lost her wits. But Burke discovered that during the two weeks before her death, Sheila Kanowski had been rather rudely escorted from places quite remote from the dockside bars and brothels where she'd lived for the past twenty years, places that had been all too well known to Lorna Dolphin.

The conclusion was inescapable. Sheila Kanowski had invaded Lorna Dolphin's world. Further inquiry revealed that on at least three occasions Sheila/Lorna had brazenly sidled up to a certain silver-haired man who'd clearly been astonished and appalled by the vulgar harridan who'd materialized before him.

The man's name was Donald Webster, a wealthy businessman who, at the time of Kanowski's murder, had been contemplating a run for Lieutenant Governor, a run which, after the murder, he'd decided not to make. He'd cited health reasons as the cause of his withdrawal from the race, but as far as Burke had been able to determine, Donald Webster had been in perfect health, played tennis every weekend at his club, took skiing trips to Switzerland, and often rode in polo matches held at his country estate.

Burke probed further, and found that a good portion of the Webster family fortune was based on the manufacture of cutlery, and that in his youth, Donald Webster's friends had called him Blade.

Burke could still recall the look on the face of the young homicide detective to whom he'd laid out his discoveries.

You're talking about a very powerful man, Tom.
Yes, I know.
And not much evidence.
All I'm asking is that you take it to Chief Dolan. If the Chief says it's not enough to bring Webster in for an interrogation, then I won't press the matter.
I've just gotten into the division. I could look like a right fool asking for something like this, Tom.
You were never afraid of that before, Francis.

Nor was he then, Burke remembered now, watching as if he were once again in the room as a twenty-eight-year-old Detective Francis O'Hearn gathered up the loose sheets of Burke's report. *All right, Tommy, but you owe me one, that's for sure, pal.*

Chief Dolan had ended Webster's interrogation after only twenty-three minutes. Webster had come alone, without a lawyer, dressed in an English suit, his shoes still smelling slightly of the freshly mowed lawns of Winchester Heights. Dolan had even shaken hands with Webster as the two men exited the room, leaving

Burke to wonder if there would be any further investigation of Donald Webster, a question Webster himself had answered the next morning when, at around five A.M., he'd climbed out of his sleek black touring car.

A witness claimed that Webster had stood absolutely erect as he'd stepped off the bridge, his arms still bolted to his sides when he pierced the icy water sixty feet below.

Error by error, Burke thought now, Webster had brought himself to that instant on the bridge. Were we all doomed to do the same? Accumulate errors and misjudgments and finally sink in a river of regret? Were there no questions you could ask at the beginning of the journey that would save you from this drowning at the end?

"I guess you teach all the detectives your method," Officer Day said, returning Burke's mind to the present.

"There's no method," Burke answered crisply as he tucked the Cathy Lake file beneath his arm. "Except to start from the beginning and go over everything again."

Did you hear her scream?

Pierce turned on the tape recorder that rested on the table. "September 12, 7:17 P.M.," he said. "Police Headquarters. Interrogation Room 3. Present are Detective Jack Pierce and Detective Norman Cohen, and Municipal Jail Inmate 1407, identified as Albert Jay Smalls. Okay, let's start from the beginning."

The prisoner nodded, and a strand of hair slid over his forehead. He raked it back through pale fingers that seemed to tremble even when they didn't.

Pierce stared at him evenly. "Okay, for the record, state your name."

"Albert Jay Smalls."

Smalls' voice was weak, a child's voice, and from the first interrogation Cohen had noticed that, like a child,

Smalls seemed uncomfortable in the presence of adults, desirous of pleasing them, afraid of what might happen to him if he didn't. There was a child's tendency to shift in his chair too, glance about restlessly, toy with whatever lay close at hand, avoid your eyes. Everything about him played at hide-and-seek. He claimed to be twenty-six but looked considerably younger. Like a child, he recalled pleasant things (seeing *The Wizard of Oz*) and unpleasant ones (the time a cat had scratched him), but everything else occupied a vague territory he "didn't keep track of." Like a child, he sometimes blurted out a truth . . . and like a child, he lied.

"And you have no permanent address, is that right?" Pierce asked.

Smalls' eyes sought the room's one dusty window. "No."

Cohen walked to the opposite corner and leaned into it, watching Smalls intently, trying to get a sense of what went on in his brain, noting the unmistakable self-loathing that surrounded him like an odor.

"How about any previous address?"

Smalls said nothing.

"Still not willing to give us any previous address, Smalls?"

"No."

Strange, Cohen thought. Why would Smalls refuse to give the police any of his previous places of residence? Pierce had always assumed it was to cover up his criminal record. But if it was not that, what could it be? Why would a young man conceal the place he came from, the people he had known, everything about himself until the moment he'd taken up residence in a filthy drainage pipe near Dubarry Playground in City Park?

"Okay, let's talk about the park," Pierce said. "You do remember living there, don't you?"

"Yes." Smalls' pale right hand fled beneath the other, like a crab scuttling under a stone.

"Tell me about that pipe the officers found you in that night."

"I live in that pipe." Smalls settled his gaze on Cohen briefly, then drew it away. It was a movement generally associated with guilt. But Cohen wondered if Smalls might not simply be a man who couldn't face other men. But why?

"You live alone, right?"

"Alone, yes."

"Do you have any relatives in the city?"

"No."

"Or anybody, for that matter?"

"Anybody?"

"Friends?"

"No," Smalls answered softly.

"Just not sociable, is that it?"

Smalls shrugged. "Never liked, that's all."

"You've cooked up a real sob story there, Smalls," Pierce said. "That nobody ever liked you."

"I stay away from people. I don't bother them."

"You ever bother a little girl?" Pierce snapped.

Smalls' body stiffened, but he gave no answer.

"Okay, tell me this," Pierce said. "What were you doing on the trail near the duck pond on the evening of September first? You remember that evening, don't you, Smalls? The time the woman saw you. You know the woman I mean, don't you?"

"Yes."

"And you remember where you were when she saw you, right?"

"Near the pond."

"What were you doing at the duck pond?"

"I was going home."

"Home? You mean that drainage pipe?"

"Yes."

Cohen stepped forward. "Okay, let me ask you this, Jay. About the little girl who was murdered. Cathy Lake. We've talked to you about Cathy quite a few times. You remember all the things we've asked you, right?"

"Sure he does," Pierce said. "He has a good memory, don't you, Smalls?"

"Good as anybody else, I guess."

"And you're a reader too," Pierce added. "We found a lot of books in your . . . home. By the way, where'd you get all those books?"

"I found them."

"Where?"

"People throw them out."

"So you pick them out of the garbage?"

Smalls sniffed softly and wiped his nose on his sleeve.

"Do you ever go into a bookstore?" Pierce asked. "Maybe slip a book under your jacket?"

"No."

Pierce eased himself around the left corner of the table where Smalls sat, hands clasped together, washed clean, the grit that had once lay caked beneath his fingernails cleared and bagged days before.

"Let me ask you something else, Jay," Cohen said. "Did you ever have any visitors at your home? Somebody who could tell us a few things about you? Things you might have done in the past."

"No."

"Okay," Pierce said. "Let's go back to the little girl. The one who was murdered in the park. Cathy Lake had something with her. Something she was wearing. A silver locket. Heart-shaped."

"Yes."

"Yes what?"

"You told me about it before," Smalls answered.

"You snatched that locket from Cathy Lake's neck," Pierce said. "You did do that, didn't you, Smalls?"

Smalls shook his head.

"Answer with your voice," Pierce said, irritated.

Smalls flinched at the sharpness in Pierce's tone. "Yes. I mean . . . no. I never saw that locket."

Cohen stepped over to the table and placed his hand on his partner's shoulder. "Jay, maybe we're moving too fast for you. So let's go back to what you were doing when those two cops found you that night. The night of Cathy's murder. When they found you in the drainage pipe. You told us you were sleeping." He offered a friendly smile. "But are you sure you were sleeping when the officers found you?"

"I was sleeping."

"But you heard them when they came up to the tunnel, right?"

"I heard them."

"What did you hear?"

"Voices."

"Okay, fine, Jay, good, tell me about those voices you heard," Cohen said gently. "What did the voices say?"

8:37 P.M., September 1, City Park, Drainage Pipe 4

"Jesus, will you look at this, Mike?"

Patrolman Pete Sanford's flashlight raked over the debris in the dark pipe, briefly illuminating empty cans and soda bottles, magazines and books, the tattered refuse of food wrappers and coffee cups, until it reached the side of a bare mattress.

"Is that a pile of . . ." Mike Zarella peered down at the mound of rags that lay on the stained mattress. "Whoa, somebody's there." He drew his pistol. "Police." His voice sharpened. "Don't move."

A groan.

"Don't move," Zarella repeated. Then to Sanford, "I'll take the other side of the pipe."

Sanford listened to the pad of Zarella's feet as he rushed to the right and over the embankment. He kept the light trained on the rustling mound. "Police," he said. "Stay where you are."

Zarella's light bobbed at the far end of the pipe, a brilliant scythe that expanded inside the tunnel until it swept up its curved concrete sides and finally curled over like a cresting wave.

"See anything?" Sanford called, afraid now, his hand wrapped around a pistol, eyes trained on some bum who slept in all this filth, maybe armed, maybe violent. "Be careful, Mike."

The mound rustled again, but no voice came from it.

"Put your hands up," Zarella ordered.

Sanford felt his breath catch, certain now that something was going to happen—a flash of light, a deafening explosion, his partner staggering backward, the light falling from his hand. He stepped forward, both hands gripped to the pistol. "I'm right behind you!" he warned the moving bundle. "Get on your feet! Slowly!"

Over the barrel of his service revolver, Sanford watched as the mound rose languidly, like it had been stirred by the fetid air inside the pipe. "Put your hands behind your head," he yelled.

The figure thrust his hands up and placed them behind his head, assuming the technical position without further instructions, Sanford noticed, clearly a guy who knew the routine, like most vagrants, used to being rousted.

Zarella kept the light aimed at the upper torso as the figure slouched toward him. He noted the ragged shirt, torn collar, the debris that clung from a long, dark beard. "That's it. Real slow now. Keep moving forward." His eyes bore in upon the shadowy figure who moved haltingly toward him. "What the hell," he whispered as the man stepped into the light.

"Keep your hands behind your head!" Sanford shouted.

"Okay, it's all right," Zarella said, calming now, convinced that it was over, that there'd be no further excitement.

Then a woman's scream pierced the stone-dark air, hard and jagged, slicing like a knife through the black vein of the tunnel.

Zarella thought of the frightened woman he and Sanford had left on the path near the pond only moments before. Terrified by what she'd seen, she'd begged one of them to stay with her, but Zarella had decided to accompany Sanford instead, make sure he got in on the action. Now he imagined the woman under attack, the ragged stranger she'd seen and reported suddenly bursting through the undergrowth, grabbing for her throat. *Why,* he wondered as he rushed back through the dark woods and up the embankment to where he'd ordered her to wait. *Why didn't I stay with her?*

7:26 P.M., *September 12, Interrogation Room 3*

"The woman, Smalls," Pierce said. "Did you hear her scream?"

"Yes."

"Did you know why the woman was screaming?"

"No."

"How about Cathy Lake?" Pierce asked. "Do you remember her screams?"

"No."

"Oh, come on, Smalls. You heard them. You know what it sounds like when a little girl screams."

Smalls' lips parted wordlessly. He seemed deeply shaken, as if suddenly overwhelmed by the knowledge of what he'd done.

"You do know what that sounds like, don't you, Smalls?" Pierce insisted.

Smalls glanced at Cohen as if pleading with him to pull Pierce off.

It was the usual reaction to the Good Cop/Bad Cop routine that Pierce and Cohen had established from the first interrogation, but this time Cohen thought he caught something else in Smalls' eyes, a hint of panic, and in that panic a desperate search for a way out.

"What's the matter, Jay?" Cohen asked. He pulled up a chair and leaned his elbow on the table. "What are you afraid of?"

"Everything," Smalls murmured. He looked like a bewildered animal with his leg in a trap, thrashing about desperately even as the cruel reality of its capture settled in.

"Tell me what happened in the park, Jay," Cohen said.

Smalls glanced toward the window, the dark city beyond it. "You want me to confess. You want me to tell you that I did it."

Cohen felt the anguish in Smalls' eyes. "Jay, wouldn't it be better to tell us?"

"It doesn't matter what I say. You're not going to believe me. So it doesn't matter what I tell you."

Cohen glimpsed a drowning man's acceptance of a watery death. "Yes, Jay, of course it—"

Pierce broke in. "Okay, let's go back to when the cops found you in the pipe. The woman screamed, then one of the cops left. The other one stayed with you. And later, the one who stayed with you brought you up to the trail. After a while there were lots of cops around. Flashing lights. You remember all that, Smalls?"

Smalls faced Pierce. "Yes."

"By then we'd found Cathy Lake by the pond and so there were lots of cops around. We brought you up to the pond. You saw her body. You remember all this, right?"

"Yes."

"What else do you remember?"

"That I was in trouble."

"Why did you think that? You hadn't been arrested yet."

"I knew I was in trouble by the way the man was talking," Smalls said. His eye shifted to Cohen. "By the way he said my name."

8:54 P.M., September 1, City Park, Duck Pond

"Smalls," Chief Burke said. "Albert Jay Smalls."

"That's right." Blunt chomped down on a thick cigar. "Only name we found. Written in some of them old books he's got."

"Has he acknowledged that this is his name?" Burke asked Blunt.

"Nope. We found crayons too. Other junk. Nothing to ID the guy though."

Burke glanced toward Smalls, noted that his head was slumped forward. He looked like a captured prisoner, helpless and defeated.

"Anything else, Chief?" Blunt asked.

"Just one thing. Find Pierce and Cohen. Tell them I want to see them."

"Okay," Blunt said.

Burke watched as Blunt lumbered away, a huge figure in his rumpled green raincoat, one of Dolan's men, kept on by Francis after he became Commissioner. Given Blunt's rank incompetence, Burke could think of no reason other than pity over the fact that Blunt's wife, Millie, had been bedridden for years, his daughter Suzy retarded, and that if he were fired from the department, it would be nearly impossible for him to find other employment. Even so, Blunt gave off such a sense of animal stupidity that it was hard to imagine a pity strong enough to keep him on the job.

Pierce and Cohen arrived six minutes later.

Burke glanced at the notes he'd taken from his earlier conversation with the medical examiner. "At this point, it doesn't appear that the child was sexually assaulted. She was strangled. That much is obvious. We also found a length of wire on the path that leads down toward the playground. The girl's body is just down that bank there. Off the trail. Behind a hedge." Floodlights had been strung all around, and in their hard white glare he could make out a small patch of pale flesh. "With that rainstorm a lot of important evidence could have been washed away." Burke looked up into the wet trees, then down the sodden path that led to where the child's body lay. "At this time we can't be sure who she is. But just after seven this evening we received a call from a woman who lives on the other side of the park. She brought her daughter to a birthday party that was supposed to be over at seven. The daughter was supposed to wait for her in the lobby of the building, but when she got there, her daughter was nowhere to be seen. The woman went to the apartment where the birthday party was held. The parents there told her that her daughter left the apartment at around six forty-five and had not come back. The mother went back downstairs and talked to the super. The super told her that he'd seen a little girl standing in the lobby at around six-forty. Then he left the lobby and returned to his own apartment. When he came back to the lobby at around seven, the little girl was gone. The mother says her daughter was wearing a red dress. So is the dead girl."

"Any other way to identify her?" Pierce asked.

"The girl in the park has a bandage on her right hand."

"The mother put that in her description?" Cohen asked.

"No," Burke answered. "So this little girl may not be hers." Again he glanced at his notes. "The mother's name is Anna Lake. She lives at 545 Obermeyer. She said she sometimes brings her daughter, Cathy, to the playground, so when Cathy wasn't waiting at the building, she looked for her there. After that Mrs. Lake circled the block, then went home and called us." He closed the notebook and tucked it into his jacket pocket. "So far we have no suspects." Burke nodded toward the bearded man in the distance. "Unless you count him."

Do you think it's real?

"How long have you lived in that pipe, Smalls?" Pierce asked. "Weeks? Months?"

"A long time."

"And before that?"

"Just places. All around."

"So, you've moved around a lot?"

"Yes."

"Why is that? Is it because you're on the run?"

Smalls lowered his head, as if offering it to the hangman.

"If you're not on the run, then why won't you tell us about other places you've lived?"

"Maybe it's because he's embarrassed, Jack," Cohen said. "Is that it, Jay? Are you embarrassed about being arrested? Don't want the people back home to know about it?"

Smalls gave no answer, but his head lifted slightly so that Cohen suspected he might actually have hit upon something.

"Your dad, maybe?" Cohen asked.

"I don't have a dad."

"Your mother, then," Cohen said. "You don't want your mother to know about you being arrested, right?"

Smalls offered no response.

"That's natural, Jay," Cohen said easily. "A guy never wants to embarrass his mother. You know what I remember most about my mother? Going to the movies. Every Sunday she took me to the movies."

Smalls smiled tentatively. "My mother took me to the Ferris wheel."

Cohen glanced at Pierce, then back to Smalls. "When did she do that?"

"Every day."

Pierce shook his head, and drew Cohen back to the rear of the room. "You're not getting anywhere with this, Norm."

Cohen walked to the door, opened it, and ushered Pierce outside. "Listen, Jack—"

"We have ten hours left," Pierce interrupted. He yanked a handkerchief from his pocket and swabbed his neck. "We don't have time to chat about his fucking mother." He returned the handkerchief to his pocket. "We're in a box here. A tight fucking box."

"Yeah, we are, but maybe we're doing better than you think."

"How you figure that?"

"Because Smalls may actually have given us a little something to work with."

Pierce stared at Cohen.

"The Ferris wheel," Cohen explained. "Smalls says he rode a Ferris wheel every day."

"So?"

"So it had to be permanent, right, this Ferris wheel? Not just coming and going with a carnival or something, but always there."

"Yeah, so what?"

"I'm thinking maybe Smalls comes from Seaview."

"Why Seaview? There are Ferris wheels all over the damn country."

"Yeah, but Smalls doesn't have an accent from some other part of the country. He sounds like a guy from around here. And the fact is, the only place around here that has a permanent Ferris wheel is Seaview. Or at least it used to have one. Remember that amusement park they had there?"

"That's a real long shot, Norm."

"Sure it is, but what do we have to lose?"

"We have ten hours left," Pierce reminded him. "You really think chasing a fucking Ferris wheel is a good use of that time?"

"If we can find out who Smalls is, maybe we can find an outstanding warrant. We could hold him on that warrant. Buy time."

"That's the problem. Time. We don't have time to go chasing around Seaview."

"Not we. You. I can keep at him here."

"You want me to drive to Seaview alone? Ask people if they remember some kid on a Ferris wheel in a park that closed ten, twelve years ago?"

"Yes."

"It's because you think I'm blowing the interrogation, isn't it? It's because you want to get me out of here. That's what all this Seaview shit is about."

"Look, Jack, I don't think we're both needed here at

the moment, that's all I'm saying. We both know the case inside out. Two of us in the same room? What's the point?"

Pierce considered the matter, then shook his head. "Not yet, Norm. I want to go at him one more time. If I don't get anywhere, then I'll go to Seaview."

Cohen knew there was no point in arguing the matter. He turned back toward the interrogation room, then stopped. "You're not coming with me?"

"I think I should cool off a little," Pierce said. "But listen, go at him hard. No more of this Good Cop bullshit. We don't have time for that. So hit him hard. I'll come in and give him more of the same. Like a one-two punch. Maybe we can shake him up that way."

Cohen nodded, then stepped inside the room. He sat in the chair opposite Smalls. For three minutes he let Smalls stew in the silence while he mapped his strategy, decided on just how friendly to be, then just how hard, the way to build the interrogation to a knife point. When he'd plotted the route, tested it in his mind, he leaned forward abruptly.

"Let's talk about the pipe, Jay. You know what I'm talking about, don't you? What they found in the pipe?"

8:55 P.M., September 1, City Park, Drainage Pipe 4

"Holy shit! Look at this."

In the tube of light the pipe had now become, Zarella slogged through the brightly illuminated debris to where Sanford stood, halfway through the length of the tunnel.

"What'd you find, Pete?" he asked as he reached his partner.

Sanford pointed down into the muck. "Look at that."

Zarella felt his stomach heave. "Oh, Jesus . . ."

"Do you think it's real?" Sanford asked.

Zarella looked closer. "I guess it could be."

Sanford bent forward and plucked the single blue eyeball from the sodden leaves.

"Jesus," Zarella moaned.

Sanford gave the eye a gentle squeeze. "Glass," he said. "Like maybe from a doll or something."

They found the rest of the doll seven minutes later at the bottom of a soggy cardboard box heaped with other toys, rubber balls, marbles, an unstrung badminton racket, a rusted cap pistol, a jump rope with one light blue plastic handle.

Sanford shined his flashlight up the length of the pipe, then beyond it. "If that little girl came up that path there, this freak could have seen her from right here."

Zarella turned to see Pierce and Cohen moving toward them.

Cohen surveyed the sides of the drainage tunnel. "Any idea how long this guy was living here?" he asked.

"We didn't question the suspect, sir," Zarella replied.

Cohen stepped closer. The wall was covered with the usual graffiti, but as his flashlight scanned it, something different emerged from the gloom. A small drawing, eight inches by eleven, no more, done with crayon, but remarkably detailed. It showed a girl draped in white, with long dark hair that tumbled nearly to her waist. Her bare arms were outstretched and imploring, as if pleading to be rescued from the tangle of green that surrounded her. Her flesh was pale, her eyes sunken. It was like some vital spark was drained from her.

"Christ," Pierce muttered.

"You think Smalls drew this?" Cohen asked him.

Pierce studied the drawing, his eyes on the terror in the child's face. "If he did, he's one sick bastard," he said.

8:07 P.M., September 12, Interrogation Room 3

"Remember the drawing, Jay?" Cohen said. "The one in the drainage pipe. Of the little girl?"

"Yes."

"She looked like Cathy, remember? Same age. Long dark hair. Did Cathy . . . pose for that drawing, Jay?"

"No."

"But it was Cathy, wasn't it?"

"No."

"Okay, fine, but tell me this. Why did you draw this little girl in that long white robe? I was just wondering how you got the idea to dress her that way. Were you ever around people who were dressed like that?"

"No."

"Never lived in any sort of institution?"

"No."

"All right, but I have to go back to the drawing, Jay. Because the thing is, my partner thinks the little girl in the robe is Cathy. He thinks you had your eye on Cathy. He thinks you'd had your eye on her for quite some time. She played in Dubarry Playground, after all. Not far from the tunnel."

Smalls leaned forward and lowered his face into his open hands.

"Is my partner right, Jay?"

Smalls straightened himself again. "I'd seen her before, that's all."

"Tell about the times you'd seen her."

"I already have."

"Let's go over them again."

"Where do you want me to start?"

"When you saw her."

"The first time?"

"Yes."

"I saw her in the playground, that's all. With other kids. She comes there on Sunday afternoons. With her mother. I've seen her there several times."

"Always with her mother?"

"Yes."

"Okay, but one time you saw her when she wasn't in the playground, right? You know the time I mean, don't you? The one you told us about."

"Yes."

"Tell me about that incident."

"She left the playground."

"And went where?"

"They have some benches. Outside the fence."

"And you were sitting on one of those benches?"

"Yes."

"When was this?"

"A few days before it happened. Before someone . . . hurt her."

"And she saw you, right?"

"Yes."

"Okay, where were you when Cathy saw you?"

"Sitting there. On one of the benches."

"Just minding your own business."

"I wasn't hurting anybody. I was just . . ."

"Watching the children in the playground."

"I wasn't hurting anybody," Smalls repeated emphatically.

"Okay, let's get back to Cathy. This time she left the playground and sat down near you. She was near you, right?"

"Yes."

"How far away would you say?"

"She was on the bench across from me."

"Did you talk to her?"

"No."

"What did she do after she saw you?"

"She didn't do anything."

"She just kept sitting there?"

"Yes."

"For how long?"

"Just a few minutes."

"Then what?"

"She went back into the playground."

"So, why do you think she left Dubarry Playground in the first place, Jay?"

"Maybe there was a man. Like I said before. A man in the playground."

"Some guy who scared her."

"Yes."

"Because this guy was creepy, or something like that."

"Yes."

"And so Cathy left the playground and went and sat on a bench outside the fence and that's where she ran into you, right?"

"Yes."

"And that's the closest she ever came to you?"

"Yes."

"So she was never in the tunnel with you, Jay?"

"No."

"Okay, where did Cathy go after she left the bench where you saw her sitting?"

"She went back to the playground."

"Why would she do that if she'd left it because some creep had scared her."

"Maybe he was gone, the . . . creep."

"What did you do after she left?"

"I went to the playground. There's a little hill that looks down on the playground. I sat there."

"On the ground?"

"Yes."

"How long did you sit there?"

"Few hours, I guess."

"That's a long time."

"I wanted to see him. I told you that."

"The man who'd scared Cathy."

"Yes."

"You wanted to spot this guy."

"Yes."

"Why, Jay?"

"So I'd know who he was."

"Why would you want to know that?"

"So I could watch him."

"Watch him," Cohen repeated. "Watch this guy."

"Yes."

"The fact is, you've been seen hanging around the playground quite a few times, right, Jay?"

"I need to keep an eye on the children."

Cohen had heard this before, but now he thought of a way of turning Smalls' answer back toward him, pressing it toward his guilt like the tip of a blade. "An eye on the children. You keep a protective eye on the children in the playground?"

Smalls looked at Cohen warily, like a man who'd suddenly felt an invisible noose tighten around his throat. "I know you don't believe me."

"Well, you have to admit, it's a little hard to swallow, Jay. I mean, you got this guy hanging around Dubarry Playground. He's creepy enough so that he scared Cathy Lake. But the thing is, nobody but you has ever mentioned this guy. Why do you think that is, Jay? Don't you think that if a lone man were hanging around the playground, someone besides you would notice him? Think about it. You got all those mothers who sit there, watching their kids on the swings and monkey bars. Don't you think one of those mothers would have noticed some creepy guy in the playground?"

"I guess."

"But no one did, Jay. No one noticed this guy you think maybe scared Cathy. But there was a guy people did notice. That guy was you, Jay. Several mothers identified you. We showed them pictures, and they picked you out as a guy they'd seen in the playground."

"I never go in the playground."

"That's right, you don't. But you hang around it, don't you? You sit on that hill and you watch the children, isn't that right?"

"Yes."

"Why do you do that, Jay? Why do you hang around that playground?"

"I told you. Because they're all in danger."

"Yes, they are in danger, Jay," Cohen said. "They're in danger of you."

"No, not me." Smalls shook his head firmly. His voice took on a strangely inconsolable tone. "I wanted to save her."

"Cathy Lake?"

"Yes."

"Okay, let's say that's true, Jay. You wanted to save Cathy. Cathy in particular, right?"

"Yes."

"But why Cathy Lake in particular? You must have seen other little girls in the park all the time. But you noticed Cathy, didn't you, Jay? You noticed her in particular. And you knew that if you noticed her, someone else might notice her too."

"Someone did," Smalls said in a pinched voice.

"This other man that no one else noticed," Cohen said, recalling the many hours he and Pierce had wasted trying to find anyone else who'd seen a man in the playground, a man who'd "noticed" Cathy Lake. "We tried to find this guy, you know. We asked everyone we could find. The cops who patrol the park and the playground. The people who bring their children there. No one noticed anyone but you hanging around the playground, Jay."

"Cathy noticed him. She was scared of him."

"Okay, let's talk about the day Cathy was murdered. You saw her that day too, didn't you?"

"She was running away. It was raining, and she just ran by."

"But you saw her, right?"

"I told you I did."

"And you recognized her as the little girl you'd seen. Before."

"Yes."

"What was she wearing that day?"

"A dress. Red."

"Was she wearing a cap?"

"No."

"A scarf?"

"No."

"Did you notice anything else about her?"

"She had a bandage on her hand."

Cohen leaned back slightly. "All that from a glimpse?" His tone was mildly accusatory. "That's a lot to notice, Jay. I'll bet you noticed that she was wearing something around her neck. You said she wasn't wearing a scarf, so you must have been close enough to see her throat, right? So, was she wearing a locket?"

"No."

"But if she were running, it would be flopping around, wouldn't it?"

"I don't know."

"Well, we know Cathy was wearing a locket that day. We know she wore it on the outside of her dress, not tucked in. And we know that someone took it from her."

"Not me. I never saw a locket."

"How could you not have seen it if you saw everything else?"

"I don't know."

"You saw it, didn't you, Jay?"

Smalls curled back in his chair and dropped his hands into his lap. "No, I didn't. I never saw a locket."

Cohen nodded. "Okay, let's go on. It starts to rain. You left the alley beside Clairmont Towers and headed for your pipe, right?"

"Yes."

"It's raining real hard. Everybody's rushing to get out of the rain, right?"

"Yes."

"You know it's possible that Cathy just wanted to get out of the rain too. I mean, she was at a schoolmate's birthday party that afternoon. We know that when she left the party she was supposed to wait for her mother in the building lobby. But Cathy didn't do that. Instead, she left the building and went over to the park entrance. What we don't know is why she went into the park, or what happened to her after that. So let's say it starts to rain, okay? Cathy starts looking for a place to get out of the rain, and maybe she spots the tunnel and she figures she can go in there and wait for the rain to stop." He leaned forward. "So, did Cathy come into your tunnel, Jay?"

"No."

"But it was raining. She needed to get out of the rain. It's a logical place for her to have gone, don't you think?"

"She never came into the tunnel."

"Okay, Cathy was just walking along, then, let's say that. She was just walking along, not paying any attention to things around her. Not even the rain. You know how kids are, right, Jay? It's not always easy to get their attention, is it?"

Smalls gave no answer, but Cohen noticed a subtle flinch in his lusterless eyes, as if he'd just been jabbed with a needle.

"Jay, have you ever tried to get a kid's attention?"

Smalls said nothing.

"I mean, you have an interest in kids, right? Hanging around playgrounds, that sort of thing. Don't you ever want to talk to a kid?"

"I don't talk to them," Smalls said.

"But you want to, don't you? You want to . . . get close to a kid."

Something in Smalls appeared to collapse slightly, like a man who'd suddenly recognized his own pathetic hollowness.

"I know how you could get a kid's attention, Jay," Cohen said. "You could throw a ball. Near a kid, I mean. We found a few rubber balls in all that stuff you had in the tunnel. You could just toss one of those balls over near a kid and ask the kid real nice to bring it back to you. Have you ever used that trick, Jay? Did you use it on Cathy? Did that happen, Jay? When Cathy came down the path, did you toss a ball at her, and did she notice it, and did she bring it back to you?"

"No."

"Think now, Jay. Think of this little girl running

down the path. The girl in the red dress. The one you'd watched before. You see her coming down the path, and so, to get her attention, you throw a ball."

"I didn't throw a ball," Smalls said fiercely.

"That's what happened, isn't it?" Cohen asked evenly, his eyes leveled on Smalls. "You saw Cathy and you . . . got her attention."

"No," Smalls answered sharply.

"And after you got her attention, you did something to her, didn't you, Jay?"

"No."

"Did you want that locket, Jay?"

"No."

"A pretty silver locket to go with the rubber balls and the toys?"

"I never saw a locket."

"Then what did you want from Cathy?"

"I didn't want anything."

"But you got scared, didn't you? Cathy wouldn't let you have her locket. Or whatever it was you wanted. She resisted you. And you got scared when she fought back. And so you killed her."

"No, I didn't."

"And after that you took the locket."

"I didn't take anything!"

"What was it, a souvenir? Is it because a guy who kills a little girl maybe wants a little souvenir?"

Smalls stared at Cohen in silence, clearly disturbed by what he'd just heard, studying Cohen intently, as if trying to see into his brain, determine exactly what information it contained.

But why was Smalls disturbed, Cohen wondered as he studied Inmate 1407. Was it because the accusation was absurd? Or was it because in a scattershot of dreadful charges, he had hit upon a truth?

8:18 P.M., *Police Headquarters, Sixth Floor Lounge*

"You break that bastard yet?" Blunt asked as he lowered himself onto the worn brown sofa.

Pierce shook his head.

Blunt lit a cigar and tossed the match on the linoleum. "I heard you got till morning or he walks."

"That's right."

Blunt pulled a handkerchief from his jacket and wiped his face. "They bake us in this fucking place." He stared about, seeking relief, then said, "A little kid, for Christ's sake."

"Anna Lake's daughter," Pierce said, and suddenly he was at Anna Lake's door as it opened to his knock, standing, oddly stricken, by the terrible question in her eyes: *Is my daughter dead?*

9:34 P.M., *September 1, 545 Obermeyer Street*

He'd known that he would soon give her the answer she dreaded, and after that, nothing would ever be the same.

"Are you Anna Lake?" he asked.

"Yes."

He reached into his jacket pocket and withdrew the badge. "My name's Pierce. Jack Pierce. This is my partner, Norman Cohen."

Cohen nodded but didn't speak.

"May we come in, Mrs. Lake?" Pierce asked.

"Miss," she said. "I'm not married." She drew open the door. "Have you found her?"

"We found a little girl," Pierce told her softly. "She was in the park. We're not sure it's your daughter."

"Why didn't you ask her?"

"I'm afraid we couldn't do that," Pierce said.

Anna Lake's face tightened. "Is my daughter dead?"

"We don't know if the girl we found is your daughter," Pierce said. "That's why we're here. To find out."

With no further word, Anna led them into the living room. "Please, sit down," she said, indicating a dark blue sofa.

Pierce sat but Cohen walked to the window and peered out into the chill autumn darkness. Anna Lake sat opposite Pierce, her eyes fixed steadily upon him.

"The little girl we found, she was wearing a red dress," Pierce told her. "You said that Cathy was wearing a red dress."

"Yes."

"Did she have a bandage on her right hand?"

Anna Lake's face grew very still. "Oh, God." She stopped as if by a wall of pain. "It's her, then."

Pierce expected her to sink her face into her hands the way Jenny had when he'd told her about Debra. But instead Anna remained upright, her face eerily still.

"We need a positive identification, Miss Lake," Pierce said after a moment.

"Yes," Anna Lake replied. "Of course." She rose and walked into an adjoining room, closing the door softly behind her. When she returned, she was wearing a black wool coat. "All right. I'm ready."

Outside the morgue, Pierce opened the car door. Anna Lake got out, and as she did so, her eyes touched him—or at least that was how it felt—not that they settled upon him, he thought, but that they touched him, like fingertips.

"This way, please," he said, directing her toward two wide metal doors.

"I'll stay here," Cohen told him, avoiding the morgue as he had since returning from the war, the cold air inside it, the stainless-steel refrigerators, knowing that the good thing he sought would never be found there.

Pierced nodded, then motioned Anna forward.

She followed him into the morgue, moving briskly, like someone determined to get the next step over with.

"Down here." Pierce led her along a brightly lit corridor to where the ME had already placed the small body on a gurney and draped it with a sheet. He stepped over to the gurney. "Are you ready, Miss Lake?"

She nodded stiffly, her eyes leveled on the covered profile.

Pierce drew back the sheet.

Anna shuddered, as if hit by a small jolt of electricity. Then she stepped closer to the gurney and pressed her hand against the dead child's cheek. "Cathy," she said softly. "Cathy." She bent forward and lifted her daughter into her arms.

Watching her, Pierce recalled how his wife had cradled a picture of Debra for days, even sleeping with it through long, tearful nights. Then he thought of Costa, who had caused Jenny such pain, then of the nameless vagrant who'd been found lurking near the duck pond only yards from the body of Cathy Lake, a man who lived like an animal, by means of animal cunning, passive in arrest but predatory, a vagrant in a crudely painted cave littered with smashed toys, peering out at the path that wound among the trees.

"I'm sorry," he said.

Anna Lake's brown eyes lifted toward him. "What will you do with her now?"

"There'll be an autopsy. Then she can be released to you."

"I want to bury her quickly," Anna said. "I don't want her . . . like this."

"I understand."

She pressed her lips to her daughter's dark brown hair, then returned the body gently to the cold steel of the gurney.

Pierce began to draw the sheet back over the girl's face, but Anna stopped him. She took the cloth from his hand. "Let me cover her," she said, and then, with what seemed to Pierce an otherworldly grace, she did.

In the car five minutes later, Pierce and Cohen drove Anna Lake back to her apartment on Obermeyer Street through a light rain, the measured thud of the windshield wipers beating softly in the silence. Through the watery glass, Pierce watched the city streets in an agony of remembrance, trying to focus on the work at hand, what needed to be done to find Cathy Lake's killer, but returning instead to Costa, his release, the sneer in his voice as he'd thanked the judge "most kindly" for unleashing him once again upon the children of the world.

"We'll find the man who did this," Pierce said. "Won't we, Norm?"

Cohen nodded.

"I'll need to ask you a few questions, Miss Lake," Pierce told her when they reached the door. "Of course, I know you need a little time to—"

"No, I don't need any time," Anna interrupted. Her voice didn't waver. "If I can help you, I want to do it."

"You mean now?" He thought of Jenny, how Debra's death had drained her of that very energy he could see building now in Anna Lake, driving her forward, as if they shared the same purpose, sought justice laced with vengeance with the same dark need.

"Yes." She opened the door and flipped on the light. "Come inside, please."

8:23 P.M., *September 12, Police Headquarters, Sixth Floor Lounge*

We'll find the man who did this.

The promise circled in Pierce's mind as Blunt pulled himself heavily from the sofa with a loud grunt. "Well, good luck cracking that fuck," he said as he lumbered out of the room.

Pierce took a restless draw on his cigarette before he crushed it in the chipped glass ashtray on the table. He could feel himself revving up for his last round of interrogation. Round, yes, like he was going into the ring, determined to defeat an opponent in a game of combat with strict rules and established time limits. He would have another round with Smalls, then if nothing came of it, he'd drive to Seaview and see what he could dig up.

He made his way down the corridor, concentrating on this final confrontation, thinking of Anna Lake, of how, for her, he had to make it work. The clock at the end of the corridor was silent but relentless, the seconds falling like stones, burying him. He opened the door and noted with pleasure the way Smalls looked up and shrank away from him. Fear, he decided as he stepped into the room, that must be his tactic. He would scare Albert Smalls to death.

Do you have to leave me here?

Cohen nodded slightly as Pierce came through the door. "All yours, Jack." He rose from the chair and stepped away from the table.

Pierce swept into the empty chair as if on a wing of fire. "Look at this, Smalls," he snapped. He drew a photograph from his jacket. "This is Catherine Lake. She was eight years old. She was murdered eleven days ago. In the park. By the duck pond. The path she took through the park went right by where you were . . . what . . . sleeping? Isn't that your story? That you were sleeping in that drainage pipe?"

"I was asleep."

"A woman found her," Pierce said hotly. "A young woman who was walking near the pond. Do you remember that woman, Smalls? The woman who found Cathy Lake's body? We told you about what she saw in the park on the night of September first. Eleven days ago. Let me tell you what she saw."

8:32 P.M., *September 1, City Park, Duck Pond*

She saw a figure, ragged and unkempt, scuttling across the shadows of the path just as she rounded the long curve at the southern tip of the duck pond, and for a moment Nancy Lisbon stopped and simply watched as the figure lumbered along the edge of the path for a few yards, then wheeled around to face her so that she saw his features clearly beneath the streetlamp, noted the snarled beard, the leaves and dirt that clung to it. For reasons she didn't quite understand, she remained still, resolutely facing the filthy, bedraggled creature who peered at her from a distance of thirty feet.

He stared at her, motionless, like some animal frozen by her gaze. Then he began to undulate in a curious slithering motion that sent a chill through Nancy Lisbon, turned her around as forcefully as a hand, sent her racing back at a dead run around the duck pond, panicked and gasping, until she saw two uniformed patrolmen and told them what she'd seen.

"He scared me," she told Zarella. "Like a snake scares you."

"Okay. Show us where you saw this man."

Lisbon led the two officers back down the path, darkness closing in around them, lacing the trees in complicated shadows. On the way, she thought of the figure who'd confronted her on the path and knew absolutely that she would never again walk in the park, that this good, healthy, relaxing thing had been stolen from her forever.

"Right there." She pointed to the curve in the path. "Just beneath the light. That's where he came out of the bushes. Then he started moving in that weird way."

"Where did he go after that?" Sanford asked. "Did you see?"

"He walked along the edge of the path," Lisbon answered.

"How far down the path?" Zarella asked.

"I don't know . . . ten yards maybe."

The two cops headed down the path together, past where Lisbon had first seen the bearded man, then ten yards beyond it to a break in the shrubs.

"About here?" Zarella asked her. "This is where he stopped?"

"Yes. He stopped and turned back toward me," Lisbon replied. "That's when I got scared."

"Okay," Sanford told her. "Just stay here on the path for a minute. We'll go take a look, make sure this guy's nowhere around."

"Do you have to leave me here?"

"Just for a couple of minutes," Zarella assured her. "We'll come back right away and escort you out of the park."

Lisbon nodded stiffly. "Please, hurry."

"If you see this guy again," Zarella told her, "yell for us and we'll be back in a flash."

"Yeah, thanks."

She watched as the two patrolmen walked down the path, turned to the right at the spot where she'd told them the bearded man had slid off into the brush. Alone now, with nothing but the light from the streetlamps to pierce the darkness, she felt her fear steadily building, a chill wave that rose like water around her, lapping first at her ankles, then rising higher and higher. *Come back*, she pleaded silently. But the officers did not return, and in their absence she began to shiver in the autumn darkness.

Then suddenly, a voice broke the silence, and she gasped.

Someone was calling in the distance, words clear and firm and full of warning.

Don't move.

Lisbon stepped backward, as if shoved there by a protective officer, told to get down, take cover.

The voice sounded again, still harsh in stern command.

Stay where you are.

Lisbon adjusted the thick glasses she wore and peered out into the darkness, listening intently to the distant voices.

Put your hands on your head.

Get to your feet.

Okay, real slow now.

She stepped back and felt something coil around her ankle. She jerked her foot from the ground, shaking at the coil, then lost her footing and tumbled backward, twisting helplessly to the right, knees buckling as she keeled sideways through the shrub, cleaving the branches until her body finally thudded hard onto the ground.

Keep your hands above your head.

She sucked in a quick breath and realized that her glasses had fallen off. She reached out, blind now, in a universe of smudged glass, and felt something hard but pliant, like a thick, soft root.

Keep your hands above your head!

In the blur, she dragged herself forward, her hands clasped to the tapered shaft until she felt a soft, rounded knob. She pressed down on the knob and lifted herself to a sitting position.

Now move forward slowly.

In the blackness she could see nothing. She fumbled along the earth until she found her glasses, then, turning back toward the root, put her glasses on . . . and screamed.

8:31 P.M., *September 12, Interrogation Room 3*

Pierce felt the flame leap triumphantly in him as he glared into Smalls' pinched eyes. "You remember all this, don't you? The woman who saw you on the path? The one who screamed?"

"Yes."

"Why did you threaten her?"

"I didn't."

"That move you made. What was that?"

"I didn't know what to do."

"You didn't know what to do? What does that mean?"

"Maybe I should run. Maybe I should just stay where I was. I couldn't tell what to do. I was afraid."

"Afraid? Of a little woman like that. That's real hard to believe, Smalls. Unless you had a reason to be scared of her. But you did have a reason, didn't you? You were scared of her because you didn't want her to get close, right? Close to you or close to the body of the little girl you'd murdered. What were the toys for? The ones we found in the pipe. Where did you get them?"

"I found them."

"Found them? Where did you find them?"

"Dumpsters."

"Why did you want to have toys?"

"To sell to Dunlap, sir."

"Yes, you told us that before."

"It's the truth."

"Yeah, when you first came up with that story we thought it might be the truth, Smalls," Pierce said. "So we went over to Dunlap's place to check it out . . . and guess what we found?"

9:00 A.M., September 2, Dunlap's Collectibles, 217 Cordelia Street

Pierce peered through the dusty glass. Inside the store, he could see a chaos of colored bottles, rusted tools, shoeboxes overflowing with yellowing photographs and old postcards. "What a shit-hole. You know the guy who runs this place?"

"Harry Dunlap," Cohen said. "The name rang a bell, so I looked him up. Turns out he was a fence until he got hammered pretty bad."

"What'd he get?"

"Three years. Out in a year and a half. He was released about five years ago."

Pierce continued to stare through the window. "And since then?"

"Clean, as far as I know."

Pierce stepped over to the door and rapped hard.

A few seconds later a short, stocky man pushed through a beaded curtain at the rear of the store. He was dressed in flannel trousers and a stained blue sweatshirt with frayed sleeves and a collar that looked as if it had been stretched by angry hands.

"That him?" Pierce asked.

Cohen nodded. "Yeah, that's Harry."

Dunlap opened the door, rubbing his eyes against the morning light.

"I ain't open till ten," he whined.

Pierce presented his identification. "We need to ask you a few questions."

Cohen smiled. "Remember me, Harry?"

Dunlap's small green eyes cut over to Cohen. "What's this all about?"

"A few questions," Cohen said easily.

"Questions? About what?"

"About a murder," Pierce said crisply.

Fear leaped into Dunlap's eyes. "A murder? Oh, Jesus, I ain't—"

"A little girl was killed, Harry," Cohen interrupted. "So, you don't mind if we come in?"

"I don't know nothing about no murder." Dunlap wiped a line of sweat from his upper lip. "A little girl. Jesus."

Pierce took out a picture that had been taken of Smalls the night before. "Have you ever seen this guy?"

Dunlap glanced at the photograph. "No." He looked at Cohen as if they were old associates, someone who might cut him a break. "Should I?"

"He says he sold you some toys," Cohen said.

"Toys?" Dunlap said. He tried to laugh, but it turned into a snigger. "Look around here. This look like a toy store?"

"Well, maybe he just offered to sell you some stuff," Cohen said. "Are you sure you've never seen him, Harry?"

Dunlap returned his attention to the photograph. "No, I ain't never seen him. Dirty-looking bastard like that, I'd remember, don't you think?"

"Could he have come into the shop when someone else was here?" Pierce plucked a postcard from a box, peered at it absently.

Dunlap handed the photograph back to Cohen.

"Nobody runs the shop but me." He tried for a joke. "What do I look like, General Motors?"

"What about when you go out buying things?" Cohen asked. "Nobody watches the place for you?"

"People bring stuff here," Dunlap answered. "I don't go out looking for it. What'd you say the guy's name was again?"

"Smalls." Pierce returned the old postcard to the crowded box. "Albert Jay Smalls."

Dunlap's hand rose to the black stubble on his jaw. "I wish I could help you. A little girl. Jesus. But I ain't never heard of the guy. I mean, the name, it ain't familiar."

"Well, the thing is, the guy's heard *your* name, Harry."

Dunlap's eyes widened. Terror covered them like a film. "Me? He's heard of me?"

Cohen nodded. "Your actual name, Harry. He came up with your actual name."

Pierce drew away and moved among the shelves of junk, eyeing the old bottles, the rusty car tags, a debris that suggested nothing but a shop whose entire stock was composed of things other people wished only to be rid of.

"He didn't mention anybody else," Cohen said, giving Dunlap a little taste of his icy stare. "Just you, Harry."

Dunlap glanced toward Pierce, then back at Cohen. "Is this a shakedown? 'Cause I ain't done nothing to deserve no shakedown."

"Shakedown?" Pierce asked.

Dunlap kept his eyes on Cohen. "You know what I mean."

"I'm afraid I don't, Harry," Cohen told him.

"A way of looking my place over without no warrant," Dunlap said cautiously.

Pierce picked up a handful of brightly colored marbles from a tin bucket. "What would we be looking for, Harry?"

"I don't know," Dunlap said. "Anything."

"Stolen property, is that what you're referring to, Harry?" Cohen asked with a slight smile.

"You got me once," Dunlap said. "I did my time on that bust. But I ain't got nothing here. Nothing . . . illegal. And so you ain't got no . . . what you call it . . . no probable cause."

"Sounds like you been hitting the law books, Dunlap," Pierce said.

Dunlap looked at Cohen imploringly. "I'm just making a point here. I don't want no trouble."

Pierce rattled the marbles back into the bucket. "So, you're sure you never had any dealings with this guy?"

Dunlap shook his head firmly. "Never. You know why? 'Cause a bum like that comes into my store, I'd figure him for a shoplifter." He glanced from one detective to another. "Know what I mean? A guy I'd keep an eye on."

"The little girl was wearing a locket," Cohen told him. "Heart-shaped. Silver. Whoever killed her took it with him. If it happens to turn up, I'd expect a call."

"Yeah, sure . . ."

"We'll be in touch," Cohen said. He turned toward the door.

"Just make sure you have a warrant next time," Dunlap chirped lightly.

Pierce wheeled, grabbed him by the shirt, and slammed him into the wall, pressing hard against him.

"Don't fuck with me, Dunlap," Pierce snarled. "A little girl is dead."

Cohen grabbed Pierce's shoulders. "Come on now, Jack. Jack—you've made your point." He drew Pierce backward, his eyes on Dunlap sternly. "I am right about that, aren't I, Harry? My partner has made his point, hasn't he?"

Dunlap adjusted his rumpled sweatshirt. His brow gleamed with perspiration. "Yeah, sure, he made his point."

Cohen studied Dunlap's doughy face, looking for some hint of conscience, but found only the usual animal rapacity, force the only thing this man would ever understand. "Because if you hold out on us, we'll come back in a real bad mood," he said.

Dunlap nodded briskly. "Yeah, okay."

"A *real* bad mood," Pierce said threateningly, then turned on his heel and slammed out the door.

8:43 P.M., September 12, Interrogation Room 3

"So, according to Harry Dunlap, you never sold him anything," Pierce said. "Harry Dunlap swore he'd never even seen you, heard of you, nothing."

"He's lying," Smalls insisted.

"No, you're lying, Smalls. You're lying about Dunlap. You never sold him a fucking thing. Toys or anything else. Look at me, Smalls. You collected those toys because you intended to use them to lure some little kid over to you. Isn't that right?"

"I never lured anybody."

"Oh, for Christ's sake," Pierce snapped. "Stop lying to me!"

Cohen stepped forward, placed a firm hand on Pierce's shoulder, a silent signal that Pierce was making no progress.

Pierce nodded reluctantly, giving in to Cohen's conclusion. He shoved his chair back, walked to the door of Interrogation Room 3, glanced back, and in that instant saw something glimmer darkly in Smalls' eyes. He had seen the same glimmer in Costa's eyes. Because of that he knew without the slightest doubt that Smalls was concealing something terrible, the murder of Cathy Lake. He started to speak, but he knew whatever he said would be a threat, so he said nothing more.

Once outside the interrogation room, Pierce took the stairs two at a time down to the garage, passing the Criminal Files Room, a single light burning inside the room. There, hunched over a table, he saw Chief Burke. He went inside.

"I wanted to let you know that I'm going to Seaview."

Burke looked up from the files. "Why?"

"Cohen thinks Smalls may have come from there. It's possible we could find something. An outstanding warrant or something we could use in the interrogation."

"It's not going well, then?"

"No," Pierce admitted. "So far, Seaview is our only lead. The rest is just the same crap we've been getting for the last eleven days."

Burke nodded. "Seaview, then."

Pierce knew he was being dismissed. "Yes, sir."

Moments later he drove out of the garage. A hard right on Madison took him around the southeast corner of the building. Most of the offices were closed now, the lower floors steeped in darkness.

At Trevor, he turned and headed toward the river, the bridge rising in the spectral mist before him. In his mind he saw Costa's body float toward it, swirl in the tidal eddies, then come to rest beneath it, bumping softly—as he knew it had—against the mossy ramparts. The body had been discovered by a passing tugboat captain the following morning, dragged on board with a grappling hook, and left to lie on the cold, wet deck until the police arrived to claim it. He could easily recall the look in the Commissioner's eyes as he'd told him of Costa's death. *Perhaps, Jack, there is some justice in this world.*

The ramp to the bridge rose in a wide loop, and at its highest point Pierce saw all the city spread out before him, the businesses and apartment houses, the stadium, the convention center, but it was the park that drew his attention, the shadows where he could still see a child's body lying faceup on the dead grass, a vision that brought back the day they'd found Debra in almost the same condition, fully clothed but in every other way horribly disheveled, her hair matted with blood, her dress wrinkled, dirty, the red velvet bracelet torn from her wrist so that nothing but the steel brace she wore on her right leg seemed still in place, its chrome sheen glinting softly in the dappled light of the culvert where she lay. Had he known rage until that moment? he wondered as he drove across the bridge toward Seaview, this consuming anger that shook him like an earthquake and whose aftershocks, despite Costa's death, still trembled inside him, cracking the hard, dry ground upon which he worked to rebuild his life? He thought of Anna Lake, and the fire that ceaselessly licked at his heart died slightly. Was that what he sought more than vengeance now, he asked himself, the cool, restoring water of this woman's love?

8:58 *P.M.*, *Criminal Files Room*

Chief Burke closed the Catherine Lake file, waited a moment, then opened it again, determined to read it through a third time . . . *go over everything again.*

And so he read the police dispatcher's record of Anna Lake's first call to Police Headquarters, this time focusing on the description she'd provided of her missing daughter.

Catherine Augusta LAKE (CAL) Eight years old. Four feet tall, 54 pounds. Dark brown waist-length hair.

Last seen wearing red dress with puffed sleeves, black shoes, a heart-shaped silver locket. Mother (Anna Lake—AL) dropped CAL off at Clairmont Towers, 490 Clairmont Street. Child to attend a birthday party in Apartment 5-G. When AL came to pick child up at 7:00 P.M., CAL was not waiting in the lobby of 490 Clairmont Street. AL questioned building superintendent, who said he saw girl fitting CAL description in lobby of building. Superintendent called away, and when he returned, the girl was no longer in lobby. AL proceeded to Apartment 5-G. Mrs. Loretta Kraft reported that CAL had left Apartment 5-G at approximately 6:45 P.M. APB issued for CAL at 7:47 P.M.

AL advised of this action, 7:48 P.M.

AFAP

AFAP. All Further Action Pending.

It was the Commissioner who'd ordered that this designation be included at various stages of any police investigation, and for Burke it added an unsettling tone to an otherwise matter-of-fact record.

In the case of Cathy Lake, AFAP meant that no further action would be taken until someone spotted Cathy wandering alone, took her hand, and led her to the nearest police precinct. If no one noticed Cathy, then a search would begin, all further action pending until she was found. And if she were found, then there would be no further action until her whereabouts for the missing hours could be ascertained. Had the child merely wandered away or gotten lost, all further action would be suspended until it could be known whether, during the course of her absence, she had been harmed by anyone. And if she had not, Cathy Lake would be returned to the custody of her mother. No further action pending . . . ever.

The door of the Criminal Files Room opened.

" 'Evening, Tom."

"I didn't expect to see you back here tonight," Burke told the Commissioner.

The Commissioner idly scanned the long rows of police files. "So, has there been any progress?"

"Not so far. Pierce is on his way to Seaview. He thinks Smalls may have come from there."

"And if he did?"

"Pierce is hoping to find something we can use. Either to keep Smalls in custody, or to help with the interrogation."

The Commissioner frowned. "I'd hoped for some sort of break. Clearly, there hasn't been one."

"Not yet, no."

"Which puts me in a difficult position." The Commissioner took a seat opposite Burke and leaned forward. "Since it looks like this last interrogation isn't going to go any better than the earlier ones, we have to think about what we're going to do with this fellow to make sure he doesn't kill another child in this city."

Burke said nothing.

"You know what I mean?" The Commissioner asked it pointedly.

"You want me to kill him, Francis?" Burke answered.

The Commissioner scowled. "No, Tom, I don't."

"When he's released, I could put a man on him."

"Surveillance? For how long? The rest of his life?" Grimly, the Commissioner shook his head. "Imagine how the Mayor would react to that budget item. One whole police officer doing nothing but following a bum around town making sure he doesn't kill some little girl."

"I don't know what else we can do. Once Smalls is released, he's free to go wherever he likes."

"Yes, he is." The Commissioner looked at Burke regretfully. "Remember Tara?"

Tara. Commissioner Dolan's name for the concrete shed where certain men, the suspects Dolan designated as incorrigible, were taken for what the old Commissioner called "correction." It was a place without windows, a brutal square of concrete covered by a piece of corrugated tin. There was no desk inside it, no chair, not even so much as a naked bulb. Dolan had designed it that way, designed it to demonstrate by its bareness the desperate nature of the case, the fact that the time for interrogation had come to an end. There would be no more questions or answers, no more coffee or cigarettes, no more cat-and-mouse games with the suspect. In Dolan's shed there was room only for the brutal application of raw force.

The only trouble, Burke remembered, was that a visit to Tara didn't work on men who were too self-destructive to be reached by fear or pain, men so mired in self-hatred, so hungry for punishment, they actually relished the beatings they underwent in Dolan's shed, men who took the worst you could give them and swallowed it like honey, spit their broken teeth into your face and grinned. Men like Scottie, Burke thought, recalling his son's degraded habit of getting drunk in Harbortown bars, insulting sailors and dockworkers twice his size, provoking them to the beatings they were more than happy to provide.

"Find a way, Tom, that's what I'm saying," the Commissioner said. "You have to find a way to keep this fellow locked up." With that he rose and exited the room.

In the silence that followed, Burke returned to Case File 90631, the murder of an eight-year-old girl with long dark hair. He saw her stroll obliviously toward her doom. In the autumn light, her hair rippled gently across her narrow shoulders. He heard the pad of her feet along the trail she'd taken that evening, then a second set of footfalls, closing in behind her, slowly at first, then faster as the festering urge broke free. A rustle in the wet leaves, one body upon another, the whimper and the gasp. A pair of hands snatched a gleaming silver locket, and it was done, no further action pending in the life of Cathy Lake.

9:03 P.M., *City Park, Drainage Pipe 4*

Terry Siddell stopped dead twenty feet from the pipe. "I don't like this."

"You don't have to like it," Eddie Lambrusco told him. "You just have to clean it."

"I don't want to go in there."

"Yeah, well, you got to," Eddie muttered. He moved toward the pipe, then noticed that Siddell remained in place. "What's the matter with you?"

"This is where that guy was living," Siddell reminded him. "The one who killed the little girl. I read about it in the paper. Strangled her."

Eddie thought of Laurie, the only little girl who mattered to him. He shoved all the others from his mind. That was how you had to think about it. Take care of your own kid and forget the rest. "Let's get to work." He took four steps forward, then stopped and looked back.

Siddell remained motionless.

"You know this kid or something?" Eddie asked.

Siddell looked offended by the question. " 'Course I didn't know her."

"So what's the big deal? You take care of your own, you don't let nothing else bother you." He waved his hand. "Come on."

Siddell did not move. His eyes remained fixed on the tunnel.

Watching him, Eddie concluded that rich kids were mostly gutless. If they didn't control things, they got scared. But none of that mattered since in the end Terry Siddell would control plenty. He would control Siddell Carting for one thing, and by that means he would also one day control Eddie Lambrusco. Eddie found this thought so troubling, he refused to dwell on it and so directed his attention to the immediate matter at hand.

"Bottom line, Terry, we got to clean this place up. So let's just get to it. Okay?"

Once again, Siddell didn't move. "I'm not going in that tunnel."

Eddie stepped toward him, ready to argue the matter, but a sudden glint in Siddell's eye stopped him cold. The look was sharp and pointed, like a fang, and Eddie knew exactly what it meant: *Get the fuck out of my face, you worthless shit, or when I take over, you'll be out on your ass!*

He stepped back. "Look, Terry, we don't have no choice in this thing. Your father made that real clear, right? We got to do it, otherwise I get fired."

Siddell stared at something in the tunnel, his eyes fixed upon it with a dark intensity.

"What are you looking at?" Eddie asked.

When Siddell gave no answer, Eddie turned, shined his light into the pipe, and saw for the first time what Siddell had glimpsed in shadow. A crayon drawing of a girl, her thin body draped in a white robe. He peered closely at the face but didn't recognize the features.

Who is this kid? he wondered. Only one thing was clear. Something was wrong with her. Terribly wrong. There was no light in her eyes. Her skin was pale and bloodless. There was no luster to the skin nor any movement in her limbs.

"She looks dead," Siddell said.

Dead.

Eddie thought of Laurie, how he'd never forgive himself for not being at her side when she got sick, for letting work come first, though he had to work, so that in the chilling silence and the darkness, there seemed no way to do the right thing, no ground a man could stand upon between fatherhood and survival, no way to support a little girl and not take something precious from her life.

PART II

You remember what we found?

Cohen took off his jacket and draped it over the chair, watching Smalls as he did so. A shadow of a man, he thought, skeletally thin, pale. Not ghostly, because a ghost, having lived, had a certain substance, the accumulated residue of a life. Smalls had nothing of this sort. He floated emptily, like no experience had ever stuck to him. Without the weight of that experience, he seemed feathery, something the most tremulous puff of air could sweep across the floor.

Every aspect of Smalls' character gave off this willowy insubstantiality but one. His steadfast denial that he'd had anything to do with the death of Cathy Lake. On that issue he had demonstrated the impenetrably opaque surface of a granite slab. Beneath that slab, enclosed in adamantine secrecy, Cohen was certain that something shameful lay hidden. He could see its guilty shape swimming behind Smalls' eyes like a fish in a tank of murky water, swift and unreachable, well-adapted to the shadowy depths.

But during the forty minutes since Pierce had left for Seaview, Cohen had failed in every attempt to bring Smalls' sunken guilt to the surface. He'd gone over all the people who'd seen Smalls in the park, hammered him with details, darted from this witness to that incident. He'd told him about talking to the Krafts, the people who'd hosted the birthday party Cathy had attended, then everyone at the party, all the parents who'd later arrived to collect their children, and that none of them, not one, could possibly have had anything to do with Cathy's death. He went through all the other stages of the investigation—the interviews with school friends, teachers, the search that had been made for any suggestion that someone might have been stalking Cathy before her murder or had any reason to do her harm, the fruitless search for the man Smalls claimed to have "scared" Cathy Lake, a search that had yielded so little, the man himself had been dubbed "invisible." All of that professional, by-the-book labor, wearing out the shoe leather, covering all the bases . . . and nothing.

During all this time, Cohen had gone over the course of the investigation with Smalls in precisely the way Pierce had wanted it, fast and furious, throwing out the time line, coming in at a slant, dodging, weaving, slashing, but at the end of it Smalls had remained unshaken, repeating again and again that he had done no harm to Cathy Lake.

For all his frail appearance, Cohen thought, Albert Jay Smalls was smart, clever, and so far he'd slithered out of every trap they'd tried to catch him in.

Even so, he might yet stumble, and for Cohen, this constituted the final hope of the interrogation, the possibility that Smalls might slip. He would never willingly swallow the bait, but he might yet be hooked.

And so Cohen decided to abandon his earlier method of interrogation in favor of one that allowed for the unexpected emergence of seemingly inconsequential facts. This was a noose that could be drawn in slowly, almost invisibly, until it was tight enough to squeeze the truth out of Albert Smalls.

But where to begin? Cohen wondered. He decided to press the simple fact that Smalls had not been randomly plucked from the park and brought to police headquarters.

"You know, Jay, we talked to a lot of people about Cathy," Cohen began. "About her murder, I mean. We didn't just pick you up and bring you in for no reason. And even after we brought you in that night, we didn't stop looking for other people. We did a full sweep, Jay, a full sweep of the park early the next morning after those first cops found you in the pipe. I was there for the sweep, so I know we looked for other people. Chief Burke made sure of that."

4:37 A.M., *September 2, City Park, Central Field*

Burke stood silently before the ranks, erect and full of authority, the pose required of him at such a moment. He well understood that his men did not look forward to carrying out the order he was about to give. There was a world no one wanted to see. It existed in the nether regions of the park, a realm populated by people broken beyond repair. This world was lit by fires made from slats and burning tires, and around those pathetic hearths, as Burke had too often seen during his years on the force, the lost ones huddled in their intractable misery, all ambition or desire reduced to the cindered hope of being left alone.

"When you go into the park," Burke told his men, "remember that although some of these people may be criminals, the vast majority have done nothing but"—he did not utter the phrase that pierced his mind—*but fall beneath the blade.* Instead, he said, "Most of them have done nothing of a criminal nature." He let his eyes drift over the uniformed officers who stood in ranks before him, then to the few plainclothes detectives who were to accompany them through the park. He noticed Detectives Pierce and Cohen just off to the side. Pierce in his dark suit, shouldering his daughter's death, and so perhaps the perfect choice, Burke decided at that instant, to track down the man who'd ripped Catherine Lake from her mother's care.

"It is unlawful for anyone to be inside the park after midnight," Burke continued. "But this is not a roust. We are not here to make arrests. We are not looking for vagrants tonight. We are looking for a murderer, someone who killed a child here in the park at approximately seven o'clock last night. We are also looking for something he might have taken from this child. A small necklace."

He stopped, waited for questions, continued when there were none.

"The locket on the necklace is silver, in the shape of a heart. It was on a short silver chain. You are to search for this locket as thoroughly as you deem necessary. Any questions? All right. Proceed."

And so they moved, the blue lines fanning out along the far perimeters of the park, then closing in, step by step, upon the unsuspecting men and women who lived, for the most part unseen, within it, sweeping down deserted lanes and under the stone bridges that arched over them, the soft beat of their footfalls drumming through the melancholy dark. Quietly, methodically, the officers pried the park's bedraggled inhabitants from beneath shrubs and out of boxes. They called them from their muttering sleep and urged them out of drainage pipes and from the woody culverts where they lay balled like infants, clinging to the roots of trees.

Once brought to their feet, the vagrants were gathered into groups of five and escorted to the center of the park, a strange, straggling herd that staggered meekly beneath the dripping trees to the designated place of concentration.

Here the men were assembled in ragged, shifting lines, then searched one by one. The officers said little to the men they searched; they rarely looked them in the eye. The method had long been established, and the officers followed it meticulously, explaining briefly that someone had been murdered, something stolen in the process, something they were looking for now in pockets and waistbands and the frayed cuffs of filthy trousers, spilling what they found onto the wet grass so that after a time curious pools began to grow at the feet of the derelicts and drunks and madmen who now stood, dazed and murmuring, a mounting detritus made up of half-gnawed crusts of bread, the milky remains of ice cream cups, wine bottles, cigarette butts.

Watching all this, Burke recalled how, at a similar sweep five years before, he'd seen Scottie stagger out of the ragged column, so thin and wizened, he'd looked more dead than alive. For a moment, Burke and his son had stared mutely at each other. Scottie had made no attempt to distinguish himself from the rest, nor had Burke intervened. They had simply faced each other during the search Burke's men were conducting, and when it was over, both had turned and walked away.

But this time Scottie was not among the vagrants, and once Burke was sure of that, he felt a curious relief wash over him, followed by a dread no less terrible. *If not here,* he wondered, *where?*

Within an hour it was over. The park's inhabitants retrieved what they wanted from the debris at their feet, then scrabbled back into the secret recesses of the park.

Burke waited until the last of them had disappeared into the misty wood and the officers once more stood before him. "Thank you," he told them. "You may go."

The policemen broke ranks immediately, and as they did so, Burke motioned for Pierce and Cohen. "I'd like the two of you to be in charge of this case," he said when the two detectives joined him.

Then he turned and walked away.

9:44 P.M., *September 12, Interrogation Room 3*

"That's when Detective Pierce and I were assigned to the case, Jay," Cohen said. "That night in the park. We've been trying to figure out what happened to Cathy ever since."

He remembered how he'd watched the helpless vagrants stagger into the ball field, and imagined his own people marched through narrow European streets and herded together in rain-soaked village squares, the trains already waiting in the distance. Had they been as faceless to their guards, he wondered, as the derelicts in the park's gaseous mist had been to him? Never again, he decided abruptly, never again this particular duty.

"Anyway," he continued. "For all that work we didn't find anything that morning. We took a few men in and questioned them, but we couldn't find any reason to believe they were connected to Cathy's murder." He waited for Smalls to respond, and when he didn't, cleared his throat. "And so we had to take a closer look at you, Jay. Do you know why? Because of all the people in the park, you were the only one who lived near the duck pond. You'd had contact with Cathy. Recognized her. And there was more. Those toys you had. Plus, you were spotted just a few yards from where her body was found." Again he waited for a response; again, Smalls offered nothing. "But even more important, we know that you were also near Cathy *before* she was murdered. Not just after she was killed, when the woman saw you. But *before* she was murdered. You know how we know that, don't you, Jay? You remember what we found?"

9:30 A.M., *September 2, Clairmont Towers,* 490 Clairmont Street

Pierce rapped resolutely at the door.

It opened seconds later. A short, stocky man stood in the doorway, absently picking his teeth with a wooden matchstick.

"What can I do for you?" he asked.

"Homicide." Pierce pulled out his badge. "You're Herman Getz, the building superintendent?"

"Yeah."

"I guess you know the Krafts?"

"Sure. They've lived here for ten years. Maybe more."

Pierce pocketed his shield. "They had a birthday

party for their daughter yesterday afternoon. One of the little girls who attended the party was murdered in the park yesterday evening."

"Jesus." The man's lips fluttered around the matchstick. "I heard a kid got killed. So that was the kid, I guess. The one her mother came looking for. The kid was supposed to wait for her in the lobby, she said."

"But she didn't wait for her," Pierce said. "Evidently she went to the park. We don't know why."

Getz shrugged. "Me neither."

Cohen surveyed the soiled wool shirt, rumpled trousers, and bare, unpolished shoes. Had Getz gotten up that morning with the idea of making himself as undesirable as possible, he could not have assembled a more fitting wardrobe.

"When did you see the little girl in the lobby?" Pierce asked.

"About a quarter to seven. She was standing close to the door. Long hair, right?"

"Yes," Pierce said.

"I just went through the lobby. On my way out. Because there was this guy in the alley next to the building. There's an overhang back there. Bums use it sometimes. A roof over their heads, you know? Anyway, I chased the bastard off."

"What did he look like?" Cohen asked.

"Ragged," Getz answered. "Beard. A bum, like I said. I went over and gave him a nudge with my shoe, told him to be on his way. He got up and done what I told him. Didn't give me no trouble. Just got to his feet, walked away."

"Where did he go after he left the alley?"

"Back to the park. That's where he lives, I bet. Anyway, he crossed the street and stood over there by the gate. Sort of leaning against it."

"He didn't go into the park?"

"Don't know. I went back inside."

"Was the little girl still in the lobby?"

"Yeah, she was." Getz nodded. "Standing right at the door, just like before."

"Was anyone else in the lobby?"

"No."

"And that was the last time you saw the girl?"

"Yeah, it was. I went through the lobby again about ten minutes later. It was raining like hell by then. Anyway, on the way out I didn't see the kid, so I figured her mother picked her up."

"Did you see anybody else in the lobby?"

"Just Mr. Stitt. He was—" He stopped.

"What?" Pierce asked.

"He was . . . straightening stuff up. Chairs and stuff. It looked like things had been tossed around a little." Getz glanced about furtively. "Look, we got all kinds in this building, you know. I wouldn't want to get nobody in trouble."

"What *kind* is Mr. Stitt?" Pierce pressed.

"He's . . . well . . . he's . . . He plays the horses, that sort of thing."

"A bookie?"

"Yeah, okay, but, look, I can't . . . I mean, I can't go telling stuff on people in the building. I'd lose my job, I started doing that."

Cohen presented a reassuring smile. "We're homicide detectives, Mr. Getz. We're looking for a guy who killed a little girl, nothing else. And if this Mr. Stitt was in the lobby when you say he was, he might have seen something."

"Okay, but don't say it came from me," Getz said, lowering his voice. "That Mr. Stitt was in the lobby, I mean. What he does. None of that came from me, okay?" He glanced about. "Apartment 14-F. That's where Stitt lives. Burt Stitt."

"Thanks," Cohen told him.

Seconds later Pierce and Cohen stood at the door of Apartment 14-F.

Pierce knocked once, then called, "Police! Open up."

The door swung open instantly. A tall, gaunt man stood before them, black hair swept back and greased down, a narrow mustache across his lip. His cheeks were sunken, like his eyes, and there was a slick snail-like quality to his skin, the sense that wherever he went, a slithery trail followed behind.

"Burt Stitt?" Cohen asked.

"Yeah."

Pierce and Cohen presented their shields.

"Homicide," Pierce told Stitt. "We're looking into the murder of a girl in the park yesterday."

"What's that got to do with me?"

"May we come in?" Cohen asked.

Stitt shrugged. "Sure, okay," he said indifferently. "But I don't know nothing about a little girl."

Pierce gave the room a quick perusal, taking in the things that told him most about Burt Stitt, the racing form on the sofa, the cheap detective novel on the floor, a torn ticket stub from a nearby strip joint. But more than these, Pierce noticed the things that weren't in Stitt's apartment. There were no family photos, no dining table, no chair that didn't face the radio. The absence of such things told Pierce that Stitt ate alone, with the plate in his lap, had no memories that meant anything to him, no wife or children he hadn't lost touch with long ago.

"We understand that you were down in the lobby yesterday evening," Cohen said. "Around seven."

Stitt nodded. "That sounds about right."

"Did you happen to see a girl in the lobby at around that time?"

"Eight years old," Pierce added. "Long, dark hair."

Stitt considered this. "Yeah, I remember a kid in the lobby."

"What else do you remember?" Pierce asked.

"I don't remember nothing else. Just some kid. That's all. Like you said, a little girl. Hair down to her waist. Dark."

"Did you notice anyone else in the lobby?"

"No."

Pierce leveled his gaze on Stitt. "Do you remember straightening up the place?"

Stitt smiled. "Yeah, sure. I was straightening up a couple of chairs. But that didn't have nothing to do with that kid I seen. I mean, she was just standing in the lobby when I came in. Looked like she was waiting around for somebody. Anyway, she didn't have nothing to do with them chairs being all thrown around."

"What did happen in the lobby, Mr. Stitt?" Cohen asked.

"A tussle, that's all," Stitt answered. "I had a tussle with this freak who followed me into the building. Bum. Most of them, they leave you alone. They ask for a handout, and if you say no, they take no for an answer. But not this guy. He went nuts. Tossed a chair right at my face. Screaming his head off."

"Where was the little girl during all this?" Cohen asked.

Stitt thought a moment. "She was there when it started, but then, I guess she left. Maybe she got scared."

"Okay, the guy you had the fight with? What did he look like?"

"A bum, like I said."

"You can do better than that."

"Not by much. I was too busy getting rid of the bastard to pay much attention to him. He was white. I can tell you that much. Twenty-five, thirty, somewhere in there. Shorter than me by maybe four, five inches. Skinny as hell."

"Do you remember what he was wearing?"

"What they all wear, baggy pants, some old ragged jacket smelled like piss. Bum clothes."

"Where did he go?"

"He just left the building. Turned right, I think. Yeah. To the right."

"What did you do after the argument?" Cohen asked.

"Nothing. I mean, straightened the place up, like you said. Then I went upstairs."

"Did you ever see this guy again?"

"No," Stitt answered promptly. "Never seen him before neither. Just a bum, like I said. A panhandler."

"There was a bum hanging around in the alley at about this time. The super chased him off. Could this have been the same guy?"

Stitt shook his head. "Nah. I know the guy you mean. I've seen him in the alley a few times. The bum who came at me was bigger than him."

"Okay, well, if you do see the guy who attacked you again, let us know," Cohen said.

"Yeah, sure," Stitt said.

Pierce gave the room a final glance, found the look of it uncomfortably like his own place, then followed Cohen out the door.

On the street, they stood, facing the park, the iron gate that led into its emerald depths.

"Cathy got scared," Pierce said. "Two guys yelling, one of them throwing things. Any kid would try to get away from something like that." He continued to stare at the gate. "But why did she go into the park, Norm? She could have just stood by the gate, watched for her mother. Why did she go into the park?"

"Maybe he went after her," Cohen answered, knowing it was sheer supposition. "The guy who threw the chair at Stitt. Maybe he came across the street and she saw him and she ran away from him into the park."

"But what about the other guy, the one Getz chased out of the alley?" Pierce turned back toward the alley that bordered Clairmont Towers. "If he were still at the gate, he would have seen Cathy cross the street at seven. He might even have seen if the other guy was after her, followed her into the park."

They walked to the alley in the hope that the man Getz had chased away might have returned, but they found only the deserted overhang and clumps of sodden newspapers that had been gathered into what resembled a bed.

Cohen peered beneath the overhang. In the murky light he saw a crayon drawing of a young girl, her body draped in white, long dark hair falling to her waist.

"Look at this, Jack," he said.

Pierce settled down upon his haunches.

"It's the same picture we found in the tunnel," Cohen said. "That bum we questioned last night."

"Questioned and let go," Pierce said. "Smalls."

They reached the tunnel six minutes later, but Smalls was not there. And so they waited, sitting on a wooden bench, the duck pond and Dubarry Playground distantly visible through the surrounding trees. An hour passed, then another. It was approaching noon before they saw him.

"Look," Cohen said, pressing his elbow into Pierce's side.

They got to their feet and watched as the man continued toward them. He was dressed in the same rags he'd been wearing the night before, and as he walked he peered left and right into the underbrush as if expecting someone to leap out of them, seize him by the throat. He was only a few feet away when he saw Pierce and Cohen rise from the bench. He stepped back fearfully, then stopped and waited as they came toward him.

"Albert Smalls?" Pierce asked.

The man nodded.

Pierce flashed his badge. "Mind coming with us?"

"No."

They led him back up the path to Clairmont Towers, then into the building and back to the apartment of Herman Getz.

"Is this the man you saw coming out of the alley yesterday afternoon?" Pierce asked Getz.

"Yeah, that's him," Getz said without hesitation.

Pierce took Smalls' wrists, brought them behind him, and cuffed them together. "Did you kill Cathy Lake?" he asked Smalls. "The dead girl we found in the park yesterday?"

"Was that her name?"

"Yes, that was her name," Pierce said impatiently.

"No. I didn't kill her."

Pierce grasped Smalls' arm and guided him forward. "Okay, come on. I want to show you something."

9:59 P.M., September 12, Interrogation Room 3

"And we led you back down to the tunnel, Jay," Cohen reminded him. "And I showed you that picture you'd drawn on the wall. The picture of a little girl. And I told you that we'd found the same picture in the alley by Clairmont Towers. You told us, Pierce and me, that you'd drawn both of those pictures. The one in the tunnel and the one in the alley. You admitted that right away."

"I drew them," Smalls admitted again. He peered at his hands as if he wished to be rid of them.

"And so we didn't let you go, Jay," Cohen told him. "Not like we did that first night when the woman saw you. Do you know why we didn't let you go? Because we found those two drawings in two different places. Places that made it clear to us that you'd been near Cathy at the time of her disappearance, and that you'd also been near the place where we found her. Still with me here?"

Smalls continued to stare down at his hands. "Yes."

"We arrested you," Cohen continued. "And since then we've been coming to talk to you, asking you questions. And during the time you've been with us, Detective Pierce and I have shown you a few things, right? Like the wire we found on the path between Cathy's body and the playground. And we've had other people come in and take a look at you. In a lineup, I mean. And one of those people identified you right away as the man she'd seen near Cathy's body."

"I scared her," Smalls said quietly.

"Yes, you did." Cohen wondered if it might actually be working, if coaxing out small, seemingly inconsequential admissions might finally lure Smalls into a trap he couldn't weasel his way out of. *Careful*, he thought. "You remember telling me that when Cathy came to the bench a couple of days before her murder, that maybe she was real scared of this guy who hangs around the playground?"

"Yes."

"How about the time in the rain? Two days before the murder. When you saw Cathy in the rain. Could she have been scared of somebody then too?"

"I don't know."

"Look, Jay, at some point Cathy leaves the building where she'd been at a party. She walks across the street and she stands at the gate at the entrance to the park. You saw her there. You told us that."

"Yes, I saw her."

Slow, Cohen thought, *very slow.* "Okay, and if Cathy saw you, she probably recognized you too, right? Maybe she nodded hello, something like that, smiled. Gave you some sign that she had seen you before. Did Cathy do that, Jay?"

"No."

"But why not? I mean, if she'd seen you before, wouldn't she naturally have given you some indication of that when she ran into you that day?"

"She didn't see me that day."

"Of course she did, Jay. You were standing right there, right by the gate. She had to have seen you."

"No. She didn't."

"Look, Jay." Cohen took a notepad from the windowsill near the table, turned to a blank page, drew a gate, then a building, and finally a line from one to the other. "You were here." He put an X by the gate. "Cathy was here." Now an X by the building. "She came this way." He drew the point of the pencil down the straight line from the building to the gate. "See what I mean, Jay? Cathy came directly toward you. She had to have seen you."

"No, she didn't."

"Why not?"

"Because she was looking behind her."

"Behind her? You mean over her shoulder?"

Smalls' eyes narrowed, like someone struggling to bring a blurry image into focus. "Yes."

Cohen saw the scene, Smalls leaning against the park gate, Cathy emerging from the building into cold sheets of rain, glancing over her shoulder as she made her way toward the park, glancing back toward . . . what?

"Why would she have been glancing back toward Clairmont Towers, Jay?" he asked.

Again Smalls appeared suddenly to grasp a detail that had previously escaped him. "It's terrible the way they look," he said, his voice very low.

"The way who looks?"

"Kids. When they're afraid."

"Are you talking about Cathy?"

"She looked afraid. When she was coming across the street." He considered something a moment, then said, "In prison, they kill them, don't they?"

"Kill who?"

"The ones who . . . hurt children."

Cohen felt a chill. "Sometimes," he answered softly.

Smalls nodded resolutely. "Good," he said. "They deserve it. And the ones who let them get away. They deserve it too."

"The ones who let them get away?" Cohen repeated. Was this Smalls' way of taunting him, mocking the fact that after ten days of interrogation neither he nor Pierce had made any progress? "They never get away with it, Jay," he told him, though he knew that he believed no such thing.

"Yes, they do," Smalls replied firmly.

"How do you know that?"

Smalls gave no answer, so Cohen supplied one of his own. They got away because there was no method of capturing them save the flawed and desperate one he and others like him used to find the guilty and put them away. They got away because at the critical moment a witness had heard a glass break, turned toward that sound, and missed the figure in the brush. They got away because knives and guns were washed clean by the indifferent rain. They got away because time ate memory and maggots ate flesh, and nothing worked to preserve the footprint in the melting snow or the tell-tale drop of blood. They got away because nothing in the spinning void gave the slightest assistance to those who sought to bring them down. The war had brought him to this grim conclusion, Cohen knew, but how, he wondered, had Smalls arrived at this same unloving place?

Is there some news?

10:37 *P.M., Seaview*

The lights of Seaview blinked from the enveloping darkness, and as he closed in upon the town, Pierce could smell the musty brine of the sea. He'd grown up in Englishtown, a riverfront village nearly fifty miles away, but as a young man he'd often come to Seaview, and he recalled now the long, lazy summer afternoons he'd spent strolling its crowded boardwalk. He'd met Jenny on one of those afternoons, and as he entered the outskirts of town, he thought of that first encounter, her quietness, how shy she'd been. At first he considered it a flirtatious pose. But later he understood that instead, it was the outward demonstration of her inner fragility. More than anything, that was the difference between Jenny and Anna Lake, he realized. In the latter, he'd felt something solid at the core. What more could he want in a woman, he wondered, than this firm ground, someone the wind could not tear, nor the tide sweep away, someone who'd fallen into the same abyss and with whom he could claw his way out again?

And so now, as he proceeded on, he recalled that firmness, the direct look in Anna's eyes when he'd shown up at her apartment three days after her daughter's murder, standing alone in the bleak hallway, not at all sure why he'd come, save that in this grieving woman he'd sensed someone with a steely capacity to endure whatever life offered. He'd seen all of that at the moment she opened the door, both the depth of her wound and her will to heal it.

5:30 P.M., September 4, 545 Obermeyer Street

The door opened and she stood, facing him, her gaze unflinching. She wore a plain green dress with narrow sleeves, and she'd pulled her long hair back and wound it into a bun. She drew her arms around her as she waited for him to speak.

"I'm Detective—"

"I remember you," she interrupted. "Is there some news?"

"No," Pierce replied. "I just wanted you to know that we still have him in custody. The man we arrested two days ago."

"Has he said anything?"

"No. They never say much at first. But in the end, we'll get it out of him."

He wanted to add something, a word of consolation, but what would that word be? How could he help her find peace when he had not found it himself? When he could not so much as imagine some future moment when Debra's murder no longer tore at his soul, releasing the unquenchable rage that drove him now.

"Thank you," Anna Lake said. "For coming by."

He felt he should leave, put on his hat, turn, and leave. He didn't. Instead, he remained, facing her, his hat in his hand, wanting to probe the curious serenity he saw in her eyes, needing to know if it might be something she could help him find.

"Would you like to come in?" she asked unexpectedly.

"I know you're . . . I mean, I wouldn't want to . . . bother you."

"You're not bothering me. I just got home from work. My first day back."

He followed her into the apartment, noticed that the door to what had once been Cathy's room was closed. He'd searched that room the day following the murder, Anna silently watching as he and Cohen went through her daughter's few possessions. They'd not really expected to find anything but had followed the established rules of investigation anyway. Even little girls had enemies, the rule book said, so they'd looked for letters, diaries, a name doodled somewhere. In pursuit of this phantom clue, they'd pawed through Cathy's desk, leafed through her school notebooks. Outside, a small brown dog had scurried along the sidewalk, raced behind a tree, spun heedlessly in the autumn air, things that Cathy Lake would never do again.

That had been the moment, Pierce recalled now, the exact instant when Cathy Lake had risen from the crowded shore of doomed children to become the singular and irreplaceable little girl she had surely been. He glanced toward her closet, the dark space where her spare wardrobe hung, clothes to play in and go to church in, clothes for all the changing seasons she would never know, clothes which, in their lifeless droop, could only suggest other clothes she would never wear, a graduation gown, a wedding dress. All of that was gone, as she was gone, this child who would never feel rain, sunlight, a warm summer breeze, this little girl whose smile would never lift anyone's spirits or change an ordinary day into something infinitely blessed. She would never toot on the little plastic trumpet she'd placed beside her bed, nor tap on the toy typewriter on her desk, nor rearrange the furniture in the doll house on the floor. She would never whisper "I love you" to her mother, or to a husband, or to the child she might have borne. Every sound, every touch, every motion of this once living little girl was now locked in stillness and silence, destined only for decay.

"Would you like a cup of coffee?" Anna asked him now.

"No. Thank you."

She sat down on a dark blue sofa beside the window. Pierce took the chair opposite her. He noted the plain dress, the ordinary shoes, the bobby pins that held back her hair, and in all of these things saw the humble nature of her life. Her deepest hope, her greatest ambition, he thought, had been nothing more than to keep and protect her daughter. When you had wished for so little, and lost even that, what was left but rage? And yet he saw nothing of his own smoldering resentment in this woman's eyes.

"I haven't gone out," she told him. Her smile was thin as rain. "For anything. I don't have anything to offer you. Cookies. Nothing."

Pierce glanced around the apartment. He knew how bare and lifeless it now seemed to her. For it was gone, all of it, abruptly and forever gone, the love and delight once added by a child. His eyes fell upon a white uniform that hung by a wire hanger from one of the doors.

"I'm a waitress," Anna told him. "I used to bring Cathy a piece of coconut pie when I came home from work. Coconut custard. That was her favorite." She glanced toward her daughter's room. "I'm giving all Cathy's things away."

Pierce saw Cathy Lake's face materialize beneath the delicate features of her mother. So it was with murdered children. They didn't elbow their way into your stranded consciousness—they bled into your entire helpless being. They never stopped reaching for you, crying for you. They crawled back into the safety of your sheltering arms and lay curled there, dead.

"Except for a few little . . . reminders," Anna continued. "You know, her first drawing. That sort of thing. The rest I thought someone else might use, so I'm going to take it down to the Salvation Army. That's where I bought most of it anyway, so it seems the right place to take it back."

So quickly, Pierce thought. So different from the way Jenny had clung tenaciously to the last thread of the last sweater their daughter had ever worn. She had kept Debra's room a shrine, so that in the end Debra's murder had consumed each memory of the child, spotted every photograph and stained every garment with her spilled blood, a need to hold on to everything Debra had ever touched that had finally become so obsessive, it lashed at him with a relentless cruelty. *Find that bracelet, goddammit, Jack. What kind of cop are you? Can't you at least do that?*

Pierce drove this from his mind and asked Anna Lake, "I was wondering about Cathy's father."

"Why?" Her eyes met his steadily.

"We need to check on everyone who was close to the . . . to your daughter. Not that he would have . . . It's routine."

"I don't know where he is," Anna replied. "But if you found him and asked him about Cathy, he wouldn't know who you were talking about." She answered the question he didn't ask. "Soldier. It was the uniform, I suppose. Anyway, I never looked him up after that . . . one night." She looked at Pierce closely. "Are you from the city?"

"I lived there before the war," Pierce answered. "Then I moved to Englishtown." It came out before he could stop it. "My daughter was murdered too. That's why I came over. To let you know that I know what you're . . . what it's like."

He had come to listen to her story but told his own instead, told Anna Lake how Debra had gone to a playground with friends for a Fourth of July cookout. At some point she'd left the group. No one knew exactly when or why. She'd not been seen again until her body was found in a culvert a hundred yards away.

"The guy who killed Debra lived in our neighborhood," Pierce said. "His name was Costa. Nicolas Costa. He had a long record of . . . being interested in children."

A local car mechanic, Pierce went on, who'd lived in the neighborhood for years, an ordinary man whom no one would have thought capable of murder. He stopped there, left out the macabre museum that had been found in Costa's basement, photographs of dead children, hundreds of children, in bloated files and taped to his basement walls.

He shrugged, embarrassed. "My wife couldn't stand living in our house anymore, our neighborhood. So she moved back to the Midwest. The little town she came from. That's when I came back to the city." He saw his small apartment, furnished with nondescript furniture, no pictures on the walls, a boxy radio endlessly droning. "I guess I wanted to keep busy."

"And the man? What happened to him?"

"He went free," Pierce answered. "There wasn't enough evidence to . . . stop him."

A silence fell between them until Anna said, "I usually take a walk before dinner."

On the street, they strolled through the chill air, an unmistakable intimacy gathering around them as though, for all the crowds and the bustle, the city had emptied suddenly, and they now walked its streets alone.

"What was she like?" Anna asked. "Your Debra."

Pierce realized that he had not actually spoken of Debra in years. "She was brave," he answered. "She had polio. Wore a metal brace on her right leg. But she took it really well. Gutsy. Smart. She'd won the spelling bee in her class. We wanted to get her something. She'd mentioned this little bracelet. Red velvet. With a piece of purple glass in the middle. So we got it for her, an award. She was wearing it the day she was murdered. Costa took it for a souvenir." Costa's face appeared in Pierce's mind, his eyes peering ratlike out of the shadows, not a man really, but a predator who'd felt no more for Debra than a fetishist feels for a high-heeled shoe, something to be used, then tossed aside. "I can't stop hating him," he blurted. "I can't stop . . . hating."

They walked on through narrow streets until they reached the harbor where, in the distance, Pierce could see the wharf from which Nicolas Costa had tumbled drunkenly into the water.

"He's not going to get away with it," Pierce had assured her, renewing with added determination his earlier pledge. "The man who killed Cathy. I promise you he won't."

But now, eight days later, as Pierce closed in upon Seaview, he was no longer sure that he could keep his promise. For days he'd tried to find some fragment of physical evidence that would nail Smalls, or, barring that, some way to break him. But neither effort had brought fruit, and now one effort seemed no less doomed to failure than the other. So what will I tell her? Pierce asked himself as he pulled into the parking lot of Seaview Police Headquarters a few minutes later. *What do I tell her if Albert Smalls goes free?*

10:42 P.M., September 12, Police Headquarters, Sixth Floor Lounge

Ralph Blunt's great bulk appeared wreathed in smoke as Cohen entered the lounge.

"Christ, Ralph," Cohen said, batting a billowing cloud away.

Blunt shifted the cigar over to the left corner of his mouth and dropped another card on the solitaire tableau he'd spread across the scarred table. "You break that bastard yet?"

Cohen poured himself a mug of coffee and slumped down opposite Blunt. "No. Sometimes I think he's about to crack, then he clams up."

"Fucking pervert," Blunt sneered. His small eyes squeezed together. "Give me five minutes with the fucking bastard and he'll tell you the whole goddamn story."

Cohen had no doubt that this was true. He'd seen Blunt in action, the brutal gleam in his eye when he threw a punch.

"Five minutes," Blunt boasted. "That's all I'd need."

It was the tough-cop swagger Cohen had always detested. But it was also the style that seemed most natural to men like Blunt, and so the only way to talk to them at all was to change the subject.

"It's sort of late for you to be hanging around headquarters, isn't it?" Cohen asked.

"Commish asked me to stick around."

"The Commissioner. Why?"

Blunt shrugged. "Didn't say." He slapped another card onto the table. "So how come you stopped drilling the bastard?"

Cohen sipped the coffee. "I'm letting him take a breather. Or maybe I'm just taking one for myself."

"Fucking freak, that guy. Is he a faggot?"

"I don't know."

"Looks like a faggot."

"Tough as nails in some ways though," Cohen said. "You ever grill a guy like that, Ralph? A guy you just couldn't get to?"

"Had a retard once. Couldn't get shit out of him."

"This is different."

"So I hear."

"Sometimes I think he wants to confess but just doesn't know how. Like it's buried so deep he can't dig it up himself."

"Bullshit." Blunt smacked another card down. "He's a freak, that's what he is. When the kid wasn't fucked, I knew it'd get weird. It's worse when the kid ain't fucked." He stared at the card a moment, then peeled another from the deck. "A guy who fucks a kid, that's just your average scum. But a guy who kills a kid he ain't fucked, that's a guy you can't never figure out."

Cohen knew that for Blunt, this amounted to a philosophical insight, though he had no intention of pursuing it. "The Chief still around?" he asked.

"Yeah, he's around." Blunt released a burst of foul smoke. "You hear about his kid? Found him in the gutter over on Cordelia five, six days ago. You knew he was a dope fiend, right?"

"I knew he had problems."

"Chief's all shook up about it."

And how, Cohen wondered, could a primitive like Ralph Blunt possibly know anything about the complicated inner life of such a man as Thomas Burke?

"He goes over to Saint Jude's," Blunt went on. He squinted down at his cards. "Every night since they picked up his kid."

"How do you know that, Ralph?"

"My cousin lives over on Cordelia. Told me he's seen the Cap coming out of Saint Jude's every night for the last few days. Always looks shook up, so my cousin says."

"Sounds like this cousin of yours is really in the know."

Blunt's eyes chilled. "What's that supposed to mean?"

"Just that he provides information to the police," Cohen replied, amazed at how sensitive the inferior were to imagined slights, how swiftly they rankled at the slightest suggestion of their vast inadequacy.

Blunt laughed. "Anyway, you ask me, talking to that bastard you got in there won't never do you no good."

"You may be right, Ralph." He glanced at the clock, and the room grew smaller, its walls pressed in by the vise of time. He gulped the last of the coffee and stood. "Take it easy, Ralph."

"Yeah," Blunt muttered. He flipped a card and stared glumly at the lengthening tableau. "Good luck."

Cohen glanced back as he left the room. *If they ever round us up again,* he realized, *it'll be men like Blunt who show up at our door.*

You're desperate, then?

10:58 P.M., Seaview, Police Headquarters

Pierce had never been in this particular building, but the look of it did not surprise him. There was the battered desk at the entrance, the overweight sergeant behind it, thumbing through a magazine. To the right, double doors opened to what Pierce assumed to be administrative offices, while just on the other side of the room, a single door was marked Records. A worn staircase led to the second floor, and there Pierce knew he'd find the shower and locker rooms, equipment offices, interrogation rooms, and, at the center of it all, a detective bull pen with a scattering of what at this hour were no doubt unmanned desks.

"Can I help you?" the sergeant asked.

"I hope so." Pierce drew out his badge. "Jack Pierce."

The sergeant closed the magazine.

"We had a murder in the city a few days ago," Pierce told him. "An eight-year-old girl. We think the guy we have in custody may have come from here. He doesn't have a record as far as we've been able to dig up, so I need to talk to somebody who knows the town. Not necessarily a cop, just somebody who's been around."

"That would be Sam Yearwood," the officer said promptly. "He worked for the local paper all his life. Knows as much as anybody about Seaview."

"Where would I find him?"

"He spends a lot of time at the Driftwood Bar." The sergeant pointed out the window to where coils of blue neon shone dully from the ocean fog. "Usually sits in the back. You can't miss him. A real old guy. Always reading some book."

Across the street, the Driftwood Bar crumbled in a murky gloom. A few old cars formed a line along the curb in front, but the streets themselves were silent and deserted, with nothing but the steady beat of the nearby surf to orchestrate the night. Everything looked as if it had been discarded years before and was now merely waiting to be hauled out to sea.

Pierce crossed the street with a determined stride, Anna Lake foremost in his mind, the promise he'd made to her, the growing fear that he would not be able to keep it, the ticking clock loud in his brain.

He stepped into the bar, and the air turned red. To his right, a swirl of neon tumbled downward in a hellish boiling wave. The air was so thick with smoke, Pierce could barely make out the hunched figures who sat at the long wooden bar or the scattered tables that rested in the sawdust on the floor.

None of the bar's patrons glanced up at him as he entered, and the murmur of their conversation continued without interruption as he angled around chairs and tables until he finally glimpsed Sam Yearwood in the back booth.

Through the smoke, Yearwood appeared bleached pale, his skin a dead white, more ghost than man. A crumpled black hat perched on his head, the brim lifted and swept back like raven's wings. His cane dangled precariously from the edge of the table, ticking rhythmically, like a clock's ruthless pendulum, at the urging of the pale, bony fingers.

"Sam Yearwood?"

The old man's eyes rose from the open book, ancient and forlorn, mirroring what they'd seen, storm and shipwreck, fire and flood and children swept from sunny beaches by rogue waves and angry currents.

"My name's Jack Pierce." He showed his badge. "I'm looking for a killer."

The old man nodded toward the bar's other patrons. "Take your pick." His voice had the quality of gnarled wood. He brought a glass of bourbon to his lips, drank, set it down. "Talk."

Pierce slid into the booth across from Yearwood. "We have a man in custody for killing an eight-year-old girl. He says his name is Smalls. Albert Jay Smalls. He looks like he might be in his late twenties, but he could be younger. He's been living on the streets, so it's hard to tell how old he really is. Anyway, he may have come from Seaview."

"What makes you think that?"

"Something he said," Pierce answered. "That when he was a kid he rode a Ferris wheel every day. Seaview's the only place around here that ever had a Ferris wheel all year round."

"Is that all you have to go on?"

"Yes."

"You're desperate, then?"

"Yes, I am."

Yearwood's jagged smile was mirthless. "I like that in a man."

Pierce reached into his jacket and came up with a mug shot. "This is Smalls."

Yearwood gazed at the photograph with what struck Pierce as an unearthly concentration. When he looked up again, something glimmered in his eye. "The lost boy," he said.

11:14 P.M., Interrogation Room 3

"This is what we call the Murder Book," Cohen told Smalls. He placed it on the table. "It has everything we've found during our investigation of Cathy's murder. I'm going to be showing you things while we talk. Pictures. Crime-scene photographs, for example, which aren't very pleasant to look at. But I want you to look at them anyway, Jay. One by one. I'm not going to rush you through this. I want you to look long and hard at the pictures."

Cohen slid the book to the center of the table, turned it so that it faced Smalls, and opened the cover to a photograph of Cathy Lake standing outside her house on Obermeyer Street. "This picture was taken five weeks ago. It's the picture Cathy's mother gave to the police when she first reported her daughter missing. Cathy's wearing the same dress she wore the day she was murdered. The same red dress. Do you recognize it?"

"Yes."

Cohen tapped the photo gently, his nail just at the nape of Cathy's slender neck. "You can't see it very well, but she's wearing a little silver locket. Heart-shaped. Cathy was wearing that locket the day she died, but we haven't been able to find it." Nothing glimmered in Smalls' eyes. Again, Cohen tapped the photograph in the Murder Book. "Concentrate on Cathy, Jay. She was only eight years old. She was in the third grade." He looked for a reaction of some kind, saw none. "She liked to dance and sing. She had a beautiful voice. Cathy was a real person, Jay. She liked chocolate ice cream best. She had an old gray cat she named Samson because its hair was long. A real person, Jay. Not some . . ." He thought of the glass eye Zarella and Sanford had found. "Not some doll you could just throw around."

Smalls said nothing, but Cohen noted that the left corner of his lips gave a tiny twitch. He drew a chair up to the table and sat down. "Tell me what you're thinking, Jay."

"I'm thinking of her. Of the last time I saw her."

"When she was crossing the street toward the park."

"Yes. I think someone was behind her."

"Who?"

"A man. Coming across the street."

"Why do you think that?"

"Because she kept looking over her shoulder. Like I said before. Maybe she was doing that because someone was following her."

"What makes you think that?"

"It would be a reason, wouldn't it? For her to be looking back over her shoulder. If someone was following her, someone who'd scared her, she'd be looking back to see where he was."

"But you didn't see anybody following Cathy, did you, Jay?"

"No."

"You only think he may have been following Cathy because she was looking over her shoulder?"

"They do that. Kids. When someone's following them."

"Sure they do, but maybe it was just that Cathy heard a car blow its horn and looked over her shoulder."

"Maybe."

"Or some guy yelling for a cab, or at his kid, or his dog. Something like that."

Smalls shrugged. "I guess."

"The fact is, anything could have made Cathy glance over her shoulder, right?"

"Yes."

"So why did you think it was a guy following her?"

"I don't know."

"There has to be a reason you thought that, Jay."

Smalls considered this, then said, "Because there was this other guy. Maybe he gave me the idea that someone was following her."

"What other guy?"

"A man I saw in the park."

"When did you see this guy?"

"The same day."

"The day of the murder?"

"Yes."

"What time?"

"I don't know for sure. Before dark."

"Where was this guy when you saw him?"

"On the path. To the playground. He was digging. Like he was burying something. And praying."

"Praying?"

"It sounded like prayer. He was saying, 'Bury me. Bury me.'"

"What did he look like?"

"Like me. Sort of . . . dirty."

"Did you ever see this guy again?"

"No."

Cohen gazed at Smalls pointedly. "Jay, this is the second guy you've come up with. First you told me about a man in the playground. A guy nobody but you ever noticed. And now, ten days later, you've come up with another guy. And you say this guy was maybe following Cathy. Or some guy was following her and maybe it was the same man you saw in the park that same afternoon."

"I know how it sounds," Smalls said. "But I did see a man. He was digging, like I said, and he—"

"Yeah, okay, let's say you did see this guy. Here's my question. Why didn't you ever mention him before?"

"I don't know."

"That's not good enough." Cohen leaned forward and fiercely stared at Smalls. "Which is why I don't really want to talk about this second guy. What I really want to talk about is you, Jay. About what you were doing the day Cathy died. Not some guy you say scared Cathy in the playground. Not some guy you saw digging a hole. You, Jay. You."

Smalls' lips pinched together.

"You know what I think, Jay? I think you followed Cathy into the park."

Smalls shook his head. "No."

"You saw Cathy come across Clairmont and go into the park, and you followed her."

"No."

"You saw that she was alone. With no one to protect her."

Smalls' head was shaking violently now. "No," he repeated. "No. No."

"You followed her and you grabbed her."

Smalls slumped forward, knocked his head against the table. "No!"

"You took a wire and you wound it around her neck and you—"

Smalls lifted his head and slammed it down against the table. "No!" He arched backward violently and brought his head down against the edge of the table in a jolting blow.

Cohen leaped to his feet, grabbed Smalls' head, and held it tight against his chest. "Stop it!" he shouted. "Stop it, Jay!" Smalls' head trembled in Cohen's tight embrace. "Stop it, Jay," Cohen repeated, softly now. He glanced at the clock, and the walls of the room closed in upon him, the air thickened and grew hotter, and he knew this was what it felt like to close slowly in on Hell.

Is it not love?

Pierce and Yearwood walked together toward the Registry Office through the misty air. Toward the sea, Pierce could hazily make out a few rotted fishing piers.

"I came here when I was a boy," he told Yearwood. "My father liked to fish off the pier. He took me to the amusement park too."

"That closed five years ago. But we may be headed out there tonight."

"Why?"

"Because if this boy turns out to be the man you have in custody, then his mother still lives in an old trailer just off the midway. The same one she came here in."

"His mother was a carnival worker?"

"She worked the county fair circuit. Had her own shooting gallery."

"The carnival circuit. Always moving from place to place. Smalls said he'd done that. Maybe that's how he's got away with it."

"You think he's done it before? Killed?" Yearwood asked.

"Probably." Pierce thought of Costa, how certain he was that Costa would have killed another child, wouldn't have stopped with Debra's murder. "One thing's for sure. They never stop once they start it. It gets easier every time."

They walked on down the street, the beat of Yearwood's cane on the cement walkway ticking like a metronome. When it stopped, they stood at the Registry door.

"Sanctum Sanctorum," the old man announced. He drew a large ring of keys from his back pocket and jangled through them until he found the one he sought, inserted it with a surprisingly steady hand, and turned it. "My whole life's in here," he muttered as he flipped the switch just inside the door.

A single line of fluorescent lamps sputtered to life, revealing eight wooden desks, all covered with the same green felt under glass. Brass lamps with green glass shades stood at the corner of each desk, along with a scattering of pencils and notepads. Small trays contained rubber bands and paper clips. The smell of ink pervaded the air.

Yearwood motioned Pierce to follow him. They scissored among the desks to where a row of metal filing cabinets stood at the back of the room. A line of books ran across the top of the cabinets, a year embossed on the side of each, running from 1849 to the present. The old man went directly to one marked 1947. "It has to have been in the fall when the boy disappeared," he said. "That's when the fair comes to town."

He led Pierce to a nearby table, placed the book on top of it, leaned forward, and blew a cloud of dust from its surface. "Sit," he told Pierce. "This could take a few minutes."

Pierce slid into the chair next to the old man and watched as he turned the yellow, crumbling pages, pausing from time to time to consider a photograph or a headline. Page by page Seaview's tragedies and disasters marched in procession beneath the sickly light, the history of a little seaside town accumulating story by story until Pierce felt something quake within him, got up quickly, walked to the front of the room, and stood, facing the window.

Down the street, the lights of the Driftwood Bar glowed out of the darkness. He thought of the people inside it and knew that whatever their stories, they could share them, something he no longer did with anyone. He'd stopped joining the other cops after a tour, stopped playing pool with them, throwing darts, listening to the game. This was what Anna had first noticed about him, he knew, the isolation in which he lived. She'd made that clear the second afternoon he'd come to visit her.

"You don't go out with the men anymore, do you?" she'd said, then sat down to hear what he'd come to tell her.

"No."

"My brother-in-law's a cop in Pittsburgh, and the cops always go out when the shift's over. You're at the end of your shift, aren't you? Right now?"

"Yes."

"So where do they get together in this city, cops after work?"

"Place called Luke's."

"Let me guess. A pool table in the back. Jukebox too. Usually playing Sinatra. Calendars with girls in striped swimsuits. The sign outside doesn't say No Women Allowed, but it might as well. Am I close?"

"On the money."

"Did you go to college?" There was a wondrous frankness in her gaze.

"No."

"I wanted to go to college, but my father said, 'Why bother, you're just going to get married.' I got even by giving him an illegitimate granddaughter." She shrugged. "But he did me one better. He loved Cathy. My father loved her and I haven't told him yet that she's dead." She glanced toward the closed door of her daughter's room, then back to Pierce. "So give me the benefit of your experience, Detective Pierce. Tomorrow, how do I tell my dying father that someone murdered his only granddaughter?"

"Take his hand," Pierce told her. "Take his hand before you tell him anything."

"Did you do that with your wife when you told her about Debra?"

"No, I didn't. That's how I know I should have." He recalled the look on Jenny's face as the blow fell, the way she'd retreated into silence. "She finally said that she couldn't feel anything anymore. And, you know, that sounded good to me. Just to feel nothing at all."

"Why?"

"Because all I felt was hatred. For Costa." He drew in a deep breath. "I even started following him. When he moved to the city, I moved here too. And I followed him. At night. When I was off duty. I did it until he died."

Anna seemed to peer into the dark well of Pierce's long sorrow. "It's a poison, isn't it?"

"Yes," Pierce replied. "When Costa died, I thought I'd get rid of it. But I didn't."

It was the tenderness he'd seen in her eyes at that moment that Pierce concentrated upon now, a tenderness he could still feel, as he stared through the dusty window of the Seaview Registry, remaining by that window until he heard Yearwood call to him, then wave him back to the book, where, it appeared from the urgent look on the old man's face, the lost boy had been found.

11:33 P.M., *Interrogation Room 3*

Cohen scratched his cheek, felt the beginning of his nightly stubble. "All right," he sighed. "Let's go over it again, Jay." He jerked at his tie, pulled down the knot. "Jay, you with me?"

Smalls' gaze was dull. "Yes."

Cohen turned the page. "Remember this?"

The photograph showed the drawing Smalls had made in the alley he'd stumbled out of only minutes before Cathy Lake's murder.

"Let's talk about this drawing." Cohen tapped the figure of the little girl in the white robe. "The girl in this drawing, she's dead, isn't she? I mean, look at the way you've drawn her. Hands folded. Like a little girl in a coffin. Why did you draw her that way?"

Smalls slumped forward as if shoved there.

"Sit up," Cohen barked. "You think you're tired? I'm tired too. But we're not through yet."

Smalls straightened himself.

Cohen tapped the photo of the drawing. "Did you know this girl?"

Smalls looked away.

"You don't want to think about her, do you?"

Smalls drew his hands to the edge of the table.

"Because you know what you did to her."

"I didn't do anything to her."

"Prove it."

"How?"

"By telling me about yourself. Where you're from. Where you grew up."

Smalls' eyes cut over to Cohen. "None of that matters." The words dropped from him like rotten morsels.

"Then why won't you tell me about any of it?"

"Because I—"

The door opened.

Chief Burke stood in the doorway.

"May I see you a moment, Detective?" Burke asked.

Cohen joined Burke in the corridor, closing the door gently behind him.

"Have you heard anything from Pierce?" Burke asked him.

"Not yet."

"And what about from your end? Is Smalls saying anything?"

"Nothing new except some guy he claims to have seen in the park a little while after the murder. Says the guy was on the path that goes from the tunnel to the playground. He didn't talk to the guy, but he swears he heard him say 'Bury me, bury me.' The guy was digging in the ground when he was saying this."

"Digging," Burke said thoughtfully. "It's worth checking out. If Smalls really did see this guy, and he was burying the locket, something like that, we wouldn't want to miss it."

"That would be a long shot, wouldn't it?" Cohen asked bleakly.

Burke stared at him. "But at this point, long shots are all we have."

11:44 P.M., Seaview, Registry Office

Pierce studied the photograph Yearwood indicated. It showed a teenage boy standing at the end of a long, narrow pier, not a killer yet, as for years Costa had not been a killer, but the horrible urge already growing in him like a tumor.

"It's him," Pierce said. "It's Smalls." The promise he'd made to Anna Lake resounded in his mind. "I have to find something, Sam."

Yearwood returned his eyes to the photograph. "His name is Eagar. James Eagar. Everybody called him Jimmy." He stroked the white gristle on his chin as he continued to stare down at the old photograph. "Messed up from the beginning. Never had a chance."

The fire blazed in Pierce's mind. "Neither did Cathy Lake," he said.

11:49 P.M., Office of the Chief of Detectives

As Burke stood in the elevator, he recalled the last five hours, how he'd worked in the old way, meticulously going over each minute detail of Case 90631. But for all his effort, the piercing light that had time and time again peeled back the curtain and revealed the truth had failed him utterly. Page by page, he'd felt the heat diminish, the light dim. A mind that had once burned so fiercely and with such fine result now seemed turned exclusively upon its own unlighted depths. What remained was his professional expertise. He had experience, long and deep. It was the one thing that remained that he could offer to the men who looked to him for guidance and support.

The elevator doors opened in the lobby. Burke strode to the front desk and picked up the phone. "Get hold of Officers Zarella and Sanford," he said when the dispatcher answered. "Tell them to meet me at the entrance to the park on Clairmont. I want them there in twenty minutes."

"Yes, Chief."

"They should bring a shovel and a couple of spades."

"Anything else, sir?"

"No," Burke answered. "That's all I have."

He strode out into the night, back toward Saint Vincent's, determined now to perform the last duties of his fatherhood. As he walked the deserted street, he could feel terrible stirrings within him, ghostly recriminations, fingers pointed directly toward the damage he had done. One of the scribblings he'd found wadded up in Scottie's smelly jacket moved like a blade across his mind. *I am the evil Evil made.* Why had he thought that line so weak and self-pitying when he'd first read it, and now so profoundly true?

11:54 P.M., Interrogation Room 3

Watching him from across the table, Cohen decided that what he desperately needed was a question Smalls couldn't anticipate. Something bold, something that firmly suggested he was closing in. He thought of the Ferris wheel, the possibility that Smalls might have lived in Seaview, and decided to take a chance. "Tell me about when you were in Seaview."

Smalls glanced away, as if from some hateful image he could not bear to glimpse.

"You did something there, didn't you, Jay?" Cohen pressed.

Smalls gave no answer.

Cohen studied the self-loathing on Smalls' face and knew that he'd hit a mark. "Something horrible."

Midnight, Seaview, Main Street

Pierce looked over to where Yearwood sat on the passenger side of the car. "I didn't remember the fairgrounds being this far from Seaview."

"It's not much farther," Yearwood assured him. "Used to be quite a lively place, our fairgrounds. Lights. Noise. Nothing left but the Ferris wheel these days, and that just sits, rusting away."

Pierce glanced at his Timex, pressed down upon the accelerator. "When was the last time you spoke to Smalls' mother?"

"About five years ago, right after the boy disappeared," Yearwood answered. "She had that look, you know, the one people get when they can't stop chewing at the bitter root."

Pierce thought he must have once had such a look, and thinking that, the foggy night returned to him, the blurred chug of the harbor boats, Costa sitting in the misty front window of the Flying Dutchman Bar, downing one whiskey after another while he joked and laughed and bought another round, the whole gang clustered around him, slapping him on the back, knowing nothing of the archive he maintained, his macabre gallery of dead children.

"She wasn't sure what had happened to him," Yearwood added. "That made it worse."

Did not knowing really make it worse? Pierce wondered. Was it really better not to know where Costa had hidden Debra's red velvet bracelet than to imagine that each night he'd drawn it from its hiding place, slid it through his fingers, or put it to some even more obscene use?

"The fairgrounds are coming up," Yearwood said.

Pierce looked to the left, where he saw the gigantic frame of the Ferris wheel just as a blast of wind abruptly rocked its rusty cars ever so slightly backward. The end of the line. If nothing comes of this, then Smalls will go free. He thought of Anna, of the moment when he would have to tell her that Smalls had been released. Would the strange composure she had so far maintained vanish at that moment, he wondered, and in that instant would she be transformed, as he had been, consumed by fury, beyond all hope of peace? To save her from that fate was his mission now, to find something on Albert Smalls that would break through his stony denial. To save Anna, he thought as he drew his eyes from the darkened Ferris wheel, this was now his one true aim for the interrogation.

PART III

Is there something else?

Burke sat at his son's bedside, Scottie's face a blur behind the plastic curtain. Even so, he was more recognizable than the withered man Burke had found in the emergency ward six days before, a deranged, shivering figure madly clawing at the bedsheet.

But in the last few hours, this thrashing had ended. There was no more ripping and tearing at the sheet or his hospital gown. Scottie's eyes were closed, lips clinched together, so that the only sign of life Burke could detect in him was the subtle heave of his chest and the saliva that bubbled briefly from the right corner of his lips, then burst.

The door opened. Burke expected to see a doctor or

a nurse on rounds, but the man in the doorway was clearly neither.

"Is this Scott Burke's room?"

"Yes, it is," Burke answered.

The man took a hesitant step forward and let the door swing shut behind him. "I wasn't sure I had the right room."

He was dressed in baggy flannel pants, a plaid wool shirt, and a rumpled parka with frayed sleeves. His hair was black and greasy and parted in the middle, with a curl that dangled just to the left and which, Burke supposed, the man believed gave him a raffish quality, when, in fact, it only added to his seediness.

Burke got to his feet. "I'm Scottie's father."

"Scottie said his dad was a cop. I figured he meant some old flatfoot, but after he got picked up, I heard it was you." The smile looked painted on the man's face, part of a crudely drawn mask. "Nice to meet you, Chief Burke."

Burke did not return the smile. "My son really isn't able to have visitors," he said.

"Oh, I know that. My name's Dunlap. Harry Dunlap. I have a store over on Cordelia. Collectibles, that sort of stuff." He looked down at Scottie. "Poor kid."

"How do you know my son?"

"We did some business."

"What kind of business?"

"He rented from me. Little room in the back of my store. Nothing much, but Scottie used to come there to sleep it off, you know? Four bucks a week, that's all I charged him. Same as some flophouse. But a better place. Warm. Dry. Nobody bothering him. I could have got ten for a place like that. Nice, like I say, clean." Dunlap toyed with the zipper of his parka with two stubby fingers. "Anyway, when a couple days went by and I didn't see him, I asked around, and that's when I found out they'd picked him up and brought him here." He shifted awkwardly. "So, how's he doing, Scottie?"

"He's dying." Burke said it flatly.

Dunlap blinked, as if against a flash of light. "Well, I just, you know, wanted to drop by, us being friends and all, me and Scottie, that is."

"How long have you known my son?"

"Like I said, a few weeks. I'd see him in that back room, you know, and we'd have a cup of coffee now and again. He was a good kid, like I said, a good—"

"I know what he was," Burke cut in.

Dunlap flinched at the coldness in Burke's voice. "Yeah. I mean, I guess it was tough. A man in your position. Big shot on the force, and all. And Scottie the way he was, a . . . well, a . . ."

Burke eyed Dunlap warily. "Is there something you want?"

"Me?" Dunlap looked as if he'd been caught red-handed.

"You didn't come here to see Scottie."

Dunlap plunged his hands into the pockets of the parka. "Well, like I said, Scottie was, you know, we was . . . well, to tell you the truth, he hadn't paid me in a couple of weeks, and I figured maybe you might . . . I mean, being a man in your position, you might want to—"

"How much does he owe you?"

Dunlap attempted a joke. "Jeez, you're just like Joe Friday."

Burke stared at him without comprehension.

"Joe Friday," Dunlap explained. "That cop on TV. *Dragnet.*"

"How much did my son owe you?" Burke repeated.

"Couple weeks, like I said, so that would be . . . eight bucks, that's all."

Burke took out the money and handed it to Dunlap.

"Thanks," Dunlap said. He sank the bills into his pocket but made no move toward the door.

"Is there something else?"

Dunlap released a short laugh, dry as a gunshot. "Me? No. I was just figuring you must be pretty busy. I mean, what with that murder. The kid they found in the park."

Burke stepped back toward the bed. "I'd like to be with my son now."

"Oh, yeah, sure, Chief," Dunlap said. He dipped one shoulder, then the other, chuckled nervously. "I can call you Chief, right?"

Burke stared at him stonily. "You got what you came for," he said evenly.

"Yeah, sure," Dunlap squeaked. "Good night, Chief. I mean, good night . . . sir." He turned and scurried out of the room, leaving nothing behind but the smell of cheap aftershave.

Burke sat in the chair beside Scottie's bed, then grew restless and stood by the window instead, watching the street below, where, like a small black insect, he could see Dunlap scuttling down the avenue, heading north toward Cordelia, with its seedy bars and pawnshops and flophouses, the dreadful world his son had inhabited for years. He looked at Scottie's hands. They were callused, the skin repeatedly scraped and scarred. He imagined his son dragging himself out of the gutter, clawing at the cement rim, already hungry for his next fix, eyeing an old woman with a purse. How far he had sunk, this boy. The depths he'd touched. A thief, a predator . . . the evil Evil made.

Dunlap's words struck him like a slap on his face.

A man in your position. Scottie the way he was.

He felt rage against Scottie, at the waste of his life, of his own humiliation at the petty criminal Scottie became, but much earlier, too, embarrassed by Scottie's boyhood failures, that he did poorly in school, never had a girlfriend, avoided all physical and mental competition, showed no interest in being a cop. Was it from the long ordeal of his father's scorn that Scottie now wanted to be released?

Released.

Burke let the word direct his mind away from Scottie and back to the comforting security of his work, back to Albert Smalls, the clear purpose at hand. He considered the transcripts of Smalls' many interrogations. Could he have failed to notice something in them? he wondered now. A crumb in the forest. In his mind he saw a little girl stroll through the park unharmed, saw his hand upon her shoulder. If he could find something in the transcripts, then Smalls would never lie in wait for this child. She would make it safely home, grow up, have children of her own. If he did not, she would die. His eyes swept over to Scottie. Too late, he thought, too late. But for some child not yet destroyed, there was still a chance.

Midnight, Ragtag Bar, 374 Trevor Avenue

Eddie Lambrusco glanced at the Schlitz beer clock. Midnight. Half the shift behind him. Halfway home to his daughter. He knew Mrs. Wilson would be looking in on her now, making sure she was all right, but the vision of her doing that gave him no comfort. It wasn't Mrs. Wilson his daughter should see when she opened her eyes in the darkness, not Mrs. Wilson's hands that should tuck her in. It should be his hands. That's what had been stolen from him, he thought. The deep satisfaction of fatherhood. Being a father. That was the one thing he was truly good at. But day by day, hour by hour, it had been ripped from him, this precious, precious thing. His anger spiked, but he choked it down. Stay calm, he told himself, remember what happens when you don't. His fingers tightened into a lethal fist, but he forced them open. He couldn't do what he wanted to do, what his rage urged him to do.

He glanced back to where Terry Siddell sat opposite him in the booth. The jukebox was playing at the back of the bar but Siddell had brought one of those small new-fangled radios. He turned it on and brought it close to his ear.

"What do you call that anyway?" Eddie asked.

"Transistor," Siddell said. He toyed with one of the radio's chrome knobs and the scratchy music increased in volume. "Transitor radio."

"Small," Eddie said.

"That's the idea," Siddell said in that superior way of his, looking peevish and resentful.

"So, what are you listening to?"

Siddell shrugged. "Anything's better than what's on the box. Fucking Perry Como. I'd rather listen to anything but that . . . or you."

Eddie wasn't surprised by what Siddell said. He knew Siddell didn't want to waste a single second of his precious life with some garbage hauler. All Siddell wanted was to bull through the rest of the shift, then disappear the way he always did after work. But there were still six hours to go, and no way was Eddie going to go straight through it without a cold beer. Siddell looked like a guy who never required cold refreshment, but that didn't matter to Eddie. He could sit and watch, the fucking twit.

Eddie took a sip from the mug. "You look like shit, Terry," he said.

Siddell shrugged.

"Like shit warmed over," Eddie added, taking another poke.

Siddell turned away, locked his eyes on the front of the bar.

They'd spent the last three hours cleaning out Drainage Pipe 4, scrubbing its walls clean of the weird drawing they'd found there. The entire time, Siddell had looked completely spooked, like a man going through another man's insides. But then, what could Terry Siddell possibly know about that kind of feeling? Siddell hadn't been in the war, hadn't seen what a man looked like after a shell had blown him inside out. What must it be like to live the way Siddell did, safe from everything, cushioned by money and his family name, with nothing to worry about, so that he never looked the way Eddie knew he sometimes looked, especially when money was tight and the holidays were coming up, a sweaty, nervous little guy, eyes peeled back, as if constantly searching for a sniper in the brush?

What the hell, Eddie thought, try one more. "Shit on a shingle," he said with an edgy laugh. "That's what you look like, Terry."

"Fuck you," Siddell said.

Eddie laughed again, satisfied that he'd done what he could to get even, taken a couple of pokes, used the only power he had, which was the power to annoy. He smiled. Charlie would have loved it, he thought, and if he'd been there, the two of them would have gone at Siddell again and again, rubbed his fucking peevish face in the creepy little shit he was. But Eddie had mouthed off to his supervisor in the Sanitation Department, then slugged him, been fired, and so he would never again work with Charlie, never again roar at his jokes or feel the warm beam of his smile. He should have taken Charlie's advice from the start. *Keep a bright smile over that black heart of yours, Eddie.* Then Charlie's impish smile. *And whistle while you work.*

"How long are we going to be here?" Siddell turned off the transistor radio and sank it into the pocket of his shirt. "Fucking hours?"

"Till I finish my beer."

Siddell frowned sullenly. "Well, don't take all night."

Eddie took a swig and studied Siddell's pale face and annoyed eyes, trying to get a fix on the young man opposite him. It wasn't that there was anything deep in Siddell, he decided, it was just that he never jawed with the other guys, never bragged about some girl he was banging or anything like that. Eddie would have felt better if Siddell were merely a guy who by nature kept his cards close to the vest. But that wasn't it at all, Eddie supposed. He could imagine Siddell talking his head off to the other young men at the Winchester Heights Tennis Club. It wasn't that Siddell didn't talk, it was that he didn't talk to people like Eddie, working stiffs who ate pork and beans out of the can and whom Siddell probably regarded as little more than pack animals.

Eddie brought the mug to his lips, wishing he were more like Charlie Sweeney. "You can do anything, Eddie," Charlie had told him, "as long as you follow it with a glad hand and a smile." And Charlie had proved that true, Eddie thought. Charlie had never been fired despite the fact that in certain ways he was lazy, even a tad deceitful, taking sick days when he wasn't sick, his way of getting even. "The art of life," he'd claimed, "is to take what you need and grin while you do it." That was the problem, Eddie realized. Eddie was no good at grinning, glad-handing, poking a guy and making him like it because at the end of the poke there was a ready smile and a hearty laugh. To hide what you really were, what you really felt, the anger that bubbled up in you, the vein of malice that ran through your soul, that was the secret. With the right grin, you could tear their hearts out, and they'd still slap you on the back, buy you a beer, say, Hey, Eddie, go home to your sick kid. If he could only swallow the anger, the sense of being totally and forever fucked, the world could be his. But he couldn't. That was the worst card he'd been dealt, he thought, that he wasn't Charlie, and never could be.

He downed the last of the beer.

"Okay," he said, wiping his hands on his trousers. "Let me give my kid a call, then we'll hit the road."

At the phone booth, Eddie dialed his home number. Mrs. Wilson answered.

"How's she doing?" Eddie asked.

"The fever didn't break yet."

"Is she still throwing up?"

"A little while ago, but she's sleeping now."

"Okay," Eddie told her. "I'll be home around six."

"It's Laurie's birthday," Mrs. Wilson reminded him.

"Yeah, I know."

"She'll be expecting a little something." Mrs. Wilson's tone grew faintly accusatory. "Mr. Sweeney brought her a birthday present."

"Don't worry, I got her something too. Nice. A nice present."

"She wouldn't open Mr. Sweeney's gift before she opened yours."

His daughter's devotion lifted Eddie's heart, but it

sank again when he recalled that he hadn't been able to buy Laurie the little Betsy McCall doll she'd asked for. All the other girls are getting them, she'd said, and Eddie had promised, but now . . .

Mrs. Wilson dragged it down again. "You need a wife, Eddie."

"The one I had didn't think so," Eddie snapped, his anger flaring. He swallowed hard, calmed himself. "Anyway, I'll get home as fast as I can."

"When she wakes up she'll ask for you."

There it was again, Eddie thought, the suggestion of failure, that if Eddie had anything between his ears he wouldn't be in this fix, so strapped for money he had to haul garbage while his sick daughter cried for him. Poor provider. So poor he might not even have a birthday present for Laurie's eighth birthday. Poor provider. The phrase his father had always used to describe the losers of this world.

"I'll get home soon as I can," Eddie assured Mrs. Wilson in a tone that made him cringe. "No beer after work, no nothing. I'll come right home." He hung up and returned to the booth where Siddell remained in his usual moody silence.

"Okay, let's get going," he told Siddell. "Six more hours and you can go home to your—" He stopped, wondering what Siddell could possibly go home to. A cat? A bird? Some sort of snake struck Eddie as more likely. Nothing dangerous though. A little green garden snake, eyes like glass, skin papery as a dead man's. "Anyway, we're in the home stretch now."

Siddell looked at him sourly but said nothing as he got to his feet.

Siddell Carting Truck 12 rested heavily at the curb, half filled with garbage, a sickening, sweet stink wafting from its open bed to poison the air inside the working-class apartment buildings that surrounded it.

"The whole neighborhood stinks," Siddell said glumly.

"Yeah, not all perfumy like it is in Winchester Heights," Eddie said. He kicked the clutch, yanked the floor shift into first gear, and stomped the accelerator.

The truck lurched forward, Eddie guiding it down the narrow street, the park on one side, a long line of dingy apartment houses on the other. For the first few blocks he saw no one. Then, out of the shadows a short little man suddenly appeared, moving rapidly along the park side of the road, the wind billowing out the sleeves of his dark green parka.

Another loser, Eddie thought as he watched the little man grow small in the rearview mirror, then disappear around a dark corner at Vandermeer and Cordelia.

Didn't stop who?

Dunlap whirled around the corner and headed down Cordelia, moving feverishly, like a small powder keg trying to outrun its own burning fuse.

So, okay, fuck the Chief, he told himself. *So, okay, I didn't learn nothing. What now?*

He stopped and tried to think it through, but the clatter of the garbage truck that had just lurched past had distracted him so that he had to get his mind around the problem once again. So, okay, I got to get somebody, he thought.

His short, squat legs scissored rapidly down the avenue while his mind reeled off a list of possibilities. There was Louis Farkus. Louis had the balls. No, not Farkus, he decided. Louis Farkus didn't have a car ever since that midnight visit from the repo man. Okay, so, all right, what about Skeeter McBride? He had a Pontiac. A Pontiac but no balls. The job required a set of balls. Not brass ones. It wasn't that tough. But a set of balls nonetheless. Other names surfaced, then fell away for various reasons, men too sick, men who couldn't be trusted, men too smart to be conned into doing it.

He reached the corner of Bradford and Cordelia, and still no one emerged who really fit the scheme. So all right, okay, the second string, guys he'd have preferred not to use but now had no choice but to consider. Ziggy, maybe? No. Bill Dexter? Forget it. Spike Patucci? Perfect save for the little matter that he was psycho. Then suddenly, a name separated from the pack. A guy with a car. A guy who had balls. Best of all, a guy who could provide a reason for being where he was. Dunlap smiled. *So, okay . . . him.*

12:17 A.M., *Interrogation Room 3*

"So, how old is she, Jay?" Cohen asked. "The girl in the picture."

"I don't know."

"It was the only picture you drew in that tunnel," Cohen said. "You could have drawn a boy. A grown-up. A dog. Anything, right?"

"I guess I could have."

"So why did you draw this little girl?"

Smalls shrugged.

"It's not a bad drawing, Jay. A lot of detail. Like she was standing in front of you. A model. It's hard to imagine that you never spoke to this kid."

Smalls said nothing.

Dead end, Cohen thought, his heart sinking. He

leaned back in his chair, placed his hands behind his head, and to his surprise Blunt's voice sounded in his head, talking about how Cathy hadn't been sexually violated, the fact that this had, in Blunt's mind, signaled a more difficult case to break.

"You know, one of the detectives has been wondering about something," Cohen said. "About why Cathy wasn't raped."

Smalls drew in a breath.

"We figured maybe she'd been killed as part of a robbery, but would a man kill a little girl for nothing more than a little silver trinket?"

Smalls remained silent.

"So this other detective thinks that the killer hadn't been a thief at all. He'd planned to rape Cathy. That was the whole idea. Of course, if that were true, why didn't he do it?"

"Maybe he got scared off." Smalls spoke with what struck Cohen as a curious assurance.

"You mean the guy heard somebody coming, something like that, and got scared off?"

"If someone saw him, then that person should have stopped him."

"I didn't say that someone saw him, Jay."

Smalls' hands spasmed on the table.

"What's the matter, Jay? You look a little . . . upset."

Smalls shrank back, glanced about, as if searching for a place to hide.

"You'd like to just disappear, wouldn't you, Jay? Become invisible. The Invisible Man. That's what we call him, you know. That first guy you told us about. The one in the playground. The one you said Cathy was afraid of. The Invisible Man."

"He wasn't invisible," Smalls muttered.

"No, he wasn't, Jay. Because Cathy saw him, didn't she? She saw him look at her, notice her, single her out."

Smalls' gaze fled to the window.

"She saw him move toward her, close in on her, reach for her. She looked him in the eye, didn't she, Jay?"

Smalls did not respond.

"She felt his hands on her throat, didn't she."

Smalls began to rock forward and backward.

"But nobody else saw this invisible man, right, Jay?"

Smalls dropped forward with a soft moan and pressed his face against the table.

"And so nobody stopped him from killing Cathy."

Smalls whispered something, but Cohen couldn't make it out. "What?" he asked.

The whispering continued, Smalls' cheek against the table, smothering the words.

"Sit up, Jay."

Smalls did not move.

"Sit up," Cohen said hotly.

Smalls' vehement whispers continued.

Cohen leaned forward, grabbed Smalls' shoulders, and forced him upright.

"Slime, slime, slime." Smalls' face was transfigured by disgust.

"Who?" Cohen asked. "Who's slime?"

"Me. Because I didn't stop him."

"Didn't stop who?"

"The man who scared Cathy."

Dead end, Cohen thought. "The Invisible Man," he murmured, his voice edged with contempt. "Bullshit, Jay. We both know who the Invisible Man was." He glared at Smalls mercilessly. "It was you."

12:21 A.M., *City Park*

Sanford and Zarella were waiting at Drainage Pipe 4 when Burke arrived.

"We have information that something pertaining to the murder of Cathy Lake might be buried at some point along the path that runs from here to the duck pond," Burke told the two cops. "So we're going to walk the path slowly, checking for any sign that the ground along the way has been disturbed. This is very important. You need to be alert to anything that looks out of the ordinary. Anything at all. Understood?"

The two patrolmen nodded.

"Okay," Burke said. "Zarella, take the left side of the path. Sanford, you take the right. I'll walk along behind both of you and recheck right and left."

And so they passed through the tunnel, flashlights on high beam as they moved along the edges of the pathway, carefully brushing back anything that got in the way of a clear view of the ground.

They'd made it halfway to the pond when Zarella stopped abruptly in front of a small marble statue of a dog. "Sir. This might be something."

Burke peered at the ground. In the gravelly earth he saw evidence of claw marks, a place where something, perhaps human fingers, had raked the earth back.

"It could just be some animal digging," Zarella said. "Dog. Squirrel."

Burke put out his hand. "Give me the spade."

Zarella instantly obeyed.

"Keep the light on the blade," Burke said. He bent forward, inserted the blade carefully, then withdrew and inserted it again. As he dug, he could feel nothing but the ground's gritty texture.

After a moment, he straightened and stepped away. "Try the shovel."

Zarella dug energetically, pressing the blade cautiously into the earth, then bringing up one small clump of ground at a time and depositing it on the path, where Sanford probed it with a gloved hand.

"Widen the hole," Burke commanded once Zarella had reached a depth of nearly a foot. "See if you can find anything around it."

Zarella did as he was told, a mound of earth growing on the pathway.

But nothing was found, and so they moved on down the path until they reached the pond.

At the water's edge Burke looked back down the path. He tried to imagine what Smalls claimed to have seen, a man digging in the earth, trying to bury something he hoped might be Cathy Lake's missing locket. It had been a long shot, of course, and now the muddy spades and empty hole suggested just how desperate their effort to hold Smalls had become, the blind leads they were forced to pursue because they had no others. During the previous twelve days, they'd dredged the pond, searched through the undergrowth, rousted the park's bedraggled population, and found nothing. But for Burke this last failure suggested that any further search for physical evidence would prove no less fruitless.

"You want us to go farther up the path, Chief?" Zarella asked quietly.

Burke handed him the spade. "No, go on with your usual duties," he replied.

The two patrolmen walked away, talking softly, leaving Burke alone in the park.

For a time, the Chief stood in place, considering this

latest failure, wondering if Smalls was capable of devising such false diversions, running out the clock one hollow lead after another.

Then, obeying a nameless impulse, he strode back along the path, through the tunnel, and up to the gate where a little girl had waited for her mother twelve days before. Across the empty street he could see the alley that ran alongside Clairmont Towers, and out of which Smalls had staggered on that fateful day, a ragged figure who'd frightened a solitary child, pressed her into the tangled folds of the park, where she'd rushed through the rain, beneath the dripping trees until, at last, she'd reached the pond's edge and there, faced with a fork in the path, allowed herself a moment's hesitation, glanced left and right, unable to decide which way to run, a fraction of a second, but long enough for Smalls to fall upon her.

A bank of clouds drew apart, and in the reverse chasm they defined, Burke could see the faint glow of the moon. He'd read somewhere that light travels infinitely through the depths of space, and wondered if, far beyond the moon, the murder of Cathy Lake flickered eternally in the nightbound sky, her killer's face eerily revealed in distant flashes of exploding stars.

Still lost, then?

They reached the fairgrounds gate, and behind the high storm fence Pierce observed what remained of the midway, a few tumbledown wooden booths, and beyond them, up a slight incline, the skeletal Ferris wheel.

Only a few years before, the midway had bustled with crowds from the city. Pierce recalled the prattle of the calliope, the crackling fire of the shooting galleries, the line of people that snaked up toward the black maw of the House of Horrors, and on the wave of that memory, he smelled cotton candy and fried onions, and yet for all the sensory vividness of these recollections, his boyhood remained like an episode from someone else's life.

It was Debra's death that had done this to him, he

knew, and now he remembered the sticky summer day when he'd first brought her here. She'd been only three years old that summer, but full of bravado as she'd clambered into the bumper car, wrestling her metal brace into position as she nestled into his lap and gripped the wheel. She'd gasped at the first collision, but after that she'd shown not the slightest fear. As the minutes passed, she'd grown ever more aggressive, happily ramming other cars, yelling "Got him, Dad!" each time she plowed into one. He'd felt a surging delight in her courage, a feeling wholly different and more intense than any he'd ever known. So this is what it feels like, he'd said to himself, to be proud of your child. Did he really have to put away such memories to reach out to life again? he wondered. Or was it possible to find a resting place for grief that did not utterly obliterate the one you'd lost?

The gate released an aching cry as Yearwood nudged it open, then glanced back to where Pierce stood staring out over the deserted grounds.

"You coming?" Yearwood asked.

"Yeah, sure," Pierce replied.

The two of them made their way across a muddy track to where a gray trailer sagged alone at the edge of the midway.

A yellow light shone from one of its small square windows, and as he grew nearer, Pierce noted a rusty car, a washing machine with a hand wringer, and a drooping clothesline from which a single unexpectedly white towel hung, its ragged edges trembling in the wind from the sea.

At the door, Yearwood paused. "Let me start things off," he warned Pierce. "Cindy might not want to talk if a stranger just starts asking her questions out of the blue."

Pierce nodded.

Yearwood rapped at the metal door. "It's Sam, Cindy. Sam Yearwood."

Something stirred inside the trailer, then the door opened and a woman stood backlit in the doorway, her body in black silhouette save for an explosion of wiry red hair that formed a glowing aura around her skull. She looked quizzically at Yearwood. "Ain't it mighty late for you to be out, Sam?"

Yearwood touched his hat. "Sorry to disturb you at this hour, Cindy."

"Been a long time since you come out this way." Her voice was raspy, a barker's voice gone to seed.

"Yes, it has," Yearwood answered. "Cindy, I have a fellow here with me. His name's Pierce. A detective from the city. He may have some news about Jimmy."

Cindy's head dropped to the right but remained in shadow so that Pierce could draw nothing from her expression. He saw only that she wore a shapeless dress that fell over her like a collapsed tent, white with overblown flowers whose colors had faded with countless trips through the wringer.

"Is he dead?" she asked Pierce.

"No," Pierce told her. "He's in trouble though."

Cindy eased back into the trailer, and its watery light washed over her, revealing a skeletally thin face, with meager eyes, a red, jagged mouth, and leathery skin that hung slackly from the bone.

"Come in," she said.

"We won't stay long, Cindy," Yearwood assured her. "Jack just has a few questions for you."

"You can stay as long as you want, Sam," she replied with a small, twisted smile. "I don't get much company."

Yearwood motioned Pierce into the trailer, then followed him inside.

It was cramped, as Pierce observed, with enough room for only a short sofa and two spindly wooden chairs. A radio perched on the narrow island that separated the living room from a second space, where a square table stood in one corner, stocked with bread, three cans of tuna, a jar of peanut butter, and an ancient hot plate. His future, he thought, and perhaps Anna's, if they did not find a way to reach beyond their respective losses. He decided that he would call her at six o'clock sharp, tell her whatever news he had, either that Smalls was still in custody or on the streets again, maybe ask if they might have breakfast together. Then, if she said yes, they'd meet at a nearby diner and he would tell her that he knew, really knew, exactly how she felt, the unbearable pain of a murderer on the loose again, the very one who'd killed your child, and that he would never stop trying to find him, and that only when he did would he himself know peace.

"Would you like a cup of coffee?" Cindy asked.

Pierce shook his head. "No, thanks."

Cindy dropped onto the sofa, then watched as Pierce and Yearwood sat down. "So Jimmy's in trouble," she said to Pierce. "Is it something real bad?"

"Yes, it is," Pierce answered. "Murder."

A short burst of air broke from Cindy's red lips. "Oh, sweet Jesus."

Her accent was southern, and Pierce imagined her as a young girl on some dirt farm, staring out over the field, yearning for the nomadic life she'd later found but which had not turned out the way she'd hoped, and so left her here, in Seaview, beached on northern shores, talking to a cop from the city about a son she could not save.

"He won't tell us anything about himself," Pierce added. "Family. Where he's lived. But my partner got the idea that he might have come from Seaview, so I drove out here to check it out."

"Poor Jimmy," Cindy muttered brokenly.

Pierce took out his notebook. "When was the last time you saw your son?"

"I ain't seen him but one time since he left. That was a little over five years ago. Didn't figure I'd ever see him again."

"Why not?"

" 'Cause he didn't want me to see him no more. He didn't want nobody to see him. Took to staying here in the trailer. Didn't want to go out. Didn't want to do nothing. Wouldn't go to school. It was like everything was took out of him. Didn't have no friends. Pushed everybody away that wanted to help him out. Like he couldn't find no way to be happy."

"When did this start, this pushing away?"

"First year of high school."

"Do you know why he began to behave this way?"

"He's just got strange, that's all." She grabbed a pack of cigarettes from the pocket of her dress, thumbed one out, lit it. "He never had nobody get close to him. Never had no job. Always jumpy. Something screwy up there." She tapped the side of her head with a nicotine-stained finger. "Made him real . . . moody. That's how I'd say it. Jimmy got real moody." She took a quick draw on the cigarette. "Still lost, then?"

"Yes," Pierce said.

"Is he out of his head? Raving? Is it like that?"

"No. It's just that he won't tell us anything about himself."

She pointed to a picture on the wall. "That's Jimmy. When he was eight."

The photograph revealed a slender boy with large eyes and dark hair parted in the middle. He wore a cowboy suit, complete with ornate holsters and two toy six-guns. There was joy in his face, and peering at it, comparing it to the timid features of Albert Jay Smalls, Pierce wondered where this joy had gone and why, as it fled, it had turned this boy into a murderer.

"Georgia," Cindy said. "We was in Georgia when that was took." A vague nostalgia touched her eyes. "Jimmy loved to draw. That's what he done the most when he was off by hisself. He'd take a drawing book down to the beach or over to the park, and he'd set and draw things all day. Kids, mostly."

"Kids?" Pierce asked.

"He loved kids," Cindy said. "Drawing 'em." She shook her head. "He was normal till he come up on thirteen, fourteen. That's when he started acting strange. Not talking. Staying in his room. Then he took to wandering off. He'd go out on the pier and just set there, staring around, like he was listening to the clouds. He didn't want to be with other kids. Just off by hisself."

"Is he wanted for anything?" Pierce asked.

"Wanted?"

"Any outstanding warrants, for example," Pierce explained. "We're trying to find something we can hold him on. It could be anything. Shoplifting. It doesn't matter as long as it's enough for us to keep him in custody."

"Because you figure he's so dangerous?"

"Yes."

"Poor thing." Her face swam in and out behind weaving curls of smoke. "He was just a kid when it come over him. I guess it got worse and worse, whatever was going on in Jimmy's mind, but he never once told me what it was."

"Did he ever do anything violent?"

"No." She started to say more, then stopped, as if

considering a question she feared to ask. "Who did Jimmy kill?"

"An eight-year-old girl," Pierce told her.

"Poor little thing," Cindy whispered. "Eight years old." Her gaze settled upon the photograph of Jimmy Eagar in his cowboy suit. "Poor little thing," she repeated. "My son."

Then the story unfolded, Cindy talking quietly in the dim light while Pierce listened intently, taking notes as she sketched the grim decline of her lost boy.

12:45 A.M., *Interrogation Room 3*

Critical as time was, Cohen decided that he would give Smalls another ten minutes to wallow in his own self-lacerating anguish in the distant hope that if it weren't an act, then it might actually urge Smalls toward confession.

And so, with no word of explanation, Cohen rose and left the interrogation room, locking the door behind him. Once in the corridor, he considered heading to the lounge but feared Blunt might still be there, playing solitaire in a cloud of rancid smoke. And so he turned to the left instead and walked down the hallway to the detective bull pen.

The desks were empty now, the phones silent, with nothing moving but the sweep of the second hand on the large clock that hung between the room's two arched windows.

Cohen walked to the water cooler, took a long drink, crushed the cup, and tossed it into the nearest can. He looked at the clock. Eight more minutes. How is it, he wondered, thinking of his forty-one years on earth, how is it that each minute can be so long and life so short?

He sat at his desk, toyed with a pencil, a paper clip, the pencil again. His eyes lit on the phone, and he thought of Ruth Green. How would she react if the phone suddenly rang in the middle of the night and it was his voice on the other end? Would she think him crazy, or would she say *Why don't you come here when you get off? I'll make a pot of coffee.* But what would happen after that? he wondered. What did he really have to offer a young woman who'd not seen the things he'd seen, and so had no way of knowing how he felt, his sense that the wheel never turned in favor of the good.

"Detective Cohen?"

Officer Day stood at the entrance of the bull pen.

"The Chief asked me to tell you that he didn't find anything in the park," Day said. "He and some other officers went along the path all the way from the gate to the pond. They found some ground that looked as if it might have been disturbed, so they dug all around it, but they didn't find anything."

Cohen nodded. "Okay, thanks."

Officer Day remained in place. "Chief Burke wants to know if anything new has come from the interrogation since he spoke to you?"

"No," Cohen answered. "Except that Smalls seems to hate himself. Really hate himself. Calls himself slime. It may be an act, of course. Or it may be a sting of actual remorse. I can't tell."

"I'll let the Chief know," Day said, then turned and exited the room.

So there was no praying beggar clawing at the ground, Cohen concluded as he sat back in his chair. No buried silver locket that might ultimately have guided them to the truth. Instead, it had all been a lie, a way for Smalls to buy time, knowing, as he probably did, that time was all he needed now, that this was the last interrogation, that at the end of it he would be set free.

He shook his head. What he needed now was a miracle. A voice from the burning bush proclaiming with incontrovertible proof, *This is the man who strangled Cathy Lake*. He looked toward the window, the empty blackness beyond it, saw no flame, heard no voice, felt only the unfeeling void.

And so it was up to him and Pierce, he told himself, himself and Pierce and others like them to go on, unaided in their quests. He glanced at the clock, felt the whirl of its hands like spinning blades. Five minutes, he thought, still resolved to let Smalls stew a little longer, five minutes that will feel like forever.

12:52 A.M., *Criminal Files Room*

Seated at the room's wooden table, Burke studied a photograph of Albert Jay Smalls, hoping to get a fix on what lay in the mind behind the man's mournful eyes. Cohen's latest remarks concerning Smalls came into Burke's mind, the ones Officer Day had reported minutes before, the fact that the suspect had referred to himself as slime.

He opened the file and once again began to read the previous interrogations, beginning with the September first interview.

And it *was* an interview, not an interrogation. Smalls was merely one of four men taken from the park the night of the murder, brought to headquarters, questioned briefly, then released. Little had been known about either Smalls or Cathy Lake's murder at that point. Smalls' two drawings had not been found, nor anything else that had connected him to the girl's killing, save the purely circumstantial fact that he'd frightened a woman near the duck pond. Thus, at the time of the interview, Smalls had not been considered a suspect. The detectives' questions had been little more than an effort to ascertain who he was and where he'd been at the time of the murder.

And yet one exchange stood out.

COHEN: *Why do you live in the park?*
SMALLS: *I have to.*
COHEN: *Why?*
SMALLS: *It's where I live, that's all.*
COHEN: *What do you do in the park?*
SMALLS: *Nothing.*
COHEN: *Just sit around? All alone in that tunnel?*
SMALLS: *I have to be on guard.*
COHEN: *Against what?*
SMALLS: *Other men.*
COHEN: *What other men?*
SMALLS: *The ones in the park.*
COHEN: *You mean other guys like you? Jay? Did you hear my question?*
SMALLS: *Yes. Other guys like me.*

Burke considered the section of the transcript he'd just read. In the initial interview, Smalls had given almost no sense of himself, his life, how or why he'd ended up in the park. He'd said only that he had to be on guard against other men who came to the park. But why? Had he been robbed? Assaulted?

COHEN: *So you're afraid of these other men?*
SMALLS: *Yes.*

COHEN: *Have any of these guys ever bothered*
            you?
SMALLS: *No.*

No.

Then what was Smalls afraid of? Burke wondered. If these other men had never harmed him, why was he on guard against them? And if he felt he had to be on guard against these men, why would he choose to live in their midst?

COHEN: *Is there some particular guy you're afraid*
            of?
SMALLS: *There's one near the playground.*
COHEN: *Has this guy ever bothered you?*
SMALLS: *Not me. Someone else.*
COHEN: *Who?*
SMALLS: *A little girl. She plays there.*
COHEN: *What's the little girl's name?*
SMALLS: *I don't know.*
COHEN: *How old is she?*
SMALLS: *I don't know for sure.*
COHEN: *You know, a little girl was murdered not*
            far from the playground this afternoon.
            That's why we're talking to you. To see if
            anybody saw anything.
SMALLS: *Murdered? She was murdered?*

Burke read Smalls' final response over again. He had asked two questions. And both appeared to have within them an element of surprise. He studied the last question, focusing on a single word: She. It seemed clear that Smalls believed that the little girl who'd been murdered was the same one who'd been frightened by a man in the playground, and clear, too, that the news of her murder had surprised him. Of course Smalls' surprise could be a ruse. What better way to suggest his innocence than by pretending to be surprised by a murder he had himself committed?

With that caution firmly in place, Burke turned the page.

COHEN: *So, if you know anything more about this guy, the one in the playground, the one who scared one of the little girls, you need to tell us.*

SMALLS: *I don't know anything else. Just that she was afraid of him.*

COHEN: *Where did you see this little girl?*

SMALLS: *I was sitting on a bench. She came up the path from the playground. She sat down on the bench across from me.*

COHEN: *Could you see the playground from where you were sitting?*

SMALLS: *No.*

COHEN: *Okay, this guy. The one in the playground. Did this little girl tell you who he was?*

SMALLS: *No.*

COHEN: *Did she describe him?*

SMALLS: *No.*

COHEN: *When did this happen?*

SMALLS: *Two days ago.*

COHEN: *Okay, what did the little girl do after you saw her?*

SMALLS: *She went back to the playground.*

COHEN: *Why? If there was a man there she was afraid of, why would she go back to the playground?*

SMALLS: *I guess he'd left the playground by then.*

COHEN: *How much time elapsed between when she saw this guy and when she went back to the playground?*

SMALLS: *I don't know for sure.*

COHEN: *Come as close as you can.*

SMALLS: *I don't know. Five, maybe ten minutes.*

COHEN: *So this guy must not have stayed very long.*

SMALLS: *No, I guess he didn't.*

COHEN: *What did you do after the girl left?*

SMALLS: *I went to the playground.*

COHEN: *Why?*

SMALLS: *I go there sometimes. I sit outside the fence. I don't go in. I don't bother anybody. I just watch the children.*

COHEN: *Watch the children?*

SMALLS: *I don't go in the playground. There's a sign. I'm not allowed. You have to have a kid with you, or you're not allowed.*

COHEN: *Okay, about what time was it when you went to the playground?*

SMALLS: *I don't know. I don't have a watch.*

COHEN: *Was it morning or afternoon? How long did you stay?*

SMALLS: *Until after dark.*

COHEN: *That's a long time.*

SMALLS: *I stay until the children leave. When it's just me at the playground. Or other men.*

Other men.

What, Burke wondered, could Smalls have possibly meant by that, save that these other men were the ones he was on guard against? He returned to an earlier exchange:

COHEN: *What do you do in the park?*

SMALLS: *Nothing.*
COHEN: *Just sit around? All alone in that tunnel?*
SMALLS: *I have to be on guard.*
COHEN: *Against what?*
SMALLS: *Other men.*
COHEN: *What other men?*
SMALLS: *The ones in the park.*
COHEN: *You mean other guys like you? Jay? Did you hear my question?*
SMALLS: *Yes. Other guys like me.*

Burke studied Cohen's final questions.

Other guys like you?
Jay?
Did you hear my question?

From the transcript it seemed clear to Burke that prior to this exchange Smalls had answered Cohen's questions quickly, directly, with no need of prompting. Then a question had suddenly stopped him: *Other guys like you?* Had Smalls answered the question immediately, Cohen would have had no need to add the next one: *Jay?* This question suggested that Smalls had not replied, that he had hesitated. The third question in the series made this even more obvious: *Did you hear my question?*

Only then, at this second prompt, had Smalls answered:

SMALLS: *Yes. Other guys like me.*

These other men were the ones Smalls had to guard against. But who were they? They were men who came to the park. And they were, in Smalls' words, "like me."
Like me, Burke repeated in his mind. *But how?*

12:47 A.M., *Ragtag Bar*

Blunt slid his large frame into the booth. "Okay, I'm here," he said gruffly.

"How's it going, Ralph?" Dunlap tried to smile but failed. "You okay, you doing all right?"

Blunt took a draw on his cigar and stared at Dunlap. "This ain't no social call, Harry."

"Yeah, I know," Dunlap muttered. Nervously, he turned toward the bar and lifted his hand. "Hey, Pete, bring us a couple of beers, huh?" Back to Blunt. "Schlitz okay?"

"Who gives a crap?"

A quick, tentative smile spasmed across Dunlap's face. "So, everything okay with you, Ralph?"

"What's on your mind, Harry?"

"Well, to tell you the truth, Ralph, I was wondering about that guy that got picked up in the park."

"What guy?"

"The one you picked up about the little girl. You know, the kid who got killed. I was wondering about that guy."

"What about him?"

"Like if it was going anywhere. Nailing him, I mean."

"They keep at him," Blunt said indifferently.

"Are they getting anywhere?"

"What do you give a shit if they're getting anywhere, Harry?"

Dunlap knitted his fingers together, his thumbs twirling. "I got an interest, you might say."

"What kind of interest?"

Dunlap leaned forward. He lowered his voice. "We're cousins, Ralph, you and me, we can talk, right? I mean, we used to do a little business, and so—"

"Shut up about that business," Blunt snarled.

Dunlap blinked rapidly. "Yeah, okay, Ralph. No sweat. History, I know."

"I don't want to hear nothing about that business," Blunt warned.

"Okay, sure, Ralph. No sweat, like I said. So, okay, about this fucking pervert they picked up. I was thinking maybe I could help out a little."

"You mean you know something?"

"I mean help *you* out."

"I don't need no help."

"Sure you do, Ralph. Everybody needs help. And us being cousins and all. One hand washing the other, you know what I mean?"

Blunt's eyes narrowed. "What's on your fucking mind?"

The bartender stepped up to the table, slapped down two beers. "Six bits."

"Run a tab, will you, Pete?" Dunlap said cheerfully.

"No way," the bartender said.

"Jesus, Pete. It ain't like I ain't good for it." He dug into his pocket, paid for the drinks. "There, feel better now?"

"Six bits better," the bartender told him as he turned and shuffled away.

Dunlap took a sip, winced, then said, "Okay, Ralph. It goes this way. I had some dealings with this fucking loony, the one they picked up. Nothing big, you understand. He'd bring shit in, you know? To sell. Junk mostly."

"What kind of junk?"

"Just the shit he brings in. Boxes of crap. Keeps it all in that tunnel where he lives."

"You been there, where he lives?"

"Yeah, couple times. Looking through whatever crap

he's got. Jesus, what shit, you know? Fucking busted up, all of it. Toys and crap. Rubber balls. Busted up, like I said." Dunlap took another hasty sip of beer, swallowed hard, and tried to offer his cousin a pair of sorrowful eyes. "Anyway, the thing is, he fingered me, Ralph."

"Fingered you? To who?"

"The cops. He give the cops my name."

"How do you know that?"

"I know 'cause not long after the killing two of 'em came over to my place, asking questions, you know, did I know this wacko. I told 'em, 'Fuck, no, I never heard of the fucking creep.' But he give 'em my name, like I said, so they got to wonder how he come up with it. I mean, I told 'em I don't know the fuck, but you know how it is, no cop ain't ever believed me. Even when I tell 'em the truth, they don't believe me."

"So what happened?"

"They go on a tour of the place. At least the young one does. Pierce. The other one, his partner, he just asks questions."

"That fuck's full of questions."

"He busted me before, you know. The bastard. Anyway, I told him I never heard of this guy they picked up. I didn't know how he got my name. They left, and I ain't heard nothing since."

Blunt took a long drink. "So how come you're so fucking spooked? Some nut says he knows you, you say he don't. That's the end of it. Who gives a shit whether Pierce and that fucking kike believe you or not?"

"Yeah, I don't give a shit about that. But there's a problem, you know, more to the story." He glanced around, his fingers drumming the table. "You hungry, you want a burger?"

Blunt glared at Dunlap. "What the fuck's the matter with you?"

"Nothing, it's just that I don't want to go over it here." Dunlap released a nervous laugh. "The walls have ears, you know. So, what I'm saying is, maybe have a burger, then we'll go to my place."

Blunt thought Dunlap's suggestion over, the wheels turning slowly. "Okay," he muttered finally, "why the fuck not."

Why do you live this way?

Cindy Eagar's story had been a long, somewhat rambling but ultimately harrowing tale of a boy whose mood had become steadily more withdrawn from the age of fourteen. He had left school at sixteen, but even before that he'd more or less stopped attending. Instead, he'd sneak back to the midway to burrow beneath it, sitting alone all day, listening to the steady drum of the foot traffic overhead. He'd been found repeatedly by truant officers and returned to school, only to flee it again at the first opportunity. Then, at the age of eighteen, he'd vanished altogether.

"But as far as him hurting somebody," she said when she'd finished her story, "I never had no reason to believe he'd do nothing like that."

Pierce looked up from his notebook. "So he never acted violently toward anyone?"

"Not that I know of. He just stopped talking or having anything to do with people. He had this look in his eyes. Not faraway, like a kid on dope or something. More like he always had this bad taste in his mouth."

"But he never gave you any idea of what he was thinking about?"

Cindy shook her head. "All I know is, it must have been bad, 'cause it eat on him so much, he finally tried to kill hisself."

"When was this?"

"About a month before he left Seaview. I seen him out on the pier. He stayed there all the time. Didn't fish or nothing. Didn't talk to nobody. Just set out there at the very end, like I told you. Anyway, I figured he'd come home when it got dark, but it got to be eight and then nine, and still he didn't show up. So I went out looking for him. I asked everybody I could find if they'd seen him, but nobody had. Then it hit me—he jumped in the ocean. That's what I figured. He just finally jumped right off the pier."

"The lost boy," Yearwood said.

"Figured the sea took him," Cindy added. "That's what we all thought. Then he just showed up all of a sudden. Said he'd walked through Titus and English-town, all the way to the city. Then he went to his room and that's when I heard it. Like a bump, something like that. I went to the door, knocked. No answer, so I shoved the door open and there he was. Hanging. He'd got up on a chair and kicked it over and he was just hanging there." She dropped the butt of her cigarette into a nearby ashtray and thumped out another. "I yelled for Carl, this guy I was living with back then." She waved out the match. "He come in and grabbed

Jimmy by the legs and lifted him up. I climbed onto a chair and got so I could get the belt loose." A wave of smoke drifted from her mouth. "Anyway, he made it. He didn't want to, kept saying how he wanted to be dead. Soon as he was able, he went off again. This time he never come back."

"Do you know why he tried to kill himself?" Pierce asked.

"He wouldn't give me no answer to that. I asked and asked, but he never give me no answer. Probably never give nobody an answer." She took another draw on the cigarette. "Unless it was Avery Garrett." Cindy's face soured. "Of all the people for Jimmy to start hanging out with, he couldn't have picked nobody worse than Avery. A guy that, you know . . . a drunkard. Anyway, after Jimmy tried to kill hisself, he took up with Avery for a few weeks. Maybe Avery felt sorry for him, I don't know. All I know is that during that last month he was here, them two spent a lot of time together."

"Is Garrett still around?" Pierce asked.

Cindy nodded. "Far as I know, he's living on the boardwalk, like he always has."

"When's the last time you saw him?" Pierce asked.

"Been over five years now," Cindy answered. "He come over a couple of weeks after Jimmy left that last time. Looking for him, you know."

"Why was Garrett looking for him?"

"Because he figured Jimmy was in some kind of trouble. I asked him. I said, 'What kind of trouble you mean?' He said he didn't know. But he was afraid Jimmy had maybe done something and didn't know how to deal with it."

"Done what?" Pierce asked urgently.

"He said he didn't know," Cindy answered. "Just that whatever it was, Jimmy seemed awful ashamed of it.

Couldn't get it out of his mind. It was chewing him up alive, Avery said. Wouldn't give him no rest. Like a dog trailing him, this thing in Jimmy's mind, like a dog trailing him, you know, biting at his heels."

12:59 A.M., *Interrogation Room 3*

"Slime," Cohen said. "Why do you call yourself that, Jay?"

"It's the way I feel, that's all."

A breeze curled in through the window, cool but not refreshing, so that Cohen felt it as little more than a cheating respite from the room's increasingly oppressive airlessness. He randomly turned a page in the Murder Book, hoping that it would give him some direction, knowing it wouldn't.

"Why do you live this way?" Cohen asked, indicating the photograph of the tunnel. "You're a smart guy. I can tell that from talking to you. You're not . . . crazy, are you, Jay?"

Smalls was silent.

"So, tell me, how did you end up living in a tunnel?"

A bitter spark fired in Smalls' eyes. "No choice."

Cohen shook his head. "You're wrong, Jay. Everybody has a choice."

"No, they don't," Smalls insisted with a force of conviction that struck Cohen as surprisingly firm, the bedrock of some understanding of life that he'd accepted without comfort or repose, like evidence he wanted to deny but couldn't, because the proof was there, stony and unimpeachable.

"Suppose I told you that I had a choice, Jay," Cohen said. "I wanted to be a cop. My father hated the idea. I was supposed to be a rabbi. Like my father. He was set on that. We broke up over it. I haven't seen him since before the war. The point is, I didn't want to be a rabbi. I wanted to be a cop. That was my choice. So what I'm telling you is, a guy can choose what he does, what he is."

"What he is?" Smalls asked softly, his tone oddly gentle and accommodating, like a parent questioning some childish illusion. "You chose not to be a rabbi, but could you have chosen not to be a Jew?"

"Why would I want to?"

"Well, suppose everything people who hate Jews say about them is true, and you *know* that it's true." Smalls' voice took on an unexpected confidence and subtle strength it had not exhibited before. "Suppose all these bad things are true about every Jew there is. True about you. Even if you knew that, could you choose *not* to be a Jew?"

"What does any of that have to do with you, Jay?"

"You couldn't," Smalls said with certainty. "You'd hate being a Jew. You'd want to be something else. Anything. You'd hate what you were, but you wouldn't be able to change it. Then you would be like me."

"How would I be like you?"

"You would want to die," Smalls answered quietly.

"Or maybe want to kill?" Cohen suggested tentatively.

Smalls shook his head. "No," he said. "But you'll never believe that."

1:35 A.M., *Dunlap's Collectibles*

Dunlap swung open the door. "Okay, come on in."

Blunt didn't move. "Not till you put on a light."

Dunlap fired up a cigarette lighter. "Better?"

"Why don't you just turn on the fucking light?"

"Please, Ralph, not till we get to the back room."

They made their way toward the back of the shop, Dunlap doing his best to guide Blunt down its cluttered center aisle.

"I can't see a fucking thing," Blunt grumbled.

"Watch your step, there."

"What the fuck is that?"

"Handlebars."

"Who the fuck's gonna buy handlebars?"

"You'd be surprised." Dunlap stopped and drew back a curtain. "Here we are."

"Now can you put on a fucking light, for Christ's sake?"

"Yeah, okay," Dunlap said. He hit a switch and a single bulb flashed on. "Have a seat."

Blunt stared around at the mountains of clutter, boxes overflowing with moldy books, chipped ashtrays, mismatched cups and saucers. "Where?"

"Just a second, I'll clear a space." Dunlap began removing boxes from a battered yellow sofa.

"This better be worth the effort, Harry, 'cause if it ain't . . ."

"It is, believe me." He tossed the last bit of debris into the nearest corner. "There. Have a seat."

Blunt surveyed the back room once again, his eyes roving from the mattress on the floor to the filthy sink to the plastic shower curtain through which he could see a rusty toilet. "You got a real dump here."

Dunlap shrugged. "You want a drink?"

"I want to get the fuck out of here is what I want." He dropped onto the sofa with a grunt. "You got five minutes."

Dunlap looked as if he'd been hit by an electric current. "Okay, okay, but you got to swear—"

"Fuck that," Blunt said. He started to get to his feet.

"No, wait," Dunlap said hastily. "It's just that this is, you know . . . it's dangerous, Ralph. It's a dangerous situation I'm in." He looked at Blunt sorrowfully. "Maybe I'm already fucked is what I'm saying."

"Fucked how?"

Dunlap hesitated, then said, "I went to see Burke."

Blunt stared at him.

"Chief Burke," Dunlap said.

"You what?"

"At the hospital," Dunlap said. "Where his kid is. The kid was a bum, Ralph. A fucking dope fiend. Slept on the steps out there till I give him a room."

"You gave Chief Burke's kid a room?"

"Well, not exactly give," Dunlap admitted. "But I didn't charge him that much. That's what I wanted to tell you before. But not in the bar, you know?"

A look of utter bafflement seeped into Blunt's eyes. "What the fuck are you getting at, Harry?"

"What I'm telling you is that I figured, okay, I knew the kid, so I can go and sort of, you know, pay my sympathies."

"Why the fuck would you do that?"

" 'Cause I figured it was a way I could maybe find out a little something. I mean, I was desperate, Ralph. I had to find out if the cops were getting anywhere with that freak, you know, about the dead kid. So the thing is, I went over to Saint Vincent's. I figured I'd tell the Chief that I was maybe friends with his kid, you know, and then maybe we'd get to talking, and I'd maybe find out a little bit about that wacko they got locked up. But the Chief, he hated my guts right off. I could see it in his eyes. The bastard. He don't even know me, and here I pay a sympathy call on that dope fiend son of his, and he don't even give a shit about that, and hates my guts right off, so he don't tell me nothing about what they got or ain't got on that fucking freak they picked up in the park. So, anyway, that's where I am with the Chief." He sighed. "Fucked."

A small light illuminated the wooly depths of Blunt's mind. "What I'm hearing is that you pulled all this dumb shit just to find out about that guy we picked up in the park."

"That's right."

"The one that killed the kid."

"Him, yeah."

"Which I still can't figure out why you give a shit anyway."

" 'Cause I got an interest, like I told you."

Blunt looked at Dunlap with cold menace. "You do something to that little girl, Harry?"

"Fuck no," Dunlap squealed.

" 'Cause if you fucking put one finger on that kid, I'll—"

Dunlap thrust his hands up. "Jesus, you think I'd do something like that? Jesus. Fuck, no, Ralph. Jesus Christ, what's the matter with you? It's just that, like I said, I lied to them cops that come over . . . and—" He stopped and struggled to calm himself. "And, well, I got this problem, you know?" He waited for Blunt to speak, but the detective only stared at him dumbly. "This problem with the cops." He walked to a splintered roll-top desk and fished around in one of its murky drawers. "He come into my store, the fucking wacko. He come in a few days before that kid got killed. I took some stuff off his hands. A box full of junk. I went through it all, and I found this." He opened his hand to reveal a tarnished metal key. "It's for a storage shed."

Blunt bent forward and looked closely at the key but did not touch it.

"It says right on the side there. Number twenty-seven," Dunlap said. "A storage shed at AJS Storage. Way back when, I used to use them sheds myself."

"When you was fencing?"

"Yeah, that's right. If something was really hot, I'd put it in one of them sheds and let it cool off before moving it. Hot, Ralph. That's the problem. I got some real hot stuff in that fucking shed."

"What shed?"

Dunlap shook the key. "*That* shed, for Christ's sake! What shed you think?"

Blunt glared at Dunlap. "You better watch your fucking mouth."

Dunlap ducked his head. "Yeah, sorry, Ralph. It's just that I'm under a lot of pressure here. I mean, this stuff I got in that shed, it's fucking hot is what I'm trying to tell you."

"What is it?"

"It's money, that's what it is."

"Money?"

"You know, fake stuff."

"Counterfeit money?" Blunt said. "You never done nothing like that."

"I didn't fucking make the stuff. I just took it off a guy's hands. He asked me could I find a place to stash the stuff, and I said yeah, sure."

"How much money we talking about?"

"Guy said it was fifty grand."

A light flickered again in Blunt's eyes. "Holy shit."

"Guy give me a grand just to stash the fucking stuff. I figured that was a good deal. But now I got to get it back. Today, Ralph. I got to get it back to him today."

Blunt stared at Dunlap dimly. "So, what's any of this got to do with me?"

"Okay, here it is," Dunlap said. "When I found this

key, I didn't say nothing to the creep. I figure, maybe one day I'll go out, see for myself what the wacko's got stashed out there. Then he gets picked up, and I know goddamn well he bumped off that kid, right? So the bastard's going down for a long time, you know, so that fucking shed, he ain't gonna have no use for it. So I figure, it's perfect, right? A shed in somebody else's name. So, I went over to check it out. And it was empty, Ralph. Plenty of room, you know, for my stuff." He shrugged. "So that's where I put the money. Fifty grand, can you believe it? I figured it's safe 'cause the word is, that pervert ain't never gonna see the light of day again, you know? So, okay, he's fucked. Better for me, right? Then the fucking cops come by. So, I get real nervous, you know, 'cause they're snooping around, nosing into this and that, and I figured they was sure to come back, and I had this stuff, you know, that I already took over to this shed I'm telling you about. So, okay, all right, I figure I'll just go back and get the money and drop the fucking key in the river and that'll be the end of it. But, you know how it is, Ralph, one idea leads to another, and so before long I'm totally rattled. I mean, you got murder in the deal here, and you got the money, which is a federal fucking rap. And me a three-time loser if they nail me. And I already got these fucking cops on my ass. So, the thing is, I freeze up, Ralph. I freeze up and so the money stays put and the cops, I figure, are getting closer and closer, you know?" His voice turned confiding. "I ain't had a wink of sleep, Ralph. Not a wink since they picked that bastard up. I keep thinking, these fucking cops must be grilling the shit out of him, and I keep thinking it's gonna come up, he's gonna spill something about how he's got this shed and all, and then the cops go over to the fucking shed and they ask around and they find out that some guy come over a few days ago. A short guy, you know? A guy that stashed some goods in this shed, see. A guy, Ralph. Meaning me and all."

Blunt blinked dully.

"So what I'm saying, Ralph, is how do I get that fucking money this guy wants, you know, today? 'Cause the guy's coming for it like I said, and this guy, he ain't to be fucked with. So what do I do, huh, to get this money?"

"You just grab your balls and go get it," Blunt answered.

"Oh, yeah, and suppose while I'm there the cops pull up?" Dunlap howled. "You got a picture of what happens to me then, Ralph?" He jabbed the air with two fingers. "Three times, Ralph. A three-time loser, that's me. They'll throw the fucking key away, you know? Plus, I got the problem I lied to the bastards, told them I didn't even know the son-of-a-bitch they're grilling. They don't like that, Ralph. Not in a murder case. And it a little kid too. You know how they get when it's a kid. They'll fuck me up, you know they will."

Blunt scratched the side of his face thoughtfully. "So, okay, what?"

"Well, the thing is, it ain't come out yet, right? I mean, you ain't heard nothing about no shed."

Blunt shook his head.

"So, okay, then, where are they at with Smalls? Are they gonna pin that kid's murder on him?"

Blunt shrugged. "There ain't enough evidence. That's what I hear. There ain't enough evidence to keep him locked up."

"So, they gonna let him go, then?"

"There ain't enough evidence," Blunt repeated. "So they got to get it out of him. They're working him over right now. They been doing it six, seven hours now."

"Oh, Jesus," Dunlap breathed. "What if he says

something about that goddamn shed? Seven fucking hours. Oh, Jesus." He swabbed his brow with a soiled handkerchief. "I'm cooked. I'm fucking cooked, Ralph."

Blunt shifted uncomfortably on the sofa. "You got a spring poking through here."

"I got worse problems than that," Dunlap said glumly. "Seven fucking hours." He considered the situation for a moment, then said, "Listen, Ralph, can you help me out here?"

"Like how?"

"Like maybe go get the money," Dunlap said. "I mean, I'd go get it myself, but, like I said, suppose they see me? What could I say, that I was over at Titus for the clams?"

"Titus?" Blunt asked.

"That's where the shed is. Where you'd have to go. It ain't that far from here, Ralph."

Dimly Blunt figured the time, the distance, what might go wrong. "Well, suppose you're right, and the cops are there, what do I say to 'em?"

"That you was sent."

"Sent? By who?"

"By fucking God," Dunlap shrieked. "Jesus, Ralph, how do I know? Somebody downtown. The Chief. I'm in deep shit here." He lowered his voice. "You got to help me, Ralph. You don't, I'm fucked. So, please, we're family, you know? Can you do this for me, Ralph? Can you go get that shit for me?"

Blunt stared at Dunlap mutely, his lips parted slightly as if airing out his brain. "What do I get out of it?"

"Twenty percent of what the guy give me for stashing it."

Blunt laughed.

"Thirty."

Blunt waved his meaty hand.

"Okay, five hundred dollars," Dunlap said. "An even split. Five hundred apiece. That's a lot of money for a little trip to Titus."

Blunt raked his fingers down his jaw. "When you need this done?"

"When?" Dunlap yelped. "Fucking now, man."

"No way."

"Why not?"

" 'Cause I got to meet somebody."

"Who?"

"What do you care? It's important."

"Important? What could be more important than making five hundred bucks for a little drive in the country?"

Blunt's face took on a bullish aggressiveness. "I ain't even said I'd do it yet."

The two men faced each other morosely, then Dunlap said, "So, what's the story, Ralph? You gonna do this thing?"

Blunt pulled himself to his feet. "I'll think about it."

"Please, Ralph. Do me this one favor and—"

"I said I'd think about it," Blunt repeated.

And as he made his way down the aisle, kicking unseen clutter from his path, Blunt did just that, the rusty cogs of his brain grinding forward, forcing the thinking part of his mind to come drowsily awake.

What's your secret?

1:51 A.M., *Criminal Files Room*

Burke returned the initial interview of Albert Jay Smalls to the file, then drew out the transcripts of the interrogations that had been done since Smalls' arrest eleven days earlier. As he reread the September fourth transcript, he was not surprised that Pierce and Cohen had begun their questioning with the salient facts they'd gathered during the previous two days of their investigation. By then they'd found two witnesses who'd seen Smalls standing at the gate of the park. A vendor had identified him, along with a man who worked at a nearby newspaper stand. The vendor had also seen Cathy Lake, though only briefly, a little girl in a red dress rushing across the street just as a rainsquall hit the city. Neither of the men had seen Smalls follow Cathy as she darted by, and no one in the park had seen him behind her once she entered it. Both Pierce and Cohen were convinced that Smalls had done exactly that, however, and they were determined to make Smalls admit it.

PIERCE: *Why were you following Cathy Lake?*

SMALLS: *I wasn't following her.*

PIERCE: *We know you saw her leave Clairmont Towers.*

SMALLS: *I saw her cross the street.*

PIERCE: *And you saw her go into the park?*

SMALLS: *Yes.*

PIERCE: *Did you know where she was going?*

SMALLS: *No.*

PIERCE: *But you were watching her?*

SMALLS: *I saw her cross the street.*

PIERCE: *And when she went into the park, you followed her, didn't you?*

SMALLS: *No.*

PIERCE: *Well, you went into the park directly after she did, didn't you? Don't bother to deny this, Smalls. We have plenty of witnesses who saw you go into the park at the same time she did.*

SMALLS: *I went in after she did, but I wasn't following her.*

PIERCE: *Where did you think she was going?*

SMALLS: *Home. She lives on the other side of the park.*

PIERCE: *How do you know where Cathy Lake lives?*

SMALLS: *I've seen her in the playground. Her mother picks her up and takes her home. They walk to the other side of the park.*

PIERCE: *Seems like you really have kept an eye on Cathy Lake.*

SMALLS: *I watch all the children.*

I watch all the children.

Burke considered the statement. Was it possible that Smalls thought of himself as a guardian of the children in the playground and the park? Someone who watched over them? But if so, why murder one of the very children he had set himself to protect?

He returned to the transcript.

PIERCE: *I'll tell you why you were watching Cathy Lake, Smalls. You were watching her because she had something you wanted.*

COHEN: *That's true, isn't it, Jay? You noticed something Cathy was wearing.*

SMALLS: *No.*

PIERCE: *A locket, right? Cathy Lake was wearing a pretty locket. Isn't that what you wanted?*

SMALLS: *No.*

PIERCE: *You saw it around her neck, and you figured you could take it from her, isn't that true?*

SMALLS: *No.*

PIERCE: *You saw this little girl, and you decided to rob her.*

SMALLS: *I never stole anything from her.*

PIERCE: *You told us before that you get things from the garbage and sell them, right?*

SMALLS: *Yes.*

COHEN: *How about Cathy's locket? Did you intend to sell it to someone?*

SMALLS: *No.*

Burke could feel the two detectives' frustration growing each time Smalls denied having anything to do with the murder. Already, he thought, Pierce and Cohen had begun to sense that in Albert Jay Smalls they had hit a wall they might not ultimately be able to penetrate. And so they'd shifted their approach, Cohen now beginning to take on the Good Cop role, his tone growing friendlier and less accusatory.

COHEN: *You know, Jay, it would go a lot better for you if you told us what happened to Cathy.*

SMALLS: *She was killed.*

COHEN: *And you understand that you're here because we think you know something about Cathy's death, right?*

SMALLS: *Yes.*

COHEN: *Why do you think we think that, Jay?*

SMALLS: *Because you found out.*

COHEN: *Found out what?*

SMALLS: *About . . .*

COHEN: *About what?*

SMALLS: *About . . . how . . .*

COHEN: *What did we find out about, Jay?*

SMALLS: *You . . . that I was there.*

Burke focused his mind on Cohen's final three questions. Smalls had answered each haltingly, as if confused or holding back. As if he'd not known how to answer, his final response merely something he'd seized upon in desperation, since the fact that he'd been in the park at the time of Cathy Lake's murder was something he already knew Cohen had "found out" days before. So why had Smalls faltered? Why had he been caught off-guard? The answer seemed clear. Smalls had momentarily believed that Cohen already knew something that Cohen did not know. Was that what he'd missed, Burke asked himself, that Smalls had something to hide, something he felt accused of and had to conceal, but that his crime was not the murder of Cathy Lake?

2:17 A.M., *Seaview, Boardwalk*

Pierce looked right and left down the deserted boardwalk. "We could be here all night," he said edgily.

Yearwood drummed his fingers along the curve of his cane. "Avery keeps strange hours," he said calmly. "You'll just have to wait for him to show up."

"I don't have that kind of time." Pierce glanced again at his watch. Less than four hours. "Where is this guy?"

A thin mist lay over the sandy beach. Pierce could make out only the jagged lines of surf that tumbled ashore a few yards away. After a moment, he wheeled and faced the weathered facade of the Boardwalk Motel, its rusty metal sign creaking in the ocean breeze. Twenty minutes before, he'd roused the motel's sleeping owner only to discover that Avery Garrett was not in his room. As to when he might return to it, the owner had had no idea, since Garrett had no set pattern for his comings and goings.

"Avery used to live under the boardwalk," Yearwood said. "But the cops were always harassing him, so I guess he finally moved indoors."

"How does he pay for his room?"

"Sells things. Scrap metal. Whatever junk he can find."

Pierce's restless gaze cut to the left, where, in the distance, the boardwalk came to an abrupt end. "Smalls had a box full of crap in that tunnel where he was living. We looked all through it, but we couldn't find anything that tied him to the murder." He paced restlessly along the rail, then back again. "This could take all night."

Yearwood leisurely slung his arm over the back of the bench. "I used to be the way you are. Jumpy."

Pierce laughed. "Well, you're calm enough now. What's your secret?"

"No secret, really. You just get old and learn that you're not as smart as you think you are, and that you never were."

Pierce kept pacing.

Yearwood watched him intently. "What happened to you, Detective Pierce?"

Pierce felt that he'd abruptly been nailed to a wall. He reached for a cigarette and lit it.

Yearwood's gaze continued to bore into him.

"You like asking questions, but you're not much on answering them, are you?" the old man asked.

Pierce said nothing.

Yearwood shrugged. "Okay, fine, no more questions from me. But here's a piece of advice you might use. Technical advice, you might call it."

Pierce blew a column of smoke into the dark air. "I'm listening."

"When you talk to Avery Garrett, don't just start firing questions at him like you're a big shot and he's nothing. Treat him with some respect. Because that's all he wants."

Pierce started to speak, but Yearwood lifted his hand and silenced him.

"So you do it the way I do it. You let Avery talk, and you don't rush him, and you listen to his story, and you listen in that story for something you can use. But more than anything, let him be a man talking to a man."

Pierce pressed his back against the rail. A breeze touched his hair, and briefly he imagined Anna Lake doing the same.

"You married?" Yearwood asked.

"Divorced."

"Kids?"

"Daughter."

"How old?"

Costa's face swam into Pierce's mind, but rather than tell the story of what had been done to Debra, he said only, "She died," and returned his gaze to the sea.

2:21 A.M., *Interrogation Room 3*

It was an odd flash of resentment, quick, bright, and unmistakable, and Cohen replayed the question that had incited it, and which he now repeated.

"You heard me, Jay. What did you have against Cathy Lake?"

Smalls sat ramrod straight, his back pressed firmly against the chair.

"You didn't have anything against Cathy, is that what you're trying to tell me, Jay?" Cohen asked. "I mean, you looked pissed when I suggested that you did."

"I didn't know her," Smalls said. "I had nothing against her."

"Well, think about how she was killed," Cohen pressed. "The wire around her neck. How tight it was. Brutal. A guy has to have a lot of hate bottled up in him to do something like that, right?" He flipped through the Murder Book until he found a photograph of the girl's crumpled body, the ligature marks visible on her throat. "A lot of hate bottled up, don't you think, to kill a little girl this way?"

"I didn't do that."

"Who did?"

"I don't know. Maybe the man in the playground. The man she was afraid of."

"The Invisible Man, right," Cohen said with a hard laugh. "Okay, let's suppose it's this guy. What can you tell me about him?"

"I never saw him."

"I don't mean what he looked like. I mean inside. What's he feel like? In his heart."

Something imprisoned deep within Smalls' mind emerged as visibly as a needle piercing through his skin. "Terrible."

"What's terrible?"

"What he wants." Smalls' voice trembled like something at the edge of a precipice.

"To kill a kid, you mean?"

"To want a . . . to feel . . ."

"What?"

"Not normal." Smalls' face was wreathed in shame.

"Not normal, how?"

"Because he wants . . ."

"A kid?"

"Yes."

Now is the moment, Cohen thought, Smalls curiously exposed, his shoulders slumped, his voice tremulous, so that he seemed suddenly exhausted and overwhelmed by his own dreadful hatred of himself, primed and ready to collapse. Now was the moment to swing his questions like a sword, drive Smalls to the wall. "What would a guy like that do, Jay? A guy who . . . wants a kid? Would he hang around playgrounds?"

"Yes," Smalls answered softly.

"Would he watch kids?"

"Yes."

"And while he watched them, would he try to be invisible?"

Smalls lowered his head.

"Would he follow a kid to some lonely place?"

Smalls said nothing.

"Would he make sure nobody was around and then . . ."

Smalls lifted his head. "I didn't do any of that," he said quietly. His earlier sense of shame dissolved and his face took on a fierce certitude that seemed itself borne upward on a wave of wounded pride. "I didn't," he repeated firmly. "I never hurt that little girl."

So is that what it finally comes to, Cohen wondered as he watched Smalls draw in a breath, that out of nowhere you suddenly believe a man you've worked so hard not to believe, believe him not because you've found something that exonerates him or because some completely different man has confessed to the crime, but because he has abruptly exhibited that unspeakable exhaustion that only the innocent may know? He thought of his own kind, the centuries of their trial, accused of devising plots, poisoning wells, killing children, and wondered how many of them had sat before their interrogators as Smalls sat before him now, silent, alone, utterly helpless. Did they, too, have nothing to declare their innocence save what he now saw in Smalls' face, the towering moral certainty that they had done no wrong?

2:30 A.M., 981 Tremont Street

Eddie Lambrusco steered Siddell Carting Truck 12 over to the curb in front of Molly's Café. "Time for lunch," he said.

Siddell sat staring straight ahead.

"What's the matter, you not hungry?" Eddie asked.

"It's two-thirty in the morning. You call that lunch?"

"It is when you work the night shift," Eddie said.

Siddell shook his head. "Just hurry up, will you?"

Eddie waved his hand. "Okay, suit yourself." He heaved himself out of the truck, slammed the door, and strode into the café. Next time, he thought, next time, no matter what, he wasn't going to get stuck with Terry Siddell as his shift partner. He thought of Charlie, wished they still worked together. A joke would save him, he thought, a joke would end this sick feeling of being small and helpless, a nothing. If he just hadn't slugged the guy in Sanitation, he'd be having a laugh now instead of . . . what he had to do.

"So, how's tricks?" Molly asked as he sat down at the counter.

"They could be better."

Molly wiped the counter with a dirty rag. "Ain't that the way of it?" She smiled her gap-toothed smile. "So what'll you have, handsome?"

Eddie watched her in amazement that such a big, ugly broad could be so happy. Didn't she know how rotten she looked, that no guy would touch her? What in all the world did Molly Pulaski have to be cheerful about? She'd lived her whole life mopping up spilled coffee, a fat, warty kid who'd expanded into a floral balloon of a woman, unmarried and unmarriageable, childless and with no hope of children, destined to be found facedown on the tenement floor, or burned to a crisp by her last cigarette. And yet she gave every evidence of being perfectly delighted with how it had all turned out. Eddie shook his head in bafflement. Did a really bad hand contain some invisible card, he wondered, one that worked like a flash of light, blinding you to the lousy cards you'd drawn?

Molly stopped wiping the counter and stared Eddie dead in the eye. "Cat got your tongue, gorgeous?"

"Uh, no. Coffee. Couple eggs."

Molly's grin expanded, revealing missing teeth on either side. "Sunny-side up?"

"Yeah, why not?"

"Comin' up, my lovely," Molly chirped, then made a surprisingly graceful turn and sashayed away, humming brightly.

Eddie watched her until she disappeared into the kitchen, the mystery of life growing more impenetrable with each oblivious sway of her huge buttocks. Then he let his attention drift out over the diner, lighting briefly on each of its early morning habitués, the fishermen and dockworkers and tugboat crewmen on their way to the river, dressed in shapeless work clothes and wool caps, the uniform of Harbortown. There were a few day laborers, though it was a full three hours before the flatbed trucks arrived to take them to worksites about town. And, as always, there was a scattering of men who'd not gone home at all, fearing, Eddie supposed, the wifely wrath that would inevitably greet them. For now they sat composing hopelessly ludicrous stories of how they'd spent the evening, careful to leave out the part about the frowsy whore they'd pounded into the grimy mattress of some buck-an-hour hotel.

"Here's your eggs and coffee." Molly slid the plate in front of Eddie with a grand flourish, then plopped the steaming mug down beside it. "Anything else, dreamboat?"

"No, thanks," Eddie said, concealing his dislike for the little terms of endearment Molly habitually tossed him. He was not a dreamboat and they both knew it. She might as easily have said "What'll you have, loser?" or "Anything else, you poor fucking jerk?" for all the comfort that it brought him in this, the final, weary portion of his working day.

He stabbed a forkful of eggs, washed it down with a gulp of coffee, his gaze now on the figure of a man in a long black coat who approached the café from across the empty street. He gave off a sense of one familiar with the night, who had no fear of it, perhaps even preferred its shadows to what the day revealed.

Eddie took another sip from the mug, watching as the man entered, then stood at the door, stripping off his gloves while he glanced about the diner's interior until his attention lit upon a large man who sat in the back corner. Then, with a nod, he strode back to the big man's booth and slid into it, taking off his hat as he did so, a great mass of hair winking silver in the light.

"Who's that?" Eddie said when Molly stepped over to him again.

"That?" Molly said with obvious pride. "Why, that's His Honor Francis X. O'Hearn. The Police Commissioner himself. You ever need anything, he's the man to see."

Eddie laughed. "What would I need from a big shot like that?"

"Protection," Molly answered without hesitation.

"From what?"

Molly glanced toward the Commissioner, then back to Eddie. "From the law, sweetheart. From what it can do to the likes of us." With that she slung the counter cloth over her beefy shoulder and moved away.

Eddie took a gulp of coffee, paid the tab, then slid off the stool. On the way to the door, he shot a final glance toward the Commissioner and the man in the green suit. The Great Man had leaned forward and was staring at the other man intently, a single finger lifted regally as he made his point. What must it be like,

Eddie wondered, to hold the reins of the city in your hands, to command other men and feel them tense at your approach, to know that all eyes turn to you when you come into the room, and that none among the throng within it can do you the slightest harm?

"Take it easy, handsome," Molly called as he opened the door of the café.

He smiled thinly. "Just call me Eddie," he said. "Just Eddie from now on."

Do you know where he was headed?

"There he is," Yearwood said. He nodded toward a figure, barely visible through the haze, walking slowly, listing to the left, like a small, badly damaged boat. "That's Avery. He's been out collecting all night, I guess." Yearwood indicated the large canvas bag flung over Garrett's shoulder. He stepped forward and waited silently for him to draw near. Then he called, "Hello, Avery."

Avery Garrett stared at him without smiling.

Yearwood motioned Pierce forward. "Remember what I told you," he murmured.

Drawing closer, Pierce saw that Avery Garrett was a man in his sixties. His jaws were covered with a scraggly graying beard. He wore thick glasses with wide black frames, and a baseball cap punched low on his brow so that his eyes disappeared in shadow.

Pierce flashed his badge.

Avery Garrett let the canvas bag drop with a hard thud onto the slats of the boardwalk. "I ain't done nothing," he declared.

"It's not about you, Avery," Yearwood assured him. "It's about Jimmy Eagar. He's in serious trouble."

"Murder," Pierce said. "An eight-year-old girl."

Garrett's eyes cut over to Pierce.

Pierce took out his notebook. "When did you see him last?"

"When he come back after being lost."

"Five years ago?"

"Yeah. He was all upset. Said he was going off somewhere. That he was leaving for good. He was gonna change his name, stash everything that identified him. Disappear, he said. Be invisible. That's what he wanted. To be invisible."

"But he didn't tell you why he wanted that?"

"No," Garrett answered.

"Did he mention anything that he might have done while he was . . . lost?"

"No."

"Did he tell you where he'd gone?"

"Said he was in Englishtown. Titus."

"Did he mention anyone he met or lived with in those places?"

"I don't think he met nobody."

"Why do you think that?"

" 'Cause he looked like me when I didn't have no place to live or nobody to help out. All ragged and dirty. Didn't have nothing but an old bag full of stuff. Papers and things. The clothes on his back, that was it. I hated to see him that way. I told him he could stay with me if he wanted to, but he said no, he didn't want to stay in Seaview."

"Do you know where he was headed?"

"Said he was going into the city. I told him I had this shed he could bed down in if he got tired. It didn't have no running water or nothing, but he could bed down in it for a night or two if he wanted."

"Did he?"

"I don't know."

"Where is the shed?"

"Off Route Six," Garrett answered. "Between Titus and Englishtown. AJS Storage. Number twenty-seven. I'd give you the key, but Jimmy never brought it back, so I figure he's still got it."

"We looked through everything he had, but we didn't find a key," Pierce told him.

Garrett shrugged. "Maybe he lost it."

"Or hid it," Pierce said.

"Why would he do that?" Garrett asked mildly.

But Pierce had already turned away and was moving rapidly down the midway toward his car.

2:51 A.M., *Interrogation Room 3*

Cohen looked at his watch and felt time as something physical, a vise squeezing out his life, making him hot and sweaty, so that he'd finally rushed to the window, cranked it open, and stuck his head into the night air.

When he turned back, Smalls was still sitting in his chair, his hands in his lap, his eyes downcast, resigned, or so it seemed to Cohen, to whatever happened to him next, broken, left with nothing more than the energy it took to proclaim by some look or gesture, the weary tenor of his voice, that he was innocent.

"You know, Jay, I've been thinking about what you said earlier. About people not having choices."

Smalls made no response.

"Take me, for example." He drew a handkerchief from his pocket and swabbed his neck. "I'm a detective. And take you. A suspect. We can't change that. So I have to go at you. Sometimes hard. Sometimes not so hard. But I have to go at you. Because that's my job." He returned the handkerchief to his pocket, went back to his chair. "But suppose we changed all that. Just the two of us. Suppose I stopped being a detective and you stopped being a guy I have to interrogate, and instead of those two guys, we just became ourselves. Norm Cohen and Jay Smalls. Just talked, like a couple of normal guys."

Smalls' gaze drifted upward as Cohen leaned back.

"Would you like that, Jay?"

"Yes."

"Okay, so what should we talk about?"

"I don't know," Smalls answered, his voice barely above a whisper. "I don't talk to people."

"Okay, how about when you were in school, what did you talk about then?"

"I didn't talk much."

"But you listened, I'll bet. What were the other kids talking about?"

"Girls mostly. The boys, I mean. They talked about girls."

"Did you ever have a girl?"

"No."

"I don't have one either," Cohen said. "I'd like to, but I don't." He waited for Smalls to respond, but Smalls remained silent. "There's this woman in my building, for example," Cohen added. "Sometimes I think of her."

What if nothing is?

"Okay, I'll do it."

"That's great, Ralph," Dunlap said excitedly. "You won't be sorry, believe me. Come in, I'll give you the details."

Blunt followed Dunlap to the rear of the store, once again stumbling through the darkness, raking whatever lay in his path before him like a huge black wave.

"Have a seat, Ralph. You want a beer?"

"I ain't got all night, Harry." Blunt's small eyes whipped back and forth. "I got to be back in town by six."

"Oh, yeah?" Dunlap asked brightly. "You got some broad waiting for you?"

"Shit," Blunt grumbled. "Broad, my ass."

"So, you want to sit down?"

"Fuck, no. Let's get on with it."

"Yeah, okay, no sweat, Ralph," Dunlap said. "Let me show you the deal."

Blunt watched glumly as Dunlap sprinted to a desk, jerked a folded map from one of its cubicles, and spread it out across a square card table. "Okay, here it is," he said. "Titus."

"I know where Titus is," Blunt growled.

"Sure you do, Ralph," Dunlap said. "But it ain't Titus I'm showing you."

"You said that fucking locker was in Titus."

"Basically, yeah. But not exactly in town." He ran his finger along a green line marked Route 6. "You go along here until you get to the outskirts of town, see?"

Blunt nodded sullenly.

"You come to Brighton Avenue," Dunlap went on. "There's an Esso station on the right. The corner, I mean. You can't miss it. You go past the station. Maybe a mile." He drew his finger toward the eastern side of the map. "You get to Covenant. There's a church there on the corner. Saint something's. Got a Madonna out front."

"Madonna out front," Blunt repeated, now with a sense that things were getting crowded inside his head. "Fucking boonies, this place."

"It's the nutcase that picked it, not me."

"All right, just go ahead," Blunt said, waving a beefy hand.

"Okay, so, you go maybe a mile, two miles down Sumpter. It gets to be like woods, you know? Like trees and shit. Nothing the fuck around. Then you come to this gate. A sign on it. AJS Storage. That's the place you're looking for. Where the goods are."

"The gate locked?"

"Nah, you just swing it open. Drive right in. At this time of night, nobody's around."

"Okay, what then?"

"There's this bunch of little houses. Like sheds, you know? Made out of wood. You're looking for number twenty-seven. The number's painted right over the door. Big black number. Twenty-seven." He reached into his pocket and drew out the key. "The creepo hadn't bothered to lock the fucking thing, but I did. So, that's it. You bring the stuff back here. I give you the five hundred bucks like I said. End of story."

Blunt folded his paw around the key. "It fucking better be the end of story, Harry."

Dunlap's hands fluttered like small pink birds between them. "Oh, it will be, Ralph. Believe me. It will be."

Blunt dropped the key into the pocket of his trousers, stepped over to the curtain, and flung it back. "This better go smooth, Harry. 'Cause if it don't—"

"It will, it will." Dunlap used all his inner strength to hold up a smile. "You can trust me on this one, Ralph."

Blunt grunted doubtfully, then stepped through the curtain and into the unlighted interior of the store.

Dunlap followed him for a few feet. "See you later, Ralph." He watched his cousin's huge frame lurch toward the door, scraping and banging all the way. Like a fucking bull, he thought, fucking bull in a china shop.

3:07 A.M., *Route 6*

The road was dark, with few lights burning in the houses or nondescript roadside shops that swept by on either side of the car. It was a bleak area, but Pierce remembered that it had been quite beautiful once, the silver waters of the tidal marshes teeming with birds, golden reeds weaving in the breeze.

"I grew up around here," Pierce said. "Met my wife here. She was from the Midwest. Just in Seaview on vacation."

"Where were you from?"

"Englishtown," Pierce answered.

"So you could just walk over to the river and look right across to the city," Yearwood said. "Did it call to you?"

"No."

"Then why did you go there?"

"I don't know," Pierce answered, though he knew quite well that he'd left Englishtown for one reason only, because Costa had left it, moved into the city, rented a house in a nice, quiet neighborhood, a house near a school and a playground, just the way his house in Englishtown had been.

"You weren't following a dream?" Yearwood asked lightly.

"No," Pierce answered. *A nightmare,* he thought.

A brief silence, then Yearwood asked, "So, what do you do in the off hours?"

"Nothing much."

"A loner, then."

Pierce imagined Anna Lake in her tidy apartment, curled up on the worn blue sofa, her legs drawn beneath her, a woolen sweater draped across her shoulders. "Not because I want to be."

"So let me ask you again," Yearwood said. "What happened to you, Detective Pierce?"

Rather than answer, Pierce said, "What do you think might be in that shed Garrett told us about?"

"What if nothing is?"

"Then I'll go back to the city."

"And give up?"

Pierce relived his long hours of stalking Costa, watching him from the distance as he drunkenly weaved down the streets of Harbortown. What would Anna think of him if she knew just how deep the poison had finally sunk? And yet, what choice did he have but to tell her how night after night he'd followed Costa to his seedy dockside haunts, then on weekends when the little mechanic had strolled to the playground near his house and sat feeding squirrels and pigeons while Pierce watched him in the distance, red-eyed with hatred, hoping with all his raging heart that once, just once, Costa would lose his grip and in that instant of lost control approach a solitary child. *Just once,* he'd thought at the time, *just once, and you're mine.*

"No, never," Pierce said.

Yearwood cracked the window, and a blast of wet air swept into the car. "But what happens when you reach the end of the line? When you've done all you can but you just can't get your man?"

"Then you have to let him go," Pierce answered. He pressed down on the accelerator. *Or cross the line yourself,* he thought.

3:11 A.M., *Interrogation Room 3*

"So, anyway, I haven't had the guts to approach her," Cohen said. "I just can't seem to work up the courage to do it. Woman trouble. You ever had that, Jay?"

"No," Smalls answered.

Before Cohen could say more, the door opened.

"I need to speak to you, Detective Cohen," the Commissioner said.

Cohen joined the Commissioner in the corridor outside Interrogation Room 3.

"It's been a long night, hasn't it?" the Commissioner asked.

"Yes, it has."

The Commissioner removed one of the white gloves of his dress uniform and examined a smudge. "So, are you making any headway?"

"Not as much as I'd like," Cohen answered. "Pierce has gone to—"

"Yes, I know," the Commissioner interrupted. He drew off the second glove. "Have you heard anything from him?"

"Not yet."

The Commissioner placed his bare right hand on Cohen's shoulder. "The race is not always to the swift, isn't that so?" The Commissioner smiled. "That being the case, I want you to understand—both you and Detective Pierce—that I know you both did your best. Not just during this last interrogation, but in the whole investigation. You found your man, Detective. This fellow. Of that there is no doubt. And you are both to be commended for it."

"Thank you, sir."

The Commissioner looked at his watch. "You've been at it for almost ten hours now. You must be tired. And so at six sharp, I want you to go home, Detective. You need rest, I can see that. I want you to get up from your chair and walk directly to your car and go home and get a full twelve hours of sleep before you come back here to headquarters. Don't worry about that fellow in there. His release will be handled by others who haven't been at him all night. The same goes for Pierce. When he leaves . . . where is it he went?"

"Seaview, sir."

The Commissioner nodded. "He should go directly home from there."

"Unless he's found something we can use," Cohen said.

"Yes, of course. In that case, he would come back. Do you expect him to call in?"

"Yes, sir."

"When he does, tell him what I said. That I'm proud of what you two men accomplished in this case, and that I know you're both dead tired, and that he should go directly home."

"Yes, sir."

"That's at six A.M. You'll leave the interrogation room."

"Smalls will need to be guarded though," Cohen said. "Otherwise he might . . ."

"Might what?"

"Might just walk out the door."

"At six o'clock, Detective, this fellow is a private citizen again. He has no warrants against him and no charges have been filed. A private citizen. Nothing else."

"Yes, sir."

The Commissioner's smile returned. "Well, good night, then, Detective." He gripped Cohen's hand. "Sleep well."

"Thank you, sir. I'll try."

With that the Commissioner turned on his heel and strode back down the corridor to his office, moving down it, Cohen thought, like something dark through an even darker vein.

3:12 A.M., *Criminal Files Room*

Burke glanced up from the transcript and glimpsed the Commissioner as he strode past the glass door, his features curiously troubled. He started to rise, follow his old friend down the corridor, but the jangle of the phone stopped him.

It was Dr. Wynn.

"I wanted to let you know that Scottie's condition has deteriorated," the doctor said. "His breathing is extremely shallow."

"So I should come there now?"

"I think so, yes."

"All right," Burke said.

On the way out, Burke saw the Commissioner standing at the window that looked out over the city.

"I have to go to the hospital, Francis," he told him.

The Commissioner did not bother to face him. "There's no need for you to come back, Tom."

"But I should—"

"Stay with Scottie. That's where you belong. I'll handle this fellow from here on out." The Commissioner turned around slowly, and Burke saw that his eyes were oddly imploring. "You know, Tommy, there's something else the nuns never taught us. That sometimes there's no way to do the right thing. If we always had choices, then we could be condemned. But we don't always have choices, do we?"

"No, we don't."

A slender smile, soft as candlelight, rose to the Commissioner's lips. "Go to your son," he said.

And so Burke did.

What'll it be?

Blunt steered the car into the dimly lighted station. He'd not planned to stop anywhere en route to Titus, but during the last few minutes Dunlap's directions had begun to blur. He needed to get his bearings, make sure he was headed in the right direction.

Through the fetid smoke trapped inside the car, he watched as the attendant lumbered forward, rubbing sleep from his eyes.

"What'll it be?" the attendant mumbled.

"Fill 'er up," Blunt answered.

The attendant staggered drowsily to the pump, snatched the nozzle from its metal cradle, and began to pump the gas.

His movements were slow, indifferent, and Blunt

thought that what this jerk really needed was a swift kick in the ass. But then, wasn't that what everyone needed?

He thought of the meeting he'd had with the Commissioner an hour before, the way the Old Man had edged around what he wanted done, never saying it straight out. Smalls needed a swift kick in the ass, that was what the message had been, but the Commissioner had delivered it at a slant, going on and on about how it was a cop's job to protect little kids from freaks like the one they'd found in the park, and how this fucking freak was going to have to be let go, and how he'd end up in the park again, and how some little girl would find herself wandering by this shit-hole the freak lived in, and how if the freak saw her, he'd do the same thing to her that he'd done to the little girl a few days before, and how that was terrible, terrible, and something should be done about it, right, Ralph, something should be done, you know what I mean, don't you?

He'd known all right, Blunt thought now, he'd known from the first words the Old Man had said to him, known that he was headed for the cement house on Lake Warren at around dawn, him and the freak, and that maybe the freak wasn't coming out of it again, at least not in shape to choke the life out of some little girl, not with his hands all fucked up the way they'd be, mangled to hell, thumbs broken. You break a guy's thumbs, Blunt thought with deep philosophical satisfaction, he never fucks with you again.

"Dollar ninety."

"Huh?"

"Dollar ninety," the attendant repeated, this time a little sharply, so that Blunt had the urge to grab him by his scrawny neck, jerk his head into the car's smoky interior, and give him the whack his smart-ass attitude was clearly begging for.

But he was a cop and so he couldn't do that. The punk would yell it to high heaven if he did, scream to some fucking lawyer that some fat-assed cop had roughed him up. How did it happen, Blunt wondered, that the pussies ran things now? They couldn't do shit without men like him. They couldn't control the first grade at Our Lady of Lourdes without people like him supplying the muscle. He wondered if the Commissioner had now joined the ranks of the pussies who ran things, a guy who couldn't do the dirty work himself anymore, afraid he might get something on those fucking pretty white gloves he'd worn in Molly's Café.

"Dollar ninety," the attendant said again.

When Blunt met his gaze, he saw something in the kid's eyes he didn't like, a vague contempt, or maybe just a question. *What's the matter with this fucking guy?*

He'd seen other people with the same look in their eyes but had never quite understood what he did that caused them to look at him that way. Maybe it was just that he didn't answer them the way they expected, that it took him a few extra seconds to get things straight. He'd broken more than a few noses over that look but decided that breaking the attendant's nose wouldn't be a good idea. After all, he had bigger fish to fry than slapping the shit out of some night-shift grease monkey. He had fifty grand waiting for him, and that thought brought a smile slithering to his lips.

"Yeah, okay," Blunt said lightly. "Dollar ninety."

He reached for his wallet, drew out two singles.

The attendant snapped them from his hand and strolled, now even more slowly than before, back inside the station.

Waiting in the car, Blunt considered his next move. Drive to Titus, find that fucking storage shed, get the money, haul ass back to the city in time to get the pervert. The last part was the easiest. The Old Man had made sure of that.

> *He'll be in Interrogation Room 3.*
> *What about the guys who are going at him?*
> *They won't be there. Pierce. Cohen. Neither one of them.*
> *They know the setup?*
> *Nobody will be there, Ralph. That's all you need to know. You just go in and get Smalls. Nobody'll stop you or question you or anything else. I'll make sure of that.*

Okay, Blunt thought now, okay, that part's easy. He'd done it before, provided the muscle. But as to what he had to do before that, this whole business of the shed and the money, he was less sure of how that might go down. Maybe he should make a plan, he thought, and immediately began to do what he always did in such situations, figure that if so-and-so does this, I do that. One by one, he clicked off the contingencies: If a guy is at the gate, fuck Harry, I won't go in. If the key don't fit, I'll snap the lock with some cutters. If the money's not there, I'll blow the place and get the hell back to town. If the money's there, I'll grab it fast and put it in the trunk. If anything goes wrong, I'll kick Dunlap's fucking ass.

"Your change."

"Whuh?"

"I said, here's your change."

The attendant's tone seemed sharp, as before, and Blunt noticed that he was looking at him that way again, giving him the once-over with the same look too many people had always had on their faces, everybody from the kids on the block to his own drunken mother, like there was some secret that everyone else knew, and that he was supposed to know but didn't.

"Yeah, okay." Blunt snatched the coins from the attendant's hand. "How far to Titus?"

The look remained in place, and for a moment Blunt wondered just how much he could get away with. Suppose he whacked the smart-ass, then sped away. Who'd know the difference, he asked himself, and after a few minutes of looking into it, who'd give a shit that some gas-pump jockey had gotten creamed at four in the morning? Nobody, Blunt decided, nobody at all. He felt his right hand curl into a fist. Just one word, you fuck, he thought, just one smart-ass word.

The attendant shrugged. "I'd say you're about twenty minutes away."

Blunt gave him another chance to fuck himself. "Twenty minutes, huh?"

The attendant didn't take it. "This time of morning, you'll have the road to yourself."

"Okay," Blunt said. He hit the ignition and pulled away, giving the grease monkey a final look in the dusty rearview mirror. Lucky bastard, he thought. He's got no idea how fucking lucky.

3:38 A.M., *Interrogation Room 3*

"Anyway, I look for opportunities to run into her." Cohen had resumed talking about Ruth Green after returning to the interrogation room following his talk with the Commissioner. "But she's young. That's the problem. Too young for me." He shook his head at his own foolish hopes, then glanced at Smalls. "Embarrassing, right? Her twenty-six and me over forty." He laughed.

"I'm a cradle-robber, that's what you're thinking. I can see it in your face, like I'm some guy after a kid, right?"

Something crawled into Smalls' eyes. Not light, but darkness, not the glimmer of innocence Cohen thought he'd recognized an hour before, but its hideous opposite, the cold, hard, unmistakable glint of guilt. He looked at Smalls' hands, the elongated fingers, delicate as reeds, the narrow wrists with their soft net of blue veins, and it rose before him in a macabre vision, full and dark and searingly real, the world of Smalls' perverse desire, the parks and playgrounds where he lurked, watching children as they laughed and frolicked, waiting for one of them to break off from the rest, to wander into his dank tunnel and be forever lost.

He felt a shudder deep inside, then a wave of self-lacerating fury at the murderous consequences of his failure, time slipping away, Smalls about to go free, how he'd fallen into Smalls' trap, been deceived by his frailty and his pose of helpless, wounded innocence, and thus been lured into a precious hour of idle talk, not interrogation at all, but idle fucking talk *about himself*!

His eyes bore into Smalls, who smiled at him softly.

You fucking bastard, Cohen smoldered, his eyes now leaping toward the window, the thick black thread of the river, the overarching bridge. *You bastard.* He saw the sprawl of small towns that spread out beyond the bridge, Titus, Englishtown, Seaview, and felt time like a burning fuse. *Find something, Jack,* he pleaded desperately. *Please.*

PART IV

Will you be with him till the end?

3:43 A.M., September 13, Route 6

Pierce gripped the wheel, looking for the turn off Route 6 that led to Titus. Time was pressure now, a swirl of ever-deepening water that would ultimately drown his promise to Anna Lake. Four years before, he'd made the same promise to Jenny but had failed to keep it. He must not fail Anna Lake, though even now he found no way to avoid the growing certainty that Smalls would go free, and thus trap Anna in the same poisonous chamber in which he had been imprisoned, and from which only Smalls' apprehension could provide escape.

Escape.

In the long weeks after Debra's murder he'd wanted escape more than vengeance. Just to escape the tormenting truth that he was condemned to breathe the same air as the man who'd killed his daughter. He saw Costa stagger out of the bar and into the fog of Harbortown, gazing blearily as he tottered forward, his red-rimmed eyes working to peel away night's black curtain, cursing the fog and the darkness and the deserted street where he could find no one to direct him home.

"You asked what happened to me," Pierce blurted out suddenly.

Yearwood looked at him but said nothing.

"A guy killed my daughter," Pierce said. "Four years ago." He expected a question from Yearwood, but none came. "I dropped her off at a park near our house. She walked over to where some of her friends were standing around. I never saw her again." He recalled his return to the park two hours later, the way his eyes had searched for her among the other children, the stab of unease he'd felt when he hadn't seen her, then the steadily building panic. "They found her three hours later. In a ditch about a hundred yards from the park."

"Did they catch the man who did it?" Yearwood asked.

"The next day," Pierce answered. "Some people had seen a guy hanging around the girls' bathroom. A couple of people recognized him from the neighborhood. But there was no physical evidence, so he got away with it. Even moved to the city. Free as a bird."

Pierce saw Costa stumble out into the fog-shrouded street, weaving drunkenly as he sought his way home.

"He fell in the river a year later though," he said. "Drowned."

"An accidental death," Yearwood said.

"Yeah."

"So in the end he didn't get away with it."

Pierce remembered Costa's body faceup on the deck of the tug, lips purple and bloated, eyes popped, a look of utter terror in his features. At that instant, he realized what he could not have known before, that vengeance was a stale bread. It did not fill the emptiness within him, nor grant him the slightest peace.

"I promised Cathy Lake's mother that Smalls wouldn't get away with it either," Pierce said. Anna appeared in his mind, and he felt something unravel within him, the hard knot of his loneliness. "Anna is her name."

Yearwood's smile came from the ages. "And you're in love with her," he said.

3:47 A.M., *Saint Vincent's Hospital, Room 704*

Dr. Wynn stood at Scottie's bed when Burke entered. He drew the curtains of the oxygen tent closed.

"Thank you for letting me know," Burke told him. "I don't want him to die alone."

The doctor toyed with the end of his stethoscope. "Will you be with him till the end?"

"Yes," Burke said.

The doctor nodded. "Well, if there's anything I can do."

"Thank you."

Once the doctor left the room, Burke was not at all sure he wanted to spend the final minutes of his son's life alone in this sterile room, Scottie little more than a blur behind the translucent plastic of the oxygen tent, a silent room save for the ragged edge of his son's breathing. But was that not how he'd always reacted to his son? Had he not always chosen flight? After that last battle, when Scottie had screamed in his face, declared that he would never, never be the son Burke wanted, had he not simply turned and walked to his car and gone to headquarters and sunk himself in whatever case first greeted his arrival? And after that, each time his wife had begged him to find Scottie, accept him, welcome him into his arms, had he not muttered that yes, yes, he would do that, and then fled downtown?

But now he felt that he had no choice but face this solitary vigil with the same fortitude with which he'd sat alone with his dying wife six years before, Scottie's whereabouts unknown, so the possibility existed that even now, in his last hours, his son did not know that his mother had died before him, drowning in a sea of worry for her wayward son, whispering his name over and over, *Scottie, Scottie*, her last plea. If she were here now, what would she say to him? Burke wondered. Only that she loved him, he supposed, always had and would, the fabled words of motherhood, older than the Virgin. But Ellen was not here, and so it was up to Burke to carry on alone.

Alone.

Burke thought of the many nights he'd left Ellen and Scottie to sit alone at the dinner table, then in front of the radio, and later still to go to their beds without his touch, then rise alone, dress and eat alone, while all that time he'd remained at headquarters or in some bloodspattered room. Had he been so deeply engrossed in the lonely death of someone far away that he had not for a moment grasped the lonely lives of those who'd been infinitely near? Had Scottie known him only for his willful absences, a father who found distasteful the very presence of his son, and so avoided contact, and by that means erased him deliberately from his life?

He walked to the end of the bed, then returned to the chair beside the bed and sat again. He was still seated at his son's bedside when Father Paddock arrived.

"Hello, Tom."

"Father."

The priest took a chair a few feet away, his hands in his lap, clasping a Bible. "Scottie will soon be home, Tom," he said.

Burke had never convinced himself of such a possibility, so he said nothing.

The priest's fingers tightened around his Bible. "It's all a wilderness, Tom, so we're bound to get lost here and there."

"I wanted a different son," Burke admitted. "That's my confession. I wanted a different son, and he knew that. And it destroyed him."

"You didn't destroy Scottie, Tom."

"Sean, as a priest, if you believed that God wished you'd never been born, wouldn't that destroy you?"

Father Paddock leaned back as if pushed by an invisible hand. "You can't eat yourself alive, that's what I'm telling you." He waited for Burke to respond, and when he didn't, got to his feet. "I'll give him the Last Rites now."

Burke listened as the priest administered the Last Rites, but the words rang hollow, and he felt a hollowness at the very center of himself. He had been given a child, a life, and had irreparably damaged that life, twisted and distorted it. That was his legacy, this brutal destruction.

"Would you like me to come back after morning Mass?" Father Paddock asked.

"No," Burke answered. "No need." He walked the priest to the door, shook his hand, thanked him, then returned to the chair beside his son's bed.

After that Burke did nothing but wait, casting his eyes toward Scottie only long enough to make out the ghastly pallor of his skin, the blue lips, eyelids that had begun to flutter in what Burke took to be a final spasm of life and which he expected to diminish quickly, then vanish behind a rigid mask of death.

But the movement only grew more violent, so that Burke finally parted the curtain and pressed his hand against his son's forehead. "You can go now, Scottie," he whispered.

Scottie's fingers clawed at Burke's hand, digging frantically as he tossed his head from side to side and began to mutter incoherently.

"You can go," Burke repeated brokenly.

But Scottie did not go. He twisted to the right, shuddered, then wheeled about, his mouth jerking wildly, the movement beneath his eyes growing ever more violent as his hands dug fiercely at the covering sheet.

"Please, Scottie," Burke pleaded. "Please go."

But still Scottie wheeled and turned, tormented, burning, twisting back and forth in an agony of stifled speech until his anguished whisper broke the air in a final plea.

Bury me.

3:55 A.M., *Route 6*

"Jesus," Blunt muttered.

He glared blearily at the black sea that churned a few yards from the car, the yellow beams illuminating tumbling lines of foam. Covenant? Brighton? Sumpter? Shit! Which one was he supposed to follow to which one?

One thing was sure; he wasn't supposed to be here, staring at the goddamn fucking ocean, with no light to be seen, not even some goddamn fisherman's hut. He was lost, goddammit, and there was no one around to help him get found again.

A steaming wave of rage washed over him, hateful

and malignant, the kind that had so often swept over him in school, especially when some bitch teacher had called on him. Called on *him,* goddammit, as if she hadn't fucking seen that his hand wasn't up. As if she hadn't noticed that his hand was never up, the bitch. Not like that fucking Weinberg kid, the puny little kike, always with the answers.

He grinned, remembering the afternoon he'd trailed Weinberg down the deserted corridor, come up behind him and nailed him with a swift ferocious blow to the back of the skull. *Now how do you feel, you little fuck? You feel smart now? Huh?* The kick had come before he'd been able to stop it, hard and vicious, then another and another until . . .

Well, he got over it, the little weasel, Blunt said to himself now. A few days in the hospital, but he got over it. Probably a good lesson for him. Probably taught him not to be such a smart-ass. And the good news was that that first whack had knocked him cold, the little pussy, and so he'd never been able to piss and moan and say it was Blunt who did it.

This final thought filled Blunt with a satisfaction so intense, it came close to ecstasy. But it was short-lived, as all joy seemed to him, and at its departure he peered out into the mute, unhelpful darkness and cursed himself for getting lost. How had he gotten to this fucking nowhere place? he wondered, now laboring to retrace the route. Had he turned left on Brighton, then right on Covenant? Or had he done the opposite of that? Maybe it was Dunlap who'd gotten it wrong. After all, the jumpy little bastard was talking so fast, whipping that pudgy finger all over the map. Sure, it could be Dunlap that fucked it up, Blunt reasoned. And if he had, he decided, then his moron of a cousin was going to get a quick kick in the ass.

He felt his mind career around a blind corner and he laughed suddenly, remembering how he'd sometimes gotten the addresses wrong on patrol, showed up at the wrong place. O'Hearn had tried to fire him for that, but Dolan always kept him on. Later Burke had tried to fire him, but by then O'Hearn had found out that he could be depended upon for certain jobs. Just like Dolan had found that out. With pleasure he recalled the words Dolan told him that he'd said to O'Hearn. He could almost hear him saying it, Dolan's voice all cheery and lilting, that twinkling smile: *There's one thing the nuns never taught us, Francis, that a hard fist can be as useful as a sharp brain.*

Blunt drew his hands from the wheel, curled his fingers into fists, and stared at them admiringly as he remembered Dolan's words. *No shit,* he thought, now imagining what those two massive fists could do to Dunlap for getting him into this fucking mess. *Take that, you little prick.*

Is this the man?

Burke knelt beside the path and ran his finger over the rough ground. Much as he hated it, he could not get the image out of his mind. Neither the image nor the words. Scottie's fingers digging into his hand, clawing at them relentlessly, repeating the same prayer over and over again.

Bury me.

He thought of the man Smalls claimed to have seen shortly after Cathy Lake's murder. The one he'd told Cohen about. A man on his knees, at this very spot where Burke now knelt, staring at the ground, muttering the same words Scottie had muttered. The question dug incessantly at Burke's mind. *Could it have been Scottie?* And if it had been Scottie, had his son committed the crime of which Smalls was accused? Could Scottie have been in the park, crouched in the rain, watching a little girl move down the sodden path, seen the silver necklace that dangled from her throat . . . and struck? In his vast neglect, in his failure to accept his son, had Burke forged the killer of a child? Was this evil his own Evil had finally made?

He looked down the path. At the end of it he could see the tunnel in which Smalls had been apprehended. It was completely cleaned out now, no longer the hovel it had once been, strewn with debris. Smalls had sat hunched in that tunnel, shivering in the chill, peering out into the park, and seen a man digging at the earth, repeating over and over the words Scottie had released on his dying breath. Again the question assailed him: *Could it have been Scottie?*

He rose and strode rapidly down the path, then through the tunnel and back out of it, toward the entrance to the park, the ornate Victorian gate where Cathy Lake had spent the last dwindling moments of her life. The unlighted facade of Clairmont Towers faced him from the opposite curb, and he recalled the interviews Cohen and Pierce had conducted first with the building's superintendent, then with a second man who'd told them about an argument he'd had with yet another man, a dope addict, desperate for money, one who'd attacked him in the lobby of the building.

He felt a jolt of urgency, walked briskly to Clairmont Towers.

The superintendent groggily opened the door of his apartment.

Burke displayed his gold shield. "Two officers questioned a man in this building regarding a murder case," he said. "He'd had some kind of argument with another man here in the lobby. Do you remember who they spoke with?"

The superintendent blinked drowsily. "Stitt," he said. "Burt Stitt, 14-F."

One minute later the door of 14-F opened. Burke saw two small brown eyes peering at him through the slit. He took out his badge.

Stitt groaned. "Jesus H. Christ, it's four in the morning." He drew the chain from its cradle and opened the door. "What's this all about?"

"You told two detectives that you were in the lobby downstairs at around seven in the evening on September first," Burke said.

"So what?" Stitt snorted. "I'm in the lobby every day at around that time. I live here."

"You told the detectives that on this particular day you had an argument with somebody."

"So that's it," Stitt said with a grim smile. "That fucking hophead again. You catch the bastard yet?"

"Tell me what happened in the lobby."

"He asked me for a handout. This was out front. I said no, and the bastard followed me inside, screaming and grabbing at me, begging for money. I said hell no, and he threw a chair at me. Desperate. Grabbing for my wallet, my briefcase, anything he could get his hands on."

"Had you ever seen this man before?"

"How would I know? He's just a hophead. You know, skin and bones. Do anything for a fix. They all look alike, dope fiends."

"Where did he go when he left the building?"

Stitt shrugged. "Last I saw, he headed up Clairmont."

Burke studied Stitt's narrow features, the feral nose

and sunken cheeks. "I have one more question." He drew out his wallet and showed him a picture. "Is this the man who attacked you?"

"Well, he didn't look all cleaned up the way he does there. But, yeah, that's him."

Burke drew the picture from Stitt's hand.

"What'd he do anyway?" Stitt asked. "I mean, you're not here over some lousy panhandler." Recognition broke like a light over his face. "It's that kid, right? The one that was killed. You think the hophead did it." He glanced at the photograph that now trembled slightly in Burke's grip. "Who is he anyway?"

"My son," Burke answered quietly.

Outside, standing in the dark air, Burke could see the iron gate that stood at the park entrance, and where he suddenly imagined Cathy Lake as she dashed through it, fleeing a man who staggered after her in the rain, frightening in his disarray, wild-eyed and desperate for money, perhaps glimpsing a way to get it in the glint of the silver locket that hung from her slender throat. The terrible question sounded a third time. *Could it have been Scottie?* And for the third time Burke forced himself to deny the terrible suspicion that was growing in his mind. *Not a little girl,* he thought, *please, not a child.*

4:22 A.M., *Interrogation Room 3*

Cohen closed the Murder Book. No more questions about Cathy Lake, he told himself. No more questions about Smalls' past either. With so little time left, none of that mattered.

The awful truth cut through his mind. *Smalls is going to go free.* If Pierce found nothing in Seaview, then

in little more than ninety minutes, Smalls would be released into the city, to prowl its parks and playgrounds,
looking for a child.

So what was left? Cohen asked himself desperately.
What could he do in ninety-eight minutes that he had
not been able to do during the last ten hours? Only one
possibility occurred to him. He might trick Smalls the
way Smalls had tricked him earlier, get him talking
mindlessly. About his goddamn feelings. The whole
self-loathing act. All that bullshit about thinking of himself as slime. If he could convince Smalls that he was
buying any of this, Cohen thought, then maybe, just
maybe, he could pry something out. A single guilty
morsel that might be enough to slam the cell door on
Smalls for a few more days.

"I'm not going to ask you any more questions about
Cathy, Jay," he said, keeping his speech measured,
holding back the anger. "Her murder, or anything about
her. So just take Cathy out of your mind. Can you do
that, Jay?"

"I'll try," Smalls said meekly.

"Good, because I want your mind clear to think
about what I'm going to say to you."

"It's hard not to think about the little girl. I know you
think I hurt her."

"Don't be so sure of that," Cohen told him, choking
back his rage, his fierce need to jerk Smalls from his
chair, slam him into the wall.

"I know you think I hurt her," Smalls repeated, his
tone, to Cohen's ear, dripping with false innocence.
"Everybody does."

"Yeah, but I want to talk about you, Jay," Cohen insisted. "Your future, I mean."

Smalls lowered his eyes delicately, let the lids flutter.
"I don't have a future."

"Sure, you do," Cohen said.

"No, I don't." He offered a short sigh. "I never had a future."

Cohen leaned in close. "Listen, Jay. There's a way out for you." He felt Smalls' breath on his face and itched to pull away, rush to the bathroom down the hall, scrub the very scent of him from his skin. But instead, he tenderly pushed back an errant strand of Smalls' long, dark hair. "You can't give up on yourself, Jay."

"I already have."

"Listen to me," Cohen said intently. "You can decide what happens to you."

"I know what's going to happen." Smalls' voice fluttered, gossamer thin, in the air between them. "I've always known."

"What? What's going to happen to you?"

"I'll be arrested again."

"For what?"

"Murder."

"Why do you say that?"

"Anytime a child is murdered, I'll be arrested for it."

"Why are you so sure of that, Jay?"

"I'm sure, that's all."

"But why?" Cohen repeated emphatically.

Smalls gave no response, but Cohen caught something move like a small candle across the otherwise motionless features of his face. "Is it because you've been arrested before?"

Smalls remained silent.

"Accused before? Is that why you won't tell us anything about your past?" Cohen's eyes probed Smalls' unrevealing features. "Jay, have you been accused of murder before?"

Smalls said nothing.

"Of the murder of a little girl?"

Smalls glanced away.

"Is that what you thought I'd found out?" Cohen pressed. "That you'd been accused before?"

Smalls returned his gaze to Cohen and the detective saw the figure of a child who was soon to die. And on that image his strategy died, his frail hope of finding a new way into Smalls, tricking him. There was no way to trick Smalls, he knew now, no way to cut through his mask of sorrow and self-pity and misfortune. Smalls was the better actor, and always would be. How long had he concealed his sickening impulses? How long had he crept through parks and playgrounds, slithered among the children he found there? Arrested perhaps, or at least accused. But free again in minutes, hours, days. Free to return to his sleazy fantasies, seek a living child upon whom to act them out.

"And after we let you go, you'll be accused again," Cohen said grimly. "Cathy wasn't the first. And she won't be the last either, will she?"

Smalls remained silent.

"Have you already picked her out, Jay?" Cohen taunted, knowing Smalls would give no answer. "The next little girl you plan to kill? Do you already know her name?"

4:24 A.M., *Phoenix and Cordelia*

"Laurie, her name's Laurie." Eddie was not sure why he was talking about his daughter, save that Siddell Carting Truck 12 was edging toward his own neighborhood. "If you look all the way down Phoenix, you can almost see my apartment. That's where Laurie is. Sick, like I said. A fever." He fished in his pants pocket and pulled out his father's battered railroad watch. "We're a little ahead of schedule. What do you say I wheel to the left and drop in on her? Check in, that's all."

"Fuck no," Siddell said.

"Come on, Terry. Two minutes."

Siddell looked at Eddie stonily. "No way. I want to get this fucking night over with."

And so Eddie guided Siddell Carting Truck 12 past Phoenix and on down Cordelia, cursing himself and Terry Siddell and vowing that no matter what, he would spend some time with Laurie when she recovered, maybe a whole day in the park, just Laurie and himself, and maybe Charlie, who'd tickle her and make her laugh in an easy, lighthearted way Eddie never could. More than anything, that was what he wanted, to see Laurie's head tilt back in laughter the way she always did when Charlie was around. Eddie had no gift for that, he realized, no gift for anything but work. He could lift and haul, but what else could he do? Nothing. Nothing at all. He couldn't even afford a birthday gift for Laurie, who was sick and had a fever and could use a nice present. He felt a searing shame wash over him, ashamed of losing his wife, ashamed of the filthy clothes he wore, but more than anything shamed by the pathetic lie he'd told Mrs. Wilson about having a "real nice" present for Laurie. There was no present, and certainly nothing "real nice." What did that mean anyway? How could he ever get his daughter anything truly nice? No, her present would be like everything else he'd ever bought her. It would be cheap, used, something with the shine already worn off it, a threadbare rag from the Salvation Army. "Real nice." He felt a terrible sting of humiliation. Poor provider, he thought, now concentrating on the other children Laurie encountered in the park, well-dressed, playing with nice new toys, while she was dressed in hand-me-downs.

4:32 A.M., *Dunlap's Collectibles*

Dunlap had to blink to convince himself that the figure before him was real. "What are you doing here, Burt? What's going on?"

"Let me in," Stitt said icily.

Dunlap drew back the door and Stitt quickly stepped into the darkened interior of the shop.

"What's going on?" Dunlap repeated.

"What's going on?" Stitt said edgily. "I just got a visit from a cop. And not just any goddamn cop. Fucking Thomas Burke. The Chief himself."

"Burke came to your place?"

"That's what I said, didn't I?"

"Why?"

"Asking about who it was I had that fight with. The one I told you about. Had a picture of the hophead, wanted to know if this was the guy. I said, yeah, that's him. Fucking hophead, grabbing stuff, spilling shit, throwing chairs. How did I know the bastard was Burke's kid?"

"It was Burke's kid grabbed your stuff?" Dunlap asked worriedly. "Oh, Jesus."

"Shit," Stitt said. "If I'd known that hophead was Burke's kid, I'd have given him a few bucks and been done with him. Written it off, you know. Business expense. Now I got the old man himself snooping around, asking questions."

"Jesus," Dunlap murmured almost to himself. "Things is getting all fucked around here."

"So, bottom line, I got to get out of town," Stitt persisted. "Fast. So where is it?"

"Where's what?"

Stitt stared lethally at Dunlap. "Don't fuck with me, Harry."

"Why would I do that, Burt?"

"To save your ass, that's why," Stitt snapped. "This is a lot more serious than you think, Harry. You fuck around with this, and you could end up . . ."

Dunlap shrank away, a line of fear scraping like a claw down his spine. "Take it easy, Burt," he said. He nodded toward the rear of the store. "Come on back, I'll pour you a drink."

"I'm not going nowhere."

Dunlap offered a tense snicker. "What do you think, Burt, I got cops waiting for you back there?"

"Where's my money?"

"It's safe, believe me," Dunlap assured him. "I got everything taken care of."

"It better be," Stitt warned. "You got no idea what lengths I'll go to."

"You don't have to be thinking that way, Burt."

"One more time. Where's my fucking dough?"

Dunlap forced a smile. "It's safe. In Titus."

"Titus?" Stitt cried. "What the fuck's it doing in Titus?"

"I took it there. So it would be safe. But it'll be here in just a few minutes. My dumb-ass cousin's bringing it in."

"It was never supposed to leave here, Harry. That was the deal."

"I know, Burt," Dunlap soothed. "But things come up, you know?" He eased backward, urging Stitt toward the rear of the shop. "It's on its way though, believe me. We can have a drink till my cousin gets here."

The two men headed toward the back of the building, Dunlap trying to decide if he should gently touch Stitt's back, do something to calm him down. But by the time he'd made the decision that maybe that would not be a good idea, they'd passed through the back curtain.

"So," Dunlap said, "how you doing, Burt?"

Stitt glared at Dunlap. "You got till six," he said.

4:38 A.M., *Route 6*

To break the long silence that had fallen between them, Pierce said, "Something has to be in that shed."

"What if nothing is?" Yearwood asked.

"Then I'll go back to the city."

"And do what?"

"The only thing I can do," Pierce said, though the very thought of it sent an ache through his soul. "Wait until he kills again."

"Are you so certain he will?"

"They always do. Costa would have done it again." Costa was in his face, blubbering about Bedford Street. Pierce saw his arm lift, his finger point through the billowing fog and beyond it, to where the pier stretched out into the river, a path slick with spray and shrouded in fog. He heard his voice, its icy malice. *That way's Bedford.*

"If he'd lived," he added now in a tone that Costa's death had done not one thing to warm.

4:47 A.M., *Dunlap's Collectibles*

Stitt's eyes shot toward the front of the shop. "What the hell is that?"

Dunlap gave his arm a reassuring pat. "Relax, Burt. It's my cousin, who else could it be?" He offered his broadest smile. "Relax, will you? Everything's fine, believe me."

He marched to the front door of the shop and opened it. "So, I guess you didn't—" He stopped and stared straight into the eyes of Thomas Burke.

"Hey, Chief, what are you—"

"When was the last time you saw my son?"

Dunlap paused, speechless, then said, "I don't know for sure."

"Did you see him a week ago last Tuesday?"

Dunlap thought a moment. "Yeah," he said. "Yeah, I seen him that day. Had that big rain, right? Yeah, I seen him last Wednesday. Scottie come after dark. I let him in and he went back to his . . . spot, I guess you'd call it."

"What did he look like?"

"Wet," Dunlap answered. "Muddy."

"Did he have anything to sell you?"

"No."

"His room," Burke said. "Have you cleaned it out yet?"

Dunlap thought fast, fear digging like a spur in his mind. "Well, yeah, I did. I cleaned it out right after I heard he was in the hospital. Not that there was much to throw out. You know. Just some old clothes. I tossed it all." He scratched his jaw and cocked his head. "You looking for something in particular, Chief?"

"No," Burke said quietly, then turned and moved back among the shadows of Cordelia Street, a shriveled figure, or so it seemed to Dunlap, hollowed out somehow.

"So, where's your cousin?" Stitt demanded as Dunlap pushed back through the curtain.

"It wasn't Ralph," Dunlap told him. "I just got the same visitor you did."

"Burke?"

"Yeah."

"What'd he want?"

"He wanted to know if I'd seen his kid a week ago Tuesday."

"Why would you have seen his fucking kid?"

" 'Cause he beds down here once in a while."

"Here?"

"In the back," Dunlap said. "Anyway, I told him yeah, I seen the kid. And what's more, he looked like shit. All wet and muddy. Like he'd been left out in the rain." He sniggered with mock delight. "Then the fucking guy wants to know what I did with the kid's shit. Threw it out, I told him. I mean, what else could I do, invite him back here to take a look for himself?" Another laugh burst from his mouth. "Let him find you here? Jesus, can you imagine that, Burt?"

Stitt's brow knit in concentration. "Week ago Tuesday," he said grimly. "That's the day that kid was iced in the park."

"So what?" Dunlap said with a dismissive wave of his hand.

"I knew it. That fucking cop figures that hophead son of his had something to do with it. The murder."

"Scottie? Why would the Chief think that?"

" 'Cause the bastard was around when it happened," Stitt replied. "When we had that fight in the lobby. That kid saw the whole goddamn thing."

"Jesus," Dunlap yelped.

"Burke probably figures that son of his iced that fucking kid."

Dunlap dropped onto the sofa, wrung his hands. "You figure Scottie would do something like that?"

"He was a fucking hophead!" Stitt shrieked.

"Yeah, but I don't know, Burt. Scottie didn't seem like no—"

"What the fuck do you know how he seemed? You should have seen him that day. Grabbing my briefcase. Out of his mind, the fucking bastard."

"You didn't tell me nothing about him grabbing the case."

"Who cares what I told you or didn't tell. The main thing, you better get rid of any crap he left behind, because the old man is poking around into that killing."

"What would he be looking for, Burt?"

"What they all look for. Some guy to pin it on. That fucking cop knows his son snuffed that kid, and now he's looking to pin it on somebody else. It's how they think, the fucking cops."

Dunlap's eyes widened in blank terror. "Somebody to pin it on? You mean, like . . . me?"

"Any fucking body. But if I were you, I'd dump whatever shit you got of that kid's. And I mean pronto."

Dunlap snapped to his feet. "Yeah, okay, Burt." He rushed into a cramped adjoining room, scooped up the smelly mound of clothes Scottie Burke had left there, hauled it outside, and dumped it beside the curb.

"Them fucking clothes was filthy," he said when he returned inside. He slapped his hands together. "That kid lived like a fucking rat, you know?"

Stitt snatched a magazine from a pile beside the sofa. "They all live like rats, fucking hopheads."

Dunlap sank down on the sofa beside him, still wiping his hands. "But, Burt, you really think Scottie killed that little girl?"

Stitt idly flipped a page. "He was out of his fucking mind that night, that's for sure."

"Jesus," Dunlap breathed. He thought a moment,

then added, "But, murdering a little girl, Burt. Was he that nuts?"

Stitt shrugged. "All I know is, a guy gets desperate enough, he'll do anything." He dropped the magazine on the floor, placed his hand on Dunlap's thigh, and squeezed cruelly. "Remember that, Harry," he said coldly. "In case you got any ideas about fucking with my money."

Why?

The gate was open, just as Dunlap had said it would be, but this gave Blunt no confidence that anything else would go according to plan. And so for four minutes he sat behind the wheel, staring at the open gate, not plotting his next move but thinking about the money, what he would do with it. He'd buy Millie some trinket, he decided, cheer her up a little. Suzy too. Something shiny. But what he really wanted was a new car, sporty, that made a guy look swell when he drove it, the kind of car that took pounds off your body and years off the calendar and caused a good-looking girl to glance your way when you cruised by. A peculiar happiness drifted over him at the thought of being behind the wheel of a sleek number, and he realized that it was all pretty simple, what a man wanted, just not to look like a fucking loser. He didn't care if the girl never strolled over to the car, got in, never went with him to some hotel. It would be enough that she'd glanced his way and didn't instantly make him for a nobody. Okay, a shiny new car, then, he decided, worth the risk. And so he hit the ignition, pressed down on the accelerator, passed through the open gate of AJS Storage, then followed a snaking gravel road that petered into a dead end before a line of wooden sheds.

Blunt brought the car to a halt and took another moment to think things through. The first unit had a white door, the number one slapped over the door in black paint. Blunt reasoned that unit twenty-seven would be near the end of the line. That part was simple. The hard part was where to hide the car. No road circled around the sheds, but the land behind them looked flat and weedy, easy enough to drive over. Worth it too, Blunt thought, in order to park the car behind unit twenty-seven just in case somebody came by, a night watchman maybe, or just some couple looking for a place to hump. He'd been around long enough to know that no place, no matter how deserted it looked, was ever really deserted. Somebody knew about it, used it for something. Just to be safe, he decided to wheel around to the back of the storage units, count them off one by one as he drove by, park directly behind twenty-seven. Good, he thought with satisfaction, that should work.

And it did.

So well that within seconds Blunt was safely inside the shed, following the beam of his flashlight along its four walls. Again Dunlap had dealt it straight. The space was empty except for a ratty old sack somebody had tossed into a corner and the brown leather briefcase Dunlap had deposited.

So far so good, Blunt thought, dividing time into the only two categories he knew, when things were going well, as they were now, and when things were going badly, which was most of the time, especially at home, where, Blunt hoped, a nice piece of costume jewelry might serve to get the old lady to put out again.

He closed in on the briefcase, his ear cocked for any sound other than the slight play of the wind on the surrounding fields, which he could hear as a steady whisper in the background.

When he reached the briefcase, he squatted and opened it.

So far, so good.

The money rested in tidy stacks held together by thick rubber bands, and to Blunt's untrained eye it looked plenty real. He jerked one of the bills from the pile and examined it in the light. How did they do it, he wondered, get it to look so a guy couldn't possibly tell it was fake without whatever the government used to tell it was phony?

He slipped the bill beneath the rubber band, then took out the first stack and ran his thumb along the edges. He'd seen people do this in movies, and pretend that after they'd done it, they knew exactly how much was in the stack. Exactly. To the buck. Blunt doubted that anyone could really do this, but he enjoyed pretending that he could. One thing was sure, they were all twenties, and there were probably forty or fifty in each stack, which came to . . . Blunt knew better than to trust his arithmetic any further, and tossed the short stack of bills back into the case. It was a lot, no doubt about it, probably the actual fifty grand Dunlap had claimed, though Blunt regretted that just to be on the safe side he hadn't grabbed his cousin's neck and squeezed. *You better not be lying to me, Harry.* That was the moment Dunlap would have hedged his bet, Blunt thought, that was the moment he'd have started sputtering about how, well, he really hadn't actually counted it, but, hey, yeah, it was a lot, probably fifty grand give or take, and on and on and on, sputtering the way punks like him always did when they were trying to wriggle out of the spot they were in. Blunt had seen plenty of people that scared. He glanced at his watch. In an hour he'd be seeing another one. Imagine that, he thought, I got fifty grand here, and I still got to take that fucking pervert for a ride.

With that thought, Blunt's mood skidded to the side and went over a cliff. Jesus Christ, he thought, fifty grand and all he was going to get out of this deal was a lousy five hundred bucks. Who could buy a roadster for that? When you got right down to it, five hundred dollars wouldn't buy shit. Chump change, he thought, his anger flaring now, feeling fucked, outsmarted even by his little junk-collecting prick of a cousin who wasn't smart enough to get out of the goddamn rain.

The idea came to him slowly, slithering into his brain. Who was really taking the big chance here? he asked himself. *He* was. After all, wasn't he the one who now squatted in a filthy storage shed in Titus? Not Dunlap. If something happened, if something went wrong, what could that prick do about it? Nothing. And what had Dunlap actually done in the whole deal but take some hot cash off somebody else's hands? Somebody who wasn't risking his own goddamn neck to get his money back. Somebody like Dunlap. Another pussy. Then who was really getting fucked in this deal? Who was taking the real chances here? Who would take the fall if it all blew up? "Fucked," Blunt snarled aloud, "I'm getting fucked in this."

Any way you cut it, he deserved more than a lousy five hundred dollars. How to get the extra bucks, that was the question. He could just tell the little prick straight out, I'm taking your five hundred too, so go fuck yourself. But Dunlap would start bawling about how he had to have the cash, how he was broke, how he couldn't feed his fucking cat. Wait a minute, Blunt thought, just how dumb did Dunlap think he was, trying to get away with that one? You can smell a cat. You can smell cat piss if a guy has a cat. Dunlap, he decided, did not have no fucking cat. And a guy who'd lie about something like that, what kind of guy was that? A guy who'd lie about how much he was getting paid to stash the cash, that's what, a guy like Dunlap, the fucking weasel.

So what to do? Blunt asked himself. How could he get a bigger share of the money without getting Dunlap all whiny and crying and talking about his goddamn cat, which he didn't have anyway, the lying bastard?

A second idea formed in Blunt's mind, and the beauty of it brought a smile that lingered happily on his face until he heard the soft rattle of a distant car.

Shit!

Hastily, he switched off his flashlight.

Who the fuck could that be?

He slunk into a dark corner and waited.

Just my goddamn luck.

An odd panic seized him as the sound of the car came closer and closer, bedeviling him with a frenzy of options that fizzled swiftly and reduced to one.

He drew his pistol and waited, listening as the approaching engine grew louder and louder until it seemed to fire and rattle inside his own combusting brain.

5:03 A.M., *Titus, AJS Storage*

Pierce stopped the car and studied the darkened shed.

Number twenty-seven was the third unit from the last, and appeared the most decrepit. The grass of the fields swept in around it, thick and high, a wall of reeds sprouting along its unpainted walls, their tips trembling delicately in the wind.

"Wait here," Pierce told Yearwood.

The old man scowled. "Why?"

"In case something happens."

"And suppose something *does* happen?" Yearwood asked. "To you, I mean. Do I still just sit here, or at that point would you like a little help?"

Pierce waved his hand. "I'll be back in a couple of minutes."

Then, with no further word, Pierce took his flashlight, got out of the car, and headed for the shed.

As he approached it, he saw that although the door was tightly closed, there was no lock, no chain. He grasped the door but didn't push it open. He did not know why he hesitated, only that something deep inside him had spoken quietly, issued in the silence of his mind a curiously tender command. *Take a moment. Look around.*

And so he did.

Standing at the door, his hand already on the handle, he stopped and peered out into the night. The fields were very dark, but in the light cast over them by the beams from his car, he could see a sweep of reeds swaying gently, their tips oddly golden in the light, and which, for all the pervading blackness, gave the fields a subtle hint of dawn, of the world rousing itself from a long night's sleep. He thought of Anna, no doubt in bed at this hour. He knew that her first waking thought would be of Cathy, then of Smalls, and finally of himself, whom she'd trusted to make sure that Smalls would not get away. If he kept his promise, she might love him, and if he could feel such love again, he knew he could endure the rest. He looked back over the moonlit fields and for the first time since Debra's death felt something good at the heart of things, earth's promise of replenishment. One more try, he told himself. One more.

He faced the door, drew it open, and stepped inside the shed.

The darkness inside was so thick it seemed syrupy, as if the air were not air at all but a heavy black oil. The light of the flashlight was a weak weapon against it, illuminating only one small area at a time, so that Pierce saw first the littered ground, then a lightbulb, and finally an old canvas sack, stained and worn, crumpled in the far corner of the shed.

Pierce strode through the darkness to the bag, knelt, and shined his flashlight inside it. Proof, he thought almost prayerfully, let it be proof. He reached into the bag, heard a sudden rustle from behind him, then a blast, a shimmer of light, his fingers opening in a spasm of release, the proof dropping away, a thud of something in the darkness, moving away from him now, then the creak of the door, something moving toward him, drawing him from the gritty floor, holding him, a flame in the shadows, a silver aura, Yearwood. He felt his strength bundle together, every muscle, tendon, sinew unite in a single desperate effort, and he said, "Tell Cohen," then his head lolled backward as he fell and fell, shattering as he fell, becoming millions of small particles, all of them tumbling in a glittering mist where there was no night, no day, but only, in the impossible distance, the silent border of dusk.

5:07 A.M., *Office of the Chief of Detectives*

Burke looked up from his desk as Cohen entered the room. "Come in, Cohen."

"You wanted to see me, Chief?" Cohen asked.

"Yes," Burke said. "The man Smalls claims to have seen after the murder. The one who was digging. Did he say anything more about him?"

"No, sir."

"No details at all? Height? Weight? Hair color? You couldn't get any more out of him?"

Cohen shook his head.

Burke reached for his wallet, opened it. "Show him this," he said as he handed his son's photograph to Cohen. "It might be the man he saw on the path, digging."

Cohen glanced at the photograph. "Who is this, sir?"

"My son," Burke answered.

"But why would—"

"Please, Detective, show it to Smalls. Let me know what he says."

"Yes, sir."

Cohen left the room and Burke slumped forward, exhausted. Within a few minutes he would know. He thought of Scottie, saw him in the depths to which he had sunk, living on the streets or in some filthy back room on Cordelia Street. It was only his son's final wrenching act he could not permit himself to imagine, a figure trudging behind a little girl, full of loathing and desperation, glancing around, looking for something to use, a limb, a brick . . . a strand of wire. He closed his eyes and with that gesture tried to seal off his mind, allow no more such images to penetrate it. For a moment he sat in that deep interior darkness. Then lights flickered and the parade began, the whole bloody chronicle of his days. They marched before him in a winding, endless line, women beaten to a pulp, children tied to beds, the whole savage course of his long career. He saw Mrs. Bennett and the ax, little Bobby Martin crouched on the stained toilet bowl. Dinah Sharpe was there, down to the broken fingernails, Stuart Bates just behind her, the child he'd knifed rotting in his arms. One by one they presented themselves, the dreary companions of his time on earth, Scottie the last of them, standing in stark relief, not as he was now, broken, dying, but as a little boy in shorts and T-shirt, lifting his empty, needful arms toward the father who had always refused him love.

5:10 A.M., *Dunlap's Collectibles*

Eddie rapped at the door, then stepped back and waited for it to open.

When it didn't, he rapped a second time, harder.

There was still no answer, and so he stomped back to where Siddell stood beside a mound of ragged clothing.

"The fuck knows he's supposed to bag this stuff," Eddie snapped. "I've told him before. You don't bag it, I don't pick it up."

"So what do you want to do, then?" Siddell asked.

Eddie shot a hostile glance at the darkened interior of Dunlap's Collectibles. "He's back there, the fuck. He just won't come out 'cause he knows I'll give him an earful."

"So go do it," Siddell said. "I don't want to stand here all night."

Eddie thought a moment, then decided. "Yeah, I will. I ain't going to take it." He strode back to the door, banged his fist hard against the doorjamb, banged it again and again, his fist red and sore by the time the door opened.

"Jesus," Dunlap whined. "Jesus Christ, keep it down, will you?"

"Look at that." Eddie thrust his arm toward the pile of clothing that lay in a sodden mass beside the curb. "You put that there?"

"Yeah. So what?"

"It ain't bagged. It's gotta be bagged."

"Look," Dunlap explained. "It's just a pile of old clothes. Some bum left them here. They were stinking up the place. So I—"

"But it ain't bagged, that's what I'm telling you. It's got to be bagged."

Behind Dunlap, a second man appeared. "Yeah, why is that, boss?" he asked mockingly.

" 'Cause that's the way it is," Eddie shot back.

"Well, tell me, boss, what if my friend here doesn't have any fucking bags?"

"Then you don't put nothing out until you got them."

"He's just supposed to sit around and smell some bum's stink?" the second man sneered.

"What I'm telling you is, everything's got to be bagged or I don't got to pick it up."

The second man laughed. "Oh, yeah, boss? And what do you think I do if you don't pick it up? Huh? I'll tell you. I call Siddell Carting, and I say some little shitbag banged on my frigging door at five in the goddamn morning and gave me hell on account of some frigging bags, and if it ever happens again, I don't pay Siddell Carting to pick up my garbage no more." He brought his face close to Eddie's. "And you maybe lose your frigging job, asshole."

Eddie stared at the man mutely.

"So, there it is, boss," the second man said. He pointed to the mound of clothing. "I don't want to see that shit here when you leave, understand . . . *boss*?"

The door slammed in Eddie's face, and for a moment he faced it brokenly. Then he turned and headed back to where Terry Siddell stood beside the curb.

"So what are we going to do, then?" Siddell demanded.

Eddie shrugged. "We'll pick it up this one time," he said quietly.

"Not me," Siddell declared. "You can smell the piss from here." He turned on his heel and stomped back to the truck.

Eddie bent down and gathered the pile of clothes into his arms. The stench of sweat and urine nearly suffocated him, rushing him to get it done, all of it, the endless night's ordeal, the clothes piled into the truck and then away from the man's humiliating taunts, and home to the daughter who loved him, respected him, called him her hero each time he drew her into his otherwise empty arms. *It's for Laurie,* he told himself as he tossed the smelly bundle into the truck. *Just for Laurie, nobody else.*

5:19 A.M., *Route 6*

"Set me up, the little prick," Blunt muttered. He felt his fingers tighten around the serrated curve of the wheel as he imagined them around Dunlap's neck. The only question was why the little prick had done it. What did he have to gain?

Blunt went over it again and again, the sound of the car as it drew near, then a beam of light he'd barely been able to step out of as the man entered the shed.

In all of this, only one thing seemed clear. No one had known that he was coming to that particular shed but Dunlap.

"Set me up," Blunt repeated in a low, vengeful murmur, "set me up, the prick."

Again Blunt tried to fathom Dunlap's angle. He saw the man step into the shed, a black silhouette behind the yellow beam of the flashlight. He'd moved cautiously, as if expecting to be jumped, directing the light left and right until it had lit upon a canvas bag in the corner of the shed. Then he'd bolted forward, as if he'd discovered a chest of gold.

An old bag? Blunt asked himself, glancing now at the briefcase that rested beside him on the front seat. What the fuck had the guy wanted with some filthy old bag?

He felt the swirling confusion of that moment in all its chaotic force. It was the darkness, he thought, the surprise. He'd never been able to deal with surprise. It was like his brain got tongue-tied, started sputtering orders faster than he could obey them. Other guys just looked surprise in the eye and dealt with whatever was in their faces. They maybe argued with it, or pushed it away, or dodged it somehow, this thing that came at them out of nowhere. If he could have done that, maybe the fucking guy would have just taken that goddamn bag and left the shed, and that would have been the end of it. But it was the surprise. He should have known better, that fucking guy. He should have known better than just bull in the way he did. Okay, so, I did what I had to, Blunt decided, okay, so, he got what he deserved.

He saw the man tumble forward, curling over the bag like he was trying to protect it, shield it with his body, like it maybe was a kid or something. Why the fuck had he done that? He considered the question briefly, then gave up and returned his attention to Harry Dunlap, the ass-kicking that now raced toward him at sixty miles an hour.

5:26 A.M., *Interrogation Room 3*

Cohen placed the photograph of Scott Burke on the table and slid it over to Smalls.

"I know I told you that I wasn't going to ask any more questions about Cathy Lake. But I have just one more."

Smalls gave no indication that he'd heard Cohen's voice. He sat, closed off, behind the high protective barricade.

"The day Cathy was murdered. You said you saw a man on the trail, right? Jay, I want you to look carefully at this picture. Study it, try to remember what the man you saw looked like, and tell me if the man you saw could be the same man as the one in the photograph."

Smalls picked up the photograph and gazed at it intently, running his finger tenderly over the surface of the picture, as if adding colors and textures, using the tip of his finger like a painter's brush.

Cohen felt a spurt of impatience. "Well?" he asked.

"It could be him."

"Could be, but you're not sure?"

"No."

Cohen snatched the photograph from Smalls' hand, shoved back his chair, and walked to Burke's office.

"I showed the picture to Smalls," he told the Chief. "He says he doesn't know if this was the man he saw in the park." He placed the photograph on Burke's desk. "Anything else, sir?"

"No," Burke told him.

Cohen eased himself back into the corridor, closing the door behind him.

Smalls had risen and was standing at the window when he walked back into the interrogation room.

"Sit down," Cohen snapped.

Smalls obeyed without hesitation, his feet scuttling across the wooden floor until they brought him once again to the table.

Cohen stepped to the window, cranked it closed, and locked it. "Stay in your seat unless you're told to leave it," he snarled.

Smalls nodded slowly. "Yes, sir."

Cohen pressed himself against the wall and glared down at the pallid, frail figure who sat, arms curled around his belly, a few feet away. What an act, he thought, the whole routine, the childlike delicacy of his features, the pale hands, the liquid blue eyes. Butter wouldn't melt, he thought angrily, butter wouldn't melt in his goddamn mouth.

He looked at the clock. Twenty-six minutes until he had to leave the interrogation room, twenty-seven minutes until someone replaced him there, took Smalls downstairs, and set him loose. Where was Pierce? he wondered. But it was not a question he could dwell upon. He had to think about Smalls. Only Smalls. So little time now. Twenty-seven . . . no, twenty-six minutes. He pulled himself from the wall. One more go, he urged himself, one more.

"Why did you kill her, Smalls?"

"I didn't."

"Why did you kill her?" Cohen repeated.

"I didn't kill Cathy."

"How about some other little girl?" Cohen asked. "That's why you won't tell me about yourself, isn't it? Where you lived before you came to the city. Where you came from. It's because you killed a kid, isn't it? Some kid in some park."

"I never killed anybody," Smalls insisted. His eyes drifted to the clock.

"Don't look at that fucking thing," Cohen raged. "Look at me. Look in my eyes."

Smalls did as he was told.

"And don't give me that sad-sack look," Cohen snapped. "I'm sick of it. Poor, sad Jay. Poor, misunderstood Jay. All the sorrows of the world on your shoulders. Do you really expect me to swallow that? That you've never done anything wrong? Poor Jay, yanked out of a tunnel where he was sleeping, just minding his own damn business. Dragged to jail, accused of murder, but so, so innocent. Well, forget that crap. You're a goddamn child-killer, and you and I both know it."

"I never killed a child."

"Just molest them, is that all you do?"

Smalls' eyes caught fire. "I didn't touch her," he insisted. "I never touched anybody."

Cohen instantly remembered an earlier moment in the interrogation. They'd been talking about Cathy's murder, how it could have been prevented if someone had chanced upon the killer before it was too late.

"If someone had been there, he would have stopped. Isn't that what you told me, Jay? That no matter how much this guy might have wanted to hurt Cathy, *he would have stopped if someone had been there*. Didn't you tell me that?"

"Yes."

"You know that's true, don't you? Because at some other point, in some other place, someone stopped you. That much wasn't a lie, was it?"

Smalls hesitated, but Cohen saw his shoulders suddenly lift, as if a great burden had just fallen from them, and knew he had struck upon the truth at last. "I wouldn't have hurt her."

"Another little girl?"

"I just wanted to draw her."

"Draw her?"

"She'd let me do it before."

"Who?"

"She let me do it before. She was . . . so pretty."

"And you . . . what, Jay?"

"I didn't touch her. Someone else did."

"Someone else?" A brutal laugh broke from Cohen. "So now we have yet another man, right? And what did this one look like, Jay? Did he look like you?"

"No."

"Not another bum, living in the park?"

"He worked in the park, but he didn't live there."

"Oh, great. Now we really have something to go on. We have us a whole lot of guys to check out, don't we? And just how do you know this guy worked in the park?"

"He had on a uniform."

"Like every other guy who works for the Parks Department."

"He wore a baseball cap."

"What kind of baseball cap? What team?"

"I don't know."

"How convenient. Okay, tell me something else about this guy."

"I thought he saved her."

"Saved her? From what?"

Smalls' admission seemed to crack his heart. "From me," he said.

"From you?"

"She saw the way I was looking at her. It scared her so she ran away. Toward this guy. He's the one who hurt her."

"What makes you so sure of that?"

"I heard her . . . cry," Smalls answered quietly.

"Ah, so that's it," Cohen said mockingly. "You didn't hurt this kid. Someone else did. Your only crime was not stopping it."

"I don't expect you to believe me," Smalls murmured.

"Well, good," Cohen snapped. "Because I don't!" He started to speak, but fell mute before the sheer weakness of mere words to do what had to be done in the minutes that remained for the interrogation. He didn't want to ask Smalls any more questions. He wanted a pair of pliers. He wanted to put Smalls' thumb between its metal teeth and squeeze the truth from him. And with that thought, Cohen realized that he'd reached the end of the road. The place you arrive at when you no longer believe that something may yet intervene on your behalf; some particle of luck or a blaze of intuition, that forestalls the death of hope.

5:29 A.M., *Route 6*

The scream of the siren, the sense of moving very fast, gave Yearwood hope that they might make it to the city in time.

Inches away, Pierce lay on a stretcher, his eyes closed, his body utterly still. A spot of blood spread out from beneath his head, but it was small and no longer growing.

Watching him, Yearwood felt the urge to take his hand. He didn't for fear of interfering with what struck him as the increasingly desperate movement of the attendants who now worked feverishly around Pierce's body. He noted the grim glances they exchanged while they talked tersely of "shock" and "decreased respiration." He had seen all of this before, and it had always signaled a deepening distress, the ebbing, ruthless and irreversible, of a human life.

5:30 A.M., *Dunlap's Collectibles*

Dunlap glanced nervously at the battered Coca-Cola clock that hung at a slant on the opposite wall, beside a poster of Elvis, which someone had decorated with kisses.

"Where's that dumb-ass cousin of yours?" Stitt demanded.

"I don't know, Burt," Dunlap said edgily. "He should have been here by now. I gave him good directions, but maybe he got lost."

"Well, he better get found," Stitt replied coldly. "And soon."

Dunlap got to his feet, walked to the curtain, and peered through the slit. Light was building on the street now, and he didn't like it. Business of this kind, he'd long ago decided, was best done in the dark. Within an hour the early risers would be on the street. Some of them would probably see Blunt when he arrived, then Stitt and Blunt when they left. Shit, he thought, goddamn.

"Sit down, Harry," Stitt barked.

Dunlap immediately did as he was told, at the same

time hating himself for it. How, he wondered, how had he become such a cringing, cowardly thing? He saw his father's eyes cut over to him. *What are you looking at—* then his massive, factory-worker hand, swift and hard, shoot out, bloodying his mouth—*that way?*

"That little fuck pick the hophead's shit up?" Stitt asked.

"Yeah," Dunlap replied. He laughed, but it didn't sound real. "You sure told him off, Burt. You sure gave it to that bastard."

Stitt grinned mockingly. "Yeah, I scared the shit out of him. Bet he had to change his shorts." The grin vanished. "You'll be changing yours, too, if I don't get my fucking money."

Dunlap turned away. How could he change his life? he wondered. In high school they'd called him Mouse, he remembered, Mouse because he was like a mouse, scurrying, frantic, panicked. Not a man, he thought, never a man. Still a virgin, for Christ's sake. At thirty-four.

He stood up again. Fuck Stitt, he thought, this is *my* place. I can fucking get up when I goddamn want to. I can walk to the curtains and part the goddamn things and stare out at the goddamn street anytime I goddamn please.

"What the hell's the matter with you?" Stitt barked.

"Nothing, I was just—"

"Sit down!"

Dunlap felt the familiar cringing fear grip him. "Okay," he said meekly as he returned to his seat. "Okay, Burt, anything you say."

5:32 A.M., *Route 6*

"How much farther?" Yearwood asked.

"We're at the bridge."

The attendant who spoke was bent over Pierce's body, tying something or inserting something, Yearwood couldn't tell.

"Okay, that's all we can do for now," the attendant announced, then drew away. "Head shots are always bad."

"I didn't know what it was at first," Yearwood told him. "The sound. Not even loud. Like snapping a dry stick."

"Any idea who did it?"

"Just his car." He saw the old gray Studebaker speed across the dark field. "So fast. The way it happened."

The attendant wrestled with a length of tubing. "So you didn't get a look at the driver?"

Yearwood shook his head. "No," he said. "Too dark. Everything."

He felt the rumble of the bridge beneath him and knew that they were passing over the river, would soon be racing down the avenue toward Saint Vincent's. "Hold on just a little longer, Jack," he told Pierce. "We're almost there."

Are you listening to me?

5:34 A.M., *Dunlap's Collectibles*

The knock at the door was brutal, like a cow kicking a barn wall, and so Dunlap knew instantly that it was Blunt.

"Jesus Christ, you don't got to wake up the whole neighborhood," he said as he swung it open.

Blunt stepped into the murky light, and Dunlap saw that he was sweating.

"Jeez, Ralph, you look like you been—"

Blunt jabbed a finger hard into Dunlap's chest. "Don't say another fucking word."

"Okay, okay," Dunlap said, raising his hands defensively. "Come on back."

The two men made their way down the shop's center aisle, and on the way, Dunlap swore to himself that he would never get his ass in this kind of sling again, that nothing was worth dealing with psychos like Blunt and Stitt.

Halfway to the curtain Dunlap stopped. "Listen, Ralph, I got a visitor," he whispered.

"A what?"

"The guy whose money you got," Dunlap explained. "He come for it a little early."

Blunt reached for his pistol. "You little prick."

Dunlap felt the barrel of the thirty-eight like the nose of a serpent, cold and deadly. "Holy shit, Ralph," he gasped. "Holy shit, put that thing away."

"Who'd you send out there?" Blunt demanded.

"Send? Who? Out where?"

Blunt jabbed the pistol into Dunlap's belly. "Who'd you send out to that fucking shed, Harry?"

"Me? Nobody," Dunlap wailed. "What are you talking about?"

Blunt shoved Dunlap hard, sending him stumbling backward through the curtain.

Stitt leaped to his feet. "What the fuck!"

"Shut up," Blunt snarled.

Stitt glared at Dunlap. "What the fuck's going on?"

"I don't know, Burt," Dunlap whined. "What's the story, Ralph? We got no idea—"

"Shut up." Blunt jerked the pistol. "Sit down. The both of you."

Stitt and Dunlap lowered themselves onto the sofa.

"You bring my money or not?" Stitt demanded.

"Yeah, I brought it," Blunt replied.

"Where is it, then?"

"It's in the car."

"Well, why don't you go get it, fatso?"

Blunt's eyes narrowed. "What'd you say?"

"You heard me."

Blunt took a short step toward Stitt. "Who the fuck are you?"

"Me?" Stitt answered coldly. "I'll tell you who I am. I'm the guy that paid this shithead cousin of yours three grand to hide my goddamn money."

Blunt's eyes cut over to Dunlap. "Three grand?"

Dunlap swallowed hard.

Stitt laughed. "You stiff this lummox, Harry? No wonder he's pissed at you."

"Shut up!" Blunt yelled.

"You don't have much of a vocabulary, do you, fat boy?" Stitt sneered.

Blunt jabbed the pistol toward Stitt. "Shut . . . you . . . you better . . ."

"Spit it out there, dumbo," Stitt cawed.

Blunt drew back the hammer.

"Oh, fuck," Dunlap gasped. "Please, Ralph. Let's all think this through, okay? This guy you saw. Let's figure this out, okay? 'Cause what I'm saying here is, I didn't send nobody."

"What guy?" Stitt demanded.

"Some guy showed up where the money was," Dunlap told him. "That's why Ralph's so pissed. Ain't that right, Ralph? So what I'm saying is, let's figure it out. Go slow, you know? Figure it out, like I said. So, please, that gun there, Ralph, you can put that way."

"I ain't puttin' nothing away."

Stitt chuckled. "Just don't shoot yourself in your big fat foot."

"Shut the—"

"Yeah, yeah," Stitt yawned. "Get the money, Harry. Send this fat . . . whatever . . . out to his fucking car and get me my money."

"Take it easy, Burt," Dunlap pleaded. "So, Ralph, this guy, what'd he look like?"

Stitt kept his eyes on Dunlap. "I don't give a shit about any of this, Harry. Are you listening to me? I want my money. Now!"

"Burt, please," Dunlap begged. "You don't know what you're dealing with here."

Stitt glared at Dunlap, then cut his eyes over to Blunt. "Your shit cousin says I don't know what I'm dealing with. Well, here's the bottom line. Nobody gets between me and my money. Anybody does, they're dead. You got that, dumbo? I don't give a fuck if some stupid bastard got in your face. I don't give a shit what you did to him."

"I shot the fucking guy," Blunt yelped.

Dunlap dropped his face into his hands. "Oh, Jesus," he moaned fretfully.

Stitt laughed. "So you shot a guy, fat boy? So what? That fucking money's already got blood on it."

Dunlap lifted his head. "Blood, Burt? You didn't tell me about no blood."

"Who cares what I told you."

"But if that money's got—"

Stitt waved his hand. "It's the hophead that fucked it up, grabbing at my stuff."

"So . . . what happened, Burt?" Dunlap probed timidly.

"He fucking grabbed my briefcase," Stitt howled. "Tossed it all the way across the room. Flew open, the fucking thing. Cash scattered everywhere."

"Jeez," Dunlap breathed.

"Then he goes out the door, and on the way snatches a chain off this kid's neck, the fuck."

Dunlap felt a blade of dread slide across his throat. "You mean . . . ?"

"Yeah, her," Stitt said. "Snaps the fucking chain right off her neck and just keeps going. And me with that goddamn money scattered all over, and that kid scared out of her fucking mind. No way she's not going to the cops."

Blunt blinked sluggishly. "Kid?"

"Yeah, what of it, fat ass?" Stitt said.

"You hurt that kid?" Blunt asked.

Stitt stared at Blunt contemptuously. "You get in my way, you get the same. It's just that simple. Real simple. So simple, a dumb-ass like you can—"

The blast was deafening, and in its explosive charge Dunlap dove frantically for the floor, covering his ears and whimpering. "Oh, shit. Jesus. Jesus. Oh, shit, man." He lay there, curled tight, his eyes squeezed shut. "Oh, Jesus," he whimpered. "Sweet Jesus."

Stitt remained in an upright position, eyes open, his head cocked to the right, as if listening for a distant sound, a neat round hole at the center of his forehead.

Dunlap cautiously opened his eyes, then drew himself from the floor, working desperately to compose himself, think things through. Blunt stood motionless, the pistol dead still in his hand, nothing moving but the curl of blue smoke that twined up from the barrel. "So what do we do now, Ralph?" he asked softly.

Blunt said nothing, but Dunlap could see the tumblers of his brain working. What, he asked himself, what was he trying to figure out? His eyes fell toward the pistol, and he wondered if he could take a short, very slow step and ease it from Blunt's fingers. He waited, thought about it a little longer, then stepped forward.

"So, Ralph, why don't you just—"

A siren wailed distantly; something glimmered in Blunt's eyes.

"I got to go," he said.

"Sure, Ralph," Dunlap agreed. "We'll figure it out, you know?" He took another small step. "You don't have to worry about me." He smiled crookedly. "I mean, we're family, right? Cousins, right? Stitt? Fuck him, you know what I mean? Imagine, a kid. Jesus Christ. So, like who's going to miss the lowlife, right?" Another short step, he thought, then touch the barrel. Don't grab. Just touch it with one outstretched finger and nudge it very gently to the side. "So, Ralph, what do you think, we get this all cleaned up, then we can—"

The second blast struck Dunlap as infinitely loud, the small piece of lead that tore into his chest infinitely large, the fall of his body to the floor infinitely swift, and the silence that followed infinitely long and dark and cold.

5:41 A.M., *Saint Vincent's Hospital, Emergency Room*

He could feel the entire fabric unraveling life's tiniest and most elemental threads, his pulse vibrating on this string of particles that only briefly united, as if drawn together on a breath, then released again, each time holding more tenuously, the lineaments more frayed, the light, when it shone, more distantly reflected until it died entirely, and the beginning and the end were the same.

5:44 A.M., *Saint Vincent's Hospital, Waiting Room*

"You brought in Mr. Pierce?" the doctor asked.

"Detective Pierce," Yearwood said. There was blood on his jacket and he kept fingering it.

"I'm sorry. Detective Pierce died at five forty-one. I'm sorry we couldn't save him."

Yearwood reached for the dusty canvas bag that rested in the chair beside him. "So am I."

Outside, the traffic had begun to build with shift workers on their way to the steel and rubber factories that huddled north of Harbortown. Yearwood took a right on Banks, and then a left on Marigold. The look of the city grew dingier amid the pawnshops and bail bondsmen. He knew that Police Headquarters lay somewhere to the east, but the name of the street eluded him.

At Cordelia he saw an old gray Studebaker beside the curb, its visor pulled down, a pasteboard sign attached: POLICE VEHICLE, OFFICIAL BUSINESS.

The man behind the wheel did not look up as Yearwood approached.

"Sir?"

The man startled violently and reached for the briefcase that rested beside him in the front seat. "Whuh?"

"I noticed the sign on the visor," Yearwood told him. "I figured you'd be able to tell me where Police Headquarters is."

The man nodded heavily, a half-dazed look in his eyes so that for a moment Yearwood took him to be drunk.

"Police Headquarters," Yearwood repeated politely.

The man looked at his pudgy fingers resting on the brown briefcase, then back up at Yearwood. "Straight down to Trevor," he said gloomily. "Turn right."

"Thanks," Yearwood said, and proceeded on until he reached the corner of Trevor Street. Before turning, he glanced back down the street, intending to wave a thank-you to the man who'd given him directions, but the car was gone.

5:59 A.M., *Interrogation Room 3*

I have no more questions, Cohen thought helplessly. There is nothing more I can do.

He watched the second hand make its final sweep of the five o'clock hour. He could not imagine why Pierce had not called in. Even if he'd found nothing that could be used in the interrogation, he had the duty to report that failure. Cohen studied the clock, considered the few seconds that remained, and summoned one more question. "Where are you going when you leave here, Jay?"

"Nowhere," Smalls said without hesitation.

"Back to the park?"

"Nowhere."

"Okay," Cohen said. He grabbed his jacket from the back of the chair. "Remember this, Jay. I'll be keeping an eye on you."

Smalls' spidery white hand crawled to his throat, then fluttered back into his lap.

Cohen walked to the door, jerked it open, then glared back into the room. "Someday I'll get you, Jay." His voice was firm and confident, but it was an act, and he knew it. Nothing would ever deliver Albert Smalls into his hands. The great engine ground on indifferently, reducing the child and the killer of that child to the same white dust, giving no sign that it cared for anything. He heard his father's words again. *God is not subject to interrogation, Norman.*

In the elevator, Cohen thought of Pierce, trying to find some reason why the night had passed without word. Then his attention turned to his own activity during the last twelve hours. What, he wondered, what could I have done differently and changed the course of things?

The doors opened on the ground floor, and he saw an old man in a black hat, clutching a soiled bag to his chest. "I'm looking for someone named Cohen," the old man said.

"You found him."

"Detective Jack Pierce wanted you to have this." The old man handed Cohen the bag.

Cohen pulled a dusty drawing pad from the bag. The cover was soiled, the edges frayed. He flipped the cover and looked at the first drawing, a girl in a dark swimsuit, the designation *Betty, Seaview* written beneath the portrait. He turned the page. Another drawing of a young girl, this one in jeans and a blouse with puffed sleeves. The caption read *Carla, Titus*.

"Pierce found the bag in a storage shed the man you're interrogating lived in for a while," Yearwood said breathlessly.

"Just pictures," Cohen said as he turned to the next page, then the next page, then the next, moving ever more quickly through the dozens of drawings, all of young girls, their names tidily inscribed beneath their portraits, along with the towns, Cohen assumed, in which the drawings had been made.

"This won't help us," Cohen said as he turned the last page, started to close the pad. Then he stopped, his eyes drawn to the dark-haired child of Smalls' final portrait. She stood in a wooded area, dressed in dark shorts and a white blouse, her bare arms dangling at her sides, smiling brightly, with nothing to suggest anything but a happy youth save the metal brace clamped around her right leg. Cohen's eyes bore into the identification Smalls had written beneath the drawing. *Debra, Englishtown.*

Cohen instantly recalled the awesome guilt he'd seen in Smalls' eyes, his terror of something that would inevitably be found out. "Debra," he whispered. "Debra Pierce."

6:05 A.M., *West Ramp, City Bridge*

Blunt pulled over, turned off the engine, and once again considered his options. What would happen to his wife, his daughter? He'd lose his pension if anybody ever found out that he'd stolen a briefcase of phony money from two lowlife crooks, then murdered the fucking bastards.

But whose fault was that? The bastards', that's who. Why couldn't Dunlap have done the whole thing himself? And the other one. The one with the big mouth. Why didn't he just keep that big mouth shut?

He hadn't meant to do it, that was the bottom line. But who'd believe that? Oh, no, they'd say, Blunt had it in mind all along. He intended all along to get the money, then come back and kill them two bastards. They'd say this was the plan from the beginning, and so his wife and daughter didn't deserve a damn bit of his fucking pension because he was a lowlife just like the scum he killed, and who'd give *their* wives and kids a fucking pension, huh? Nobody, that's who.

So back to square one. The options.

Each time he revisited them, a few dropped away. Like go to Mexico. Shit! How had that one ever gotten on the list anyway? Throw away the money. Well, sure, but that didn't do a thing about them two dead bastards. And he'd been seen. Jesus Christ. His fucking car sitting there right in front of the junk shop, with the visor down, *Police Vehicle, Official Business,* while in the meantime he's inside blowing two bastards away. And the street a bus route on top of it, with every nosy bus driver who passed while he was inside noticing how there was this big old gray Studebaker parked out front of Dunlap's Collectibles with the goddamn visor down and a cardboard sign, *Police Vehicle.* Christ, he might as well have put a sign in the window that said "Blunt's inside killing two worthless bastards."

He shook his head. What's the point, he asked himself, what's the point of thinking about it? He was fucked no matter what. So really, for all the thinking, he had no options at all. Except one. Just go to the bridge and heave the briefcase off it. Then do the rest quick and clean. He reached for his pistol, and for just a moment, as it rested affectionately in his grip, warm and silent, it was as close as he had ever known to the handshake of a friend.

He placed the barrel against the side of his head, felt his hand begin to shake, and decided, no, just a second, just one goddamn second. He had to get rid of the money.

He grabbed the briefcase, got out of the car, and walked to the side of the bridge. Far below, the brackish water moved turgidly, glutted with the vomit and swill of the factories to the north. He leaned over, and with no further thought tossed the briefcase over the side. He watched as it plummeted away from him, falling and falling with a strange silent grace. Not a bad way to go, he thought. Better than the big mess he'd make with that fucking gun. Okay, then, he decided, okay. He tucked the pistol in his belt and with a heavy grunt hauled himself up onto the concrete side rail. For a moment he felt like a statue on a pedestal, a figure of stone, towering and dignified. Then the truth hit him. He was not like that. He was Blunt. And Blunt was nothing. He leaned forward, thrust out one leg, then another, and stepped into the waiting air, falling hard and unexpectedly fast, thinking only, in his last instant, that Stevie Weinberg, the fucking kike, would never have gotten his ass in a fix like this.

6:07 A.M., *Interrogation Room 3*

Cohen burst through the door of the interrogation room. Smalls' chair was pushed back from the table, but there was no other sign that he'd ever been there. Cohen looked around, half expecting to find him curled in a corner. But the room was empty, and so he dashed back into the corridor, then down it to the detectives' bull pen. Empty. Then the lounge, the other two inter-rogation rooms, the Criminal Files Room. Nothing.

Only the bathroom at the end of the corridor re-mained. Cohen felt a bony finger rake his spine. *In there,* he decided. *He has to be in there.*

He moved toward the door like a man toward the entrance to the dreaded cavern where he knows it waits for him, that part of life that is indifferent to his hopes, sneers at his plans, lies forever beyond his control. At the door, he reached for his pistol, then let it go, and grasped the cold brass knob instead.

The door opened like a door in a nightmare, without being pushed. It glided across the stained tile floor, revealing first a metal can bristling with mops and brooms, then the urinals, the dark green stalls, a line of stained sinks, the last one gurgling softly, steam rising toward the cracked mirror that hung above it, a shard of glass removed, the door still moving in its ghostly trance until it finally came to rest against a bare, blood-spattered hand.

What do we know for sure?

9:45 A.M., *Bickford's Restaurant, 1284 De Paul Street*

Anna Lake stood on the sidewalk, wearing her white waitress uniform. Her features had grown increasingly taut as Cohen told her the details.

"So what Pierce found in Titus," she said. "It was proof."

"Yes," Cohen answered. "I mean, there's no way to prove that Smalls murdered the little girl he'd drawn. But she was murdered. And Cathy . . . well, for one man to be in the same place where two little girls were murdered, that's evidence of a kind. Maybe not enough in a trial, but Smalls is dead, so there won't be a trial."

He didn't tell her that the murdered child was Debra Pierce, that regardless of how right Pierce had been about Smalls' guilt, he had been wrong about Nicolas Costa, that it was Smalls who'd tightened the wire around Debra's neck, stripped off the red velvet bracelet with its winking purple glass adornment, left her broken in the matted grass.

"Pierce promised me that Smalls wouldn't get away," Anna said.

"And he didn't," Cohen told her.

He recalled the details of Yearwood's account, the way Pierce had found him in the Driftwood Bar, found Cindy Eagar and Avery Garrett, how he'd paused before entering the storage shed, looked out over the fields, and "gone somewhere deep within himself," as Yearwood said. After that, the single shot, Pierce's body curled around the canvas bag, the fleeing car Yearwood could not identify, nor the man behind its wheel.

"Well, thank you for coming here," Anna said. She offered her hand.

Cohen took it. "Jack cared about you."

She smiled mutely, then went back inside the restaurant, leaving Cohen alone on the street.

The drive to his apartment carried him back along the downtown streets, past Police Headquarters, and toward the west ramp of the bridge, where the Department's other tragedy had occurred. Well, not really a tragedy, he thought as he swept by the ramp, Blunt's old Studebaker now hauled onto the back of a police tow truck. Not like Pierce.

Suddenly Pierce's death fell upon him with annihilating force. He had shouldered the shock of his partner's murder resolutely until then, played the hardheaded detective, taken the news stoically. But now he felt something die as he recalled the look of Pierce's body at the hospital, inert beneath the sheet, eyes closed, the terrible stillness of his limbs, so different from the stirring care that had made him such a good cop. So what is death, then, Cohen wondered, but a profound indifference?

He thought of Smalls' body on the tiled floor, blood pooled beneath his pale white throat. The Invisible Man. Still invisible. Beyond knowing, and now beyond any further probing. Thus had it ended, the interrogation.

He reached his apartment six minutes later. Going up the stairs, he passed Ruth Green's door and paused, hoping to hear something rustle beyond it, then realizing that she was no doubt already at work, teaching, surrounded by little girls and boys. So once again there'd be no one waiting for him, no one to sit and listen. No one to hear about Pierce's murder, or Smalls' suicide, or of the long, desperate night he'd journeyed through.

He turned back toward the stairs, and as he did so, her door opened and she stood before him, dark and beautiful, peering at him strangely, as if instantly comprehending what the night's ordeal had etched into his face.

"Not at work?" he asked with a quick, sad smile.

"It's Sunday," she answered quietly.

"Oh," Cohen said.

"Are you just coming in?"

"Yes."

"Long night, then?"

"Long night."

She studied him, then drew back the door. "Would you like to come in?"

"Yes," he said, "I *would* like to come in." *From the night and the cold,* he thought, *and the uncaring void.*

9:54 A.M., *Office of the Chief of Detectives*

The Commissioner sat in the leather chair in front of Burke's desk. "What will be the final report, then?" he asked, tapping his fingers together.

"That we don't know," Burke said. "The fact is,

Smalls may have left some drawings in that shed, but we still don't have any actual evidence that he murdered Cathy Lake."

The Commissioner scowled. "That won't do, Tom. We can't tell the papers or the Mayor that we don't know if this fellow killed that child. There'll be lots of questions about all of this."

"But there won't be many answers," Burke told him flatly.

O'Hearn waved his hand. "All right. Let's drop the matter of this fellow for now. What about Blunt?"

"He's your man, not mine."

"His wife's illness, then?"

"I don't know."

"His wife's illness," the Commissioner said decisively. "The man was distraught about his wife. That's the reason we'll give. And Pierce. He'll be the hero of the day. We'll do it up right. The funeral, I mean." He got to his feet. "I believe we're done."

Burke nodded firmly. "Yes, I believe we are," he said quietly.

O'Hearn walked to the door, opened it. Then he turned back to Burke. "I haven't asked you about Scottie."

"He died."

"Dear God, Tommy, I had no idea," the Commissioner said. He started to say more, but Burke raised his hand to stop him, and so the Commissioner only nodded, then eased himself out the door.

For a time, Burke remained behind his desk, thinking of Scottie, the dreadful possibility that Smalls had gotten it right, had actually seen a man in the rain, digging in the earth. But he could not be sure of that, and besides, even if the man Smalls had seen there were Scottie, it didn't mean that Scottie had strangled Cathy

Lake. There was no evidence to suggest that. After all, it wasn't as if he'd been found with Cathy's locket in his clothes.

Burke rose and turned toward the window, peering down at the city's busy streets, standing as he had hours before, his arms behind his back. At the corner of Trevor and Madison, he watched the Commissioner's car come to a stop and imagined his old friend in its plush backseat, working to compose what he would tell Blunt's wife about her husband's death. Lies, he hoped, lots of lies. For in the end, faced with life's cold truths, what else warmed our self-deceiving hearts?

10:07 A.M., 7305 *Phoenix Avenue*

Eddie Lambrusco started to rise, then felt his daughter's small, pale fist curl tightly around his little finger. "Papa."

"I'm here, princess." He forced a smile. "I've been right here for hours."

"You should have waked me up."

"No, no," Eddie said. "I love to watch you sleep."

He thought of the child who'd died in the park nearly two weeks before, the picture he'd seen in the paper. Just eight years old. How lucky he was that Laurie was still with him. That she was getting better, that she would recover, that she was alive, alive to hold his finger in her small hand. What other warning did we need, what other guide and caution than how easy, how very, very easy it is to lose the one thing you love? "I can stay home with you all day today," he said.

Laurie smiled softly.

Eddie leaned forward and kissed her cheek. "So, get

a little more rest, then maybe this afternoon I'll take you to the park."

12:17 P.M., 1272 Hilton Street, Apartment 5-B

Rest, Cohen told himself. Close your eyes and rest.

But his eyes remained open. And he could not rest.

For the past hour he'd tossed on the bed, unable to sleep, or even calm the inner turmoil that boiled within him. He'd spent an hour with Ruth Green, but for all her kindness, the way she'd listened to him attentively, he felt no less burdened than when he'd first entered her apartment. Could he really have believed that a few minutes with Ruth Green would change things?

He closed his eyes, tried to relax, but felt only a steady tightening of the spring. During the interrogation he'd felt the walls of the room close in upon him. But now the interrogation was over. Murder solved. Case closed. Then why were the walls still moving in? Why did it seem even harder now to draw a breath?

He rose, paced, opened the refrigerator, closed it. He parted the curtains, gazed out the window, drew them together again without looking out. He saw Pierce beneath the sheet, Cathy on the wet ground, Smalls floating lifelessly in his own blood, and the whole unfathomable wash of life, its random ebb and flow, the chaotic currents that swept over us, drew us down, tossed us here, deposited us there; all of it seemed nothing more than a vast disorder.

He sat down, leaned forward, sank his face into his hands, and thought again of the long night's effort. Smalls' interrogation was over, but he couldn't let go of it, didn't want to let go of it, and he wondered suddenly if this were the one thing he could offer the world, not marriage, family, enduring love, all the noble vestments of a stable life, but this seething conviction that there had to be an answer.

The passion of his discontent lifted him to his feet, propelled him down the stairs and out into the bustling street, bits of the night's interrogation swirling in his head. He recalled silences and evasions. Words and images circled in his mind, rocking him this way and that, at times certain that Smalls had murdered Cathy Lake, at times doubtful and wondering if it might have been someone else, the man in the rain, the man in the park, some man Smalls had never seen, someone who was still there, under the trees, lurking. A thousand suspects swept through his mind, the mug shots of humanity, a dark gallery from which no one face emerged, so that with each passing second Cohen felt his helplessness deepen, felt destitute and beggarly, his hand open and pleading for some intervention, a cosmic play of chance that would drop into his hand just one small morsel of the truth.

2:36 *P.M.*, *City Park*

"Park's crowded today," Eddie said as he led Laurie through the gate and down the path toward the playground.

Normally, Laurie would have released his hand and skipped ahead, but today she clung firmly to him.

"You sure you want to walk all the way to the playground?" Eddie asked.

"Yes," Laurie said.

Eddie glanced at the gift Charlie had brought over a few hours before. "It's really pretty."

Laurie touched it delicately. "I like it," she said brightly.

They walked on down the path, through the tunnel Eddie had cleaned out hours before. Kids could run and bicycle through the tunnel now, he thought, with no fear of glass or metal. They could do this because of him, because he'd done his job. "I cleaned that tunnel this morning," he told his daughter. "We can walk through there now."

They reached the playground four minutes later. For a time they remained outside the fence, while Laurie surveyed the people beyond it with a curious intensity, as if seeking a favorite playmate.

"Well, do you want to go in?" Eddie asked finally.

"Yeah," Laurie said. She ran along the fence with a sudden burst of energy, then around its far corner and into the playground. Eddie followed behind, giving her the distance he knew she craved, already needing to feel independent, grown-up, in charge of herself. That was the first step in leaving him, he knew, but that was part of the deal, wasn't it?

Laurie moved swiftly to the swings, climbed on one, and began pumping herself upward. Her smile was radiant, and Eddie found himself dreading the day when the limits of childhood mushroomed into the burdens he carried. Maybe he could teach her a few things, he decided, to go slow, be careful, marry in something other than a fever, stick things out when you had to, hold on to what you cared about.

Laurie leaned forward and sailed out of the swing so suddenly that Eddie reached for her across the impossible distance between them, then gasped when she landed safely on her feet. That she had done so filled him with delight, and he did the parent's trick of finding in these early feats evidence of later triumph. If she could land on her feet in this way, might not she do so in all other ways as well, survive, beat the odds, win?

Laurie glanced to the right, where a swarm of children noisily climbed the monkey bars while their mothers watched, talking idly among themselves. Slowly, one by one, the conversations grew less animated as each mother drew her eyes over toward Eddie. They did not stop talking, but their gaze remained disconnected from their conversations, directed somewhere over Eddie's right shoulder.

He turned and saw a tall man enter the playground. He wore a dark blue suit and black trench coat. A cigarette dangled from his fingers, and as he took a seat on one of the empty benches, he lifted his head slightly and let his gaze sweep out over the yard. For a while he eyed the children with an eerie attentiveness, his eyes roaming from the swings to the monkey bars, then to the sandbox, until at last, as it seemed to Eddie, they came to rest on Laurie.

Through it all, the mothers watched the stranger warily, Eddie noticed, their eyes sliding over to him, then back to their children as if they half expected their son or daughter to be snatched away by the sheer reach of the newcomer's piercing gaze.

Eddie thought of the little girl who'd been murdered here twelve days before. But they'd caught the man who'd done that, hadn't they?

He continued to watch the man in the trench coat, his eyes following him as he rose, walked to another part of the playground, and sat down again. The mothers' attention settled upon him briefly, pulled away, then returned, always warily, as if he were a wolf who stalked them from just beyond the firelight.

Eddie glanced back to Laurie, watched as she abruptly burst from the crowd of children and dashed gleefully across the playground, past the swings, the slide, the monkey bars, and over to the place where the man in the trench coat sat silently, his long legs drawn beneath the bench, locked at the ankles, his features shadowed by the hat.

If he talks to her, Eddie thought, if he makes the slightest move . . .

3:01 P.M., *Dubarry Playground*

"Hi," the man said, the word pushed from the corner of his mouth like a body from a car.

"Hi," Laurie answered.

"What's your name?"

"Laurie."

The man smiled. "My name's Norm."

Laurie offered a tentative smile. "I'm not supposed to talk to strangers."

"Good idea," Cohen told her. "You're not alone, are you?"

"No. Here comes my dad."

Cohen turned to see a man in work clothes striding toward him from across the playground, a little bantam rooster of a guy, quick, fierce, the type Cohen had seen plenty of in the army, the kind that if you took a swing, you'd probably have to kill him, because he'd never stop getting up, coming at you, never, never stop until he was dead.

"You know my kid, mister?" Eddie asked sternly as he came up to Cohen.

Cohen shook his head.

"You got a kid here?"

"No, I don't."

"There's a sign, you know? You got to accompany a kid. That's what it says. If you don't have no kid here, you ain't supposed to be here neither."

"I know there's a sign," Cohen told him. He reached for his badge. "I'm a cop."

"Jeez, I'm sorry." Eddie sat down beside Cohen and drew Laurie into his lap. "What with that other little girl . . . you know . . . I . . . but you got that guy, right? The bum?"

"Yeah." Cohen gazed over the playground. "He always said there was another man. A guy who scared the little girl when she was in the playground, but we never found anybody else who'd seen him. The Invisible Man, we called him."

"A guy alone, people notice," Eddie said.

"Yeah," Cohen agreed. "But I just thought I'd test the theory to be sure." He shrugged. "Turns out we were right. Everybody in the place noticed me."

"Maybe he done it somewhere else," Eddie said. "Not in the playground. Scared that kid, I mean."

"Maybe."

"You should talk to a friend of mine," Eddie suggested. "He works the whole park. He might have seen something."

Cohen noticed a workman as he entered the playground. He was dressed in a bright orange Parks Department uniform and carried a large canvas bag over his shoulder. The mothers' eyes flicked toward him, then away.

"Cleans the playground every Monday, Tuesday, and Friday," Eddie added. "My friend does. He's off today though."

The worker moved methodically from one area of the playground to the next, picking up litter with a spiked stick, filling his bag, then emptying it into the nearest garbage can.

"Name's Sweeney," Eddie said. "Charlie Sweeney."

The workman continued his rounds, unobtrusively

edging around the swings and the monkey bars, retrieving candy wrappers and paper cups while the children frolicked without care all around him and the mothers chatted obliviously, paying him no heed.

"The Invisible Man," Cohen said.

"Uncle Charlie gave me a birthday present," Laurie chirped. She lifted her hand to display it. "See?"

Cohen drew his eyes to the child's wrist, the red velvet bracelet tied delicately around it, weighted with a purple stone. Smalls' words sounded in Cohen's mind, telling a story Cohen hadn't believed before. A story about a man Smalls had once encountered. A man who worked in the park. But not *this* park, for Smalls had seen this man years before, and in a different place, this man, Smalls claimed, who'd killed a little girl. He saw Debra Pierce through Smalls' pale blue eyes, moving away from him haltingly, the metal brace glinting in the sun as she turned and headed down the path, toward the wooded ravine where they would later find her.

The purple stone winked in the light, summoning Cohen to its proof. "Has this friend of yours always worked in the city?" he asked.

"No," Eddie said. "Charlie came here about four years ago."

A man appeared at the end of the ravine, wearing the work clothes that made him invisible, Debra limping toward him now, away from Smalls, feeling safe as the uniformed man turned and caught her in his eye.

"From where?" Cohen asked.

"Englishtown," Eddie answered.

Cohen saw the man in uniform let his canvas bag drop from his shoulders as he lowered himself to the ground, eye level to a child, his arms stretching toward the frightened little girl who limped toward him, dragging her dead foot through the clutching bramble, relieved to see him waiting there, warmed by his smile.

"Does he wear a baseball cap?" Cohen asked. "Your friend Charlie?"

Eddie peered at Cohen oddly. "Yeah, he does."

From somewhere in the scheme of things, Cohen heard a wheel turn, a gear unlock, felt something fall like a coin into his needful hand. His eyes glistened.

"Where is this man?" he asked.

About the Author

THOMAS H. COOK is the author of fifteen novels, including *The Chatham School Affair*, winner of the Edgar Award for Best Novel; *Places in the Dark; Instruments of Night; Breakheart Hill; Sacrificial Ground* and *Blood Innocents*, both Edgar Award nominees; and two early works about true crime, *Early Graves* and *Blood Echoes*, which was also nominated for an Edgar. He lives in New York City and in Cape Cod, where he is at work on his next novel of psychological suspense, *Peril*.

If you enjoyed Thomas H. Cook's THE INTERROGATION, you won't want to miss any of his award-winning novels of suspense. Look for them at your favorite bookseller's.

And turn the page for an exciting preview of his next novel, PERIL, coming soon in hardcover from Bantam Books.

PERIL

A NOVEL OF SUSPENSE

THOMAS H. COOK

Sara

Okay, she thought, do it.

She headed up the stairs to the bedroom she'd shared with Tony for the last fifteen years. With every step she crumbled a little. Her ankles felt like sawdust, and she half expected parts of her body to fall away as she continued up the stairs, a tuft of hair on the third step, a hand on the fourth, until there'd be nothing left of her by the time she reached the second floor. But she moved on up the stairs despite the sensation of breaking apart, and step by determined step, the forward movement knit her together so that by the time she reached the top of the stairs she was once again resolved to do it.

Tony's underwear lay crumpled at his side of the bed. The rest of his clothes were strewn haphazardly about the room, lifeless as pelts. He could have easily tossed his underwear into the hamper and draped his shirt and trousers over the bedpost. But he'd thrown them on the floor, probably because his father had told him that that was what a man should do. She could hear the Old Man going at him, laying down the law, daring him to disobey it. *A woman has to be taught certain things, Tony.* One of them, she thought, was to stoop.

But on this morning she had not stooped to retrieve Tony's clothes. That they'd still be lying where he'd tossed them would be his first clue that things had changed. When he got home that night, he'd notice that his clothes had not been picked up, and there'd be a click in his head, audible as a pistol shot, *She's gone.*

She walked to the closet, pulled the suitcase from the top shelf, and began to pack. She took no shorts or swimsuit or sandals, and leaving such things behind confirmed the irrevocable nature of what she was doing. She was packing not for a few days away, but for the rest of her life, and she made sure there was nothing temporary about the clothes she selected, nothing that suggested she might change her mind, return to the sun-drenched house, the glittering pool. The clothes she chose were decidedly simple, the colors gray and black, appropriate camouflage for the hidden life she would live from then on. She selected them like one readying for nocturnal battle, and as she packed each item, she tried to think of herself as one of the women warriors she'd read about, armored, mounted, broadsword in hand, brave in a way she'd never been but now had to be if she was going to climb out of the sucking quicksand of her life.

Once packed, she took a moment to observe the room. Everything in it looked frilly. Lacy pillows. Fringed draperies. All the colors were pastels. It was a little girl's room with muted hues and caressing fabrics, a vision of safety where there were no shadows or sharp corners, and nothing ever grabbed you from behind.

She returned downstairs, called a cab, and waited by the door, watching the morning light build over her neighbors' houses. Again the dangerous and irrevocable nature of what she was doing settled over her. She would never see this street again, never wave to her friend Della across the cul de sac or shop with her in the local supermarket. Della, like everything else on

Long Island, was already disappearing from her life, growing translucent in her memory. She would call her when she got to the city, let her know that she'd made it, but all the rest, whatever job she got, where she lived, all of that she would have to keep secret. Especially from the Old Man. She felt his hand groping at her thigh as it had on that Saturday a week before, smelled his drunken breath, heard his brutal whisper, *You should try a real man for a change.*

The phone rang but she didn't answer it. She was afraid it might be Tony and she didn't want to hear his voice because she knew she'd feel sorry for him, the way she always did, sorry for the little boy with the bullying father who'd never really grown into a man. She knew that some part of her still loved him, but that this love was mostly made of pity for how weak he was, how baffled he would be by her leaving him, and how wounded. But if she stayed with him it would be guilt that kept her there, and no one in the end, she thought, should build a life on that. You needed substance in a marriage, each person firm enough to hold the roots of the other. You needed to be able to work out your differences without interference, and in the face of interference you needed to act. That was what Tony had finally been unable to do, and so the Old Man's malicious goading had grown steadily more poisonous and uncontrolled, until he'd finally crossed the line, reached for her as some sweaty lout in a sleazy bar would. He'd done it not because he was drunk, or crazy, but because he knew he could, knew she'd be afraid to tell Tony, and perhaps even knew that Tony, faced with such an affront, might actually do nothing about it. That was the moment when she'd realized that it was over, that she had no choice but to leave. It had taken her a week to finally do it, but now, as she did it, the act itself seemed inevitable, something long ago foretold but only now brought to fruition, everything before it oddly weightless and insubstantial, the years of her marriage suddenly rising from her like the final bubbles of a dead champagne.

Caruso

"How did this fucking happen?" Labriola demanded. His eyes glowed hotly in the murky darkness of the living room.

Caruso gripped the arms of the worn Naugahyde chair and shifted nervously. "He's always been good for it before."

"And so you let him get in this deep?" Labriola thundered. "Fifteen grand."

"Like I say, he was good for it before, and so—"

"Before?" Labriola's mouth twitched violently, spitting words like stones. "You mean before he suddenly wasn't good for it no more?"

"Yes, sir," Caruso admitted weakly.

Labriola's eyes narrowed menacingly. "Well, here's my question, then, Vinnie. Why the fuck do I care what he was before if he ain't good for it now?" He stood up, his massive frame blocking Caruso's view of the street outside, the gabled row houses of Sheepshead Bay. "Can I spend the money this guy ain't good for?"

"No, sir," Caruso answered meekly. Beyond the window, children played on the sidewalk and women stopped to chat, their arms filled with grocery bags or the latest baby. He wondered what it would be like to live on such a street, have a house, a wife, kids, be complete and on his own. His cramped apartment surfaced in his mind, the soiled sheets and unmade bed. He called it his bachelor's pad, but it was no such thing. A bachelor pad was a place a guy fixed up nice and kept clean because he might meet a girl and bring her home. The room he rented in Bay Ridge wasn't like that at all. It was just the place where he slept and ate pizza from the box and waited for the phone to ring, summoning him here, to stand before the towering figure of Leo Labriola.

"You listening to me, Vinnie?"

"What?"

"Are you fucking listening to me?"

"Yes, sir."

Labriola ticked off all the things he couldn't buy with money he didn't have—fancy cars and whores, and diamonds for Belle, his longtime mistress. If stiff dicks were for sale, he couldn't buy one. And if "some broad" wanted a sawbuck for a blow job, he'd have to pass on that, too, because Caruso had let this deadbeat fuck get in over his head, which wasn't going to stand, because nobody came up empty on Leo Labriola. No-fucking-body. Ever.

"So what I'm saying is, make him good for it," Labriola fumed. "You don't make him good for it, Vinnie, then I'll make *you* good for it."

"Yes, sir," Caruso said. His fingers rose to the knot of his tie. "Don't worry, Mr. Labriola. I'll get the money."

"You fucking better. Because I don't make threats, right? I make promises."

Labriola had told him about other promises he'd made to people who crossed him or disappointed him or simply failed him in some way. They'd ended up at the bottom of the East River or curled into the trunks of old sedans on President Street, he said. And always the stories about Russian roulette, how if you wanted to face down a guy, you offered to play it with him, took the first turn yourself, proved you had the balls to look death in the fucking eye. You did that, Labriola said, nobody ever questioned who was boss.

Caruso wasn't sure that any of Labriola's gangland tales were true. Years before, when Labriola had given him a job, he'd believed the Old Man was a big-time mobster. Later he'd learned that in fact, he was little more than a nickel-and-dime shylock. But by then it didn't matter whether Labriola was big or small. He was the guy who'd taken him in after Caruso's father had vanished, the guy who'd given him work and patted him on the head when he did things right and yelled at him when he did things wrong, and in doing that had pulled him from the boiling rapids he'd been shooting down before Labriola had yanked him from the water, given him something to do besides boost cars and raid vending machines for a few lousy bucks. Mr. Labriola had brought him into his organization, given him real work, so that he wore a suit now and looked respectable, and if you didn't know better, you might even think he was legit.

"So, you gonna straighten this fucker out?" Labriola barked. " 'Cause nobody screws Leo Labriola and gets away with it." He slashed the air, his hand like a cleaver. "Now get outta here."

Caruso rose and headed for the door. He'd already opened it, when the Old Man's voice drew him back.

"By the way, what did you think I'd tell you, Vinnie?" Labriola demanded. "Huh? To just forget it? Write this fucking deadbeat a ticket? Merry Christmas. Some shit like that?"

"I just thought you should know that in the past. . ."

Labriola laughed loudly. "You know what the past is, Vinnie?" he sneered. "A dead body. It fucking stinks."

Caruso nodded, walked out of the room, and closed the

door behind him. He knew that he should be pissed at the Old Man for talking to him like he was a jerk, but each time his anger flared, he remembered how much he owed him, along with how much he looked forward to those moments when Labriola seemed to like him, seemed to want him around, even to think that he did a good job.

He knew that if he did enough good jobs, he'd get the Big Assignment. Labriola had never told him what the Big Assignment was, but Caruso had seen enough movies to know that it was a hit that made a guy big. Someday, he thought, Mr. Labriola would put his arm over his shoulder, give him the Big Assignment, then kiss him once on each cheek. At that point it would have all been worth it. The waiting by the phone, the times he'd been chewed out. At that point it would be worth it because he'd know that he was something important, the one guy the Old Man trusted to carry out the ultimate big deal.

He knew that moment would one day come, and because of that, he couldn't get mad at the Old Man, and so immediately shifted his anger to the deadbeat bastard who'd landed him in this fix, lulled him into false trust by always being good for it before, and in that way set him up to get hauled over the coals by Labriola. It was, he concluded, all that fucking Morty's fault.

Della

She rinsed the coffee urn while Mike ate his breakfast and thumbed through the paper. Nicky gurgled happily in his high chair, his small, pink fingers dunking in the milk, reaching for a Cheerio.

"Where's Denise?" Mike asked.

She turned and saw that he'd folded the paper and placed it on the table beside his plate. "Upstairs. Primping."

"Primping? Jesus. She's twelve years old."

"They start early now," Della said. "More coffee?"

Mike shook his head and got to his feet. "No. I'd have to piss halfway into the city if I had another cup." He shrugged. "Probably will anyway." He smiled that boyish smile of his, the one she'd fallen in love with twenty years before. Then he turned and trudged up the stairs, his big, hulking shape a comfort to her, like living with Santa Claus. Once he'd made it upstairs, she listened as he moved from the bedroom to the adjoining bathroom and back again. He'd misplaced something. His keys probably. What a lug she'd married. What a kind, sweet lug.

She walked to the bottom of the stairs. "Look in the hamper," she called. "They're probably still in your pants."

She listened as he did as he was told.

"Got 'em," he said loudly. "Thanks, babe."

She felt a modest surge of accomplishment, a sense of being useful, then returned to the kitchen and began clearing the table. She'd just finished wiping milk from Nicky's mouth, when she saw Denise fly down the stairs and bolt out into the yard. Kids, Della thought, they're so crazy now.

"Okay, I'm off," Mike said as he lumbered back into the kitchen. He glanced out the window to where Denise stood waiting for a bus. "She okay?"

"Getting to be a teenager, that's all."

"Anything I should know about?"

"She talks to you as much as me." She drew Nicky out of the high chair. "Say bye to your dad."

Mike kissed Nicky on the cheek. "You be a good boy

now," he said brightly. He looked at Della, and his big, clownish face warmed her. "See you tonight."

"We're having tuna melts," she told him. His favorite.

He kissed her, walked to the car, and got in. Denise offered a grudging, halfhearted wave as he drifted backward into the cul de sac.

Della returned Nicky to his high chair, then began to load the dishwasher. The school bus arrived and Denise bounded into it. Then the bus pulled away, and Della glimpsed her friend Sara's house across the cul de sac. It looked cold and cheerless and abandoned, everything *her* house was not, and she felt a sudden vaulting gratitude that unlike Sara, she'd married a good guy, one who'd always take care of her, make sure she had everything she needed, provide a life that was truly safe.

Stark

He thought of time, then death, then the sweetness of oblivion and of how much he yearned for the end of days. So easy, he told himself, so easy just to let it go, this chain of days that stretched ahead of him. He imagined the moment, the feel of the pistol in his mouth, the shattering impact, and felt himself instantly disintegrate, burst like a vase of air, leaving nothing behind.

Literally nothing save the few luxurious items he'd purchased because the high craft employed in making them lifted his spirits and took his mind off Marisol.

But now, as he approached the grim anniversary of her death, he realized that the power of a beautifully cut piece of glass, or a perfectly woven scarf, to change his mood had waned enormously during the preceding twelve months. He suspected that his getting older was part of it, though he was only fifty-three. The rest was loneliness, and the fading hope that there would ever be an end to it while he lived on earth. He'd loved once, and overwhelmingly, lost that love in a whirl of violence, then lived on in the aftermath of that explosion, its echo forever in his mind, the earth forever trembling beneath his feet. Now more than ever, he admitted to himself this morning, he wanted an end to memory, to all sensation, an end to light and movement. Beyond life he saw a world of utter stillness and eternal dark, and yet he harbored the hope that somewhere in that darkness the soul of Marisol waited for him patiently. The nurturing of this hope, he knew, was an act of will. But if he abandoned it, Henderson would win and Lockridge would win, and they could win only at the cost of Marisol.

"Beautiful, isn't it?"

Stark faced the dealer, noted the small rosebud in his lapel, thought it foppish.

"It's sixteenth century," the dealer added with a nod toward the crystal goblet at which, Stark realized, he must have been gazing while thinking of Marisol.

"Not my thing," Stark said coolly.

The dealer looked as if he'd been gently pushed away, perhaps with the nose of a pearl-handled derringer. "Well, if I may be of help. . ."

"I'll let you know," Stark said.

"Of course," the dealer said, then vanished.

Alone again, Stark strolled back down the aisle toward the shop's front door. Finely wrought objects lined his path, but nothing called to him, and because of that he knew that he'd slipped out of the old reality, the one that had held him for so many years. Even though Mortimer would arrive that night with the latest payment, he would never spend another dime on what he now suddenly dismissed as "collectibles."

Once out of the shop, he headed south down Madison Avenue. He knew that dressed as he was, in a fashionably cut black suit, he looked like a successful Manhattan business executive. It was a look he'd cultivated over the years, and which he carefully maintained. It went with the phony name and the secret life, the elegant bars where, if he sat long enough, a woman would finally approach him.

Woman.

The very word returned him to the sunny afternoon he'd first seen Marisol, and whose anniversary was in three days. For years he'd tried to tell himself that she was just a woman, that if she'd lived, and they'd remained together, they would have grown apart, their passion faded. But she had died horribly and this death had immortalized her. She was Helen still on the walls of Troy, and he had never been able to bring her down from that mythic height. He'd tried to find another woman, fall in love again, but the ghost of Marisol lingered in the air around him. She slithered between himself and any woman he caressed. Her breath was on every kiss. He'd tried to resist her by finding someone else. Year after year, he'd cast his line into a sea of women, but never reeled in more than an empty hook.

And so for the last few years he'd pursued sex alone, sex without affection, and except for Kiko, always with strangers. He'd withheld all emotion, cut off any information about himself, and tried simply to enjoy the purely physical pleasures of the act. But he could sense that this was just another detour from the road he truly sought, and which he now imagined leading off into the shadowy and impossible distance, Marisol at the end of it, willowy and perfect and unchanged, her arms opening to receive him. He could almost hear her whisper, *Welcome home*.

Mortimer

Sitting in Dr. Langton's office, he felt small and uneducated, both of which he knew he was, a dull, pudgy little man with a mind that had precious little in it, at least precious little of the stuff educated people had in their minds—dates and names, and bits of poetry. If he had it all to do over, he thought, he'd have gone to college, even if nothing more than Bunker Hill Community College, gotten a little polish, a little class, so that he could look a doctor in the eye and not feel the way he did now, two pegs up from a bug.

"Good afternoon," Dr. Langton said as he came into the office.

Mortimer nodded.

Dr. Langton sat down behind his desk, a wall of diplomas arrayed behind him. He placed the folder he'd brought with him on his desk and opened it. For a moment he flipped through the pages, then he lifted his eyes and Mortimer saw just how bad it was. His stomach emptied in the way it had during the war, when someone yelled, "Incoming!"

"I have the test results," Dr. Langton said. "It's not good news, I'm afraid."

"How long?" Mortimer asked. He didn't want to be curt, but he didn't want to string it out either, because he knew that if he didn't get it quick and straight, he'd end up feeling even worse than he already did.

"That's always a guess," Dr. Langton answered. "But I'd say we're probably looking at around four months."

To his surprise, Mortimer felt a screwy sense that it couldn't be true, that a man couldn't sit in an office feeling more or less okay and hear a death sentence like that, four lousy months. My God, he was only fifty-five. "You're sure?" he asked.

"I wish I had a treatment for you," Dr. Langton added. "But in this case. . ."

"Okay," Mortimer said. The incoming round exploded somewhere deep inside him, and he suddenly felt already dead. Then his mind shifted to the living, to Dottie, the wife he'd leave behind . . . with nothing.

"I'm sorry," Dr. Langton said.

"Me too," Mortimer said, though it was not for himself he felt sorry now, but for how little he'd accumulated. Nothing in the bank. Nothing in the market. Not even a little row house in Flatbush. All of that had galloped away from him one horse at a time, galloped away on the back of some nag that finished fifth on the track at Belmont. Leaving him with nothing. No. Worse than nothing. In hock fifteen grand to a guy Caruso claimed was capable of anything. Breaking thumbs. Cutting out your tongue. And if Mortimer were, so to speak, beyond reach. What would Labriola do then? Was it really unthinkable that he might go after Dottie?

"Is there anything else?"

Mortimer looked at Dr. Langton. "What?"

"Is there anything else I can do for you?" the doctor asked.

"No," Mortimer answered. Not you. Not anybody.

Once on the street, Mortimer glanced down Eighty-fifth Street, trying to decide what would do him the most good now, the bustle of Broadway or some secluded corner of Central Park.

He decided on the park, and after a few minutes found himself seated on a large gray stone, watching dully as the park's other visitors made their way down its many winding paths. Not far away, a large black woman bumpily pushed a wheelchair across the lawn. An old man sat in the chair, his legs wrapped in a burgundy blanket. The old man's eyes were blue, but milky, and little wisps of white hair trembled each time the wheelchair rocked. He was deathly thin, his long, bony fingers little more than skeletal. *Even that fucking guy*, Mortimer thought, *ninety if he's a day, but even that poor, sick bastard will probably outlive me.*

But it was not the speed of his approaching death that rocked Mortimer now. It was how little time he had to make things right with Dottie, leave her something. He had no illusion that she would miss him. He had not been an attentive husband. In fact, he'd hardly been around at all. Was that not reason enough to leave her something to make up for the thirty wintry years she'd spent with him, a guy who had never taken her out, taken her dancing, or even given her a little kiss when he left in the morning or came back at night. What could her life have been, he wondered, without that kiss? And now, after so many dull, dead years, the only kiss he had to leave her was his kiss of death.

No, he decided. No, he couldn't do that. He had to find a way. That, he concluded, was his mission now.